Sweet Nothing

Sweet Nothing

Alison May

Book 1 – 21st Century Bard series

Where heroes are like chocolate – irresistible!

Published 2015 by Choc Lit Limited
Penrose House, Crawley Drive, Camberley, Surrey GU15 2AB, UK
www.choc-lit.com

A CIP catalogue record for this book is available
from the British Library

ISBN 978-1-78189-241-1

Printed and bound by Clays Ltd

For Paul, because dedicating my first romance novel to someone who isn't my husband would be at least six different sorts of wrong.

Acknowledgements

All the friends and family who selflessly put up with me being perpetually broke, intermittently morose and occasionally manic during the writing of this novel. Particular thanks to Holly, Lisa, Helen, Rich, Julie and the members of Pen Club who read some or all of the book before it got to the 'ready for public consumption' point.

Everyone at the RNA, for being generally lovely, and for having the most excellent New Writers' Scheme, and the best parties in Writer World (which is an actual definite real place where all the writers sit on their chaises longues and talk about literature, darling).

My utterly lovely editor and everyone at Choc Lit including Choc Lit Tasting Panel members: Emma, Jo, Avril, Margay, Terry, Lou, Lucie, Sonya B, Caroline, Jane O. I'm still pinching myself about the whole 'finished published book' notion.

Thank you all.

All the stars in the sky; all the grains of sand on the shore; all the cells of your body; every thought you've ever had; every emotion you've ever felt; they all had their origins in the heart of a Zero. Before there were stars, before there were planets, before there was life, before the first human being walked the earth, there was Nothing.

Everything begins, everything ends, with Nothing.

Chapter One

A Beginning

Henrietta

'Right, then.' Claudio has come back from the bar and is sounding suddenly businesslike. I sit up to attention. 'If this is our first date, there are certain conventions that must be adhered to.'

This is a little bit worrying. Actually, this is a massive bit worrying. So far we are having a perfect day. We met at the Minster and then walked from town along the River Ouse, all the way out to Rowntree Park, and then to Fulford to this pub for lunch. It's the sort of day that reminds me why I love living in York. I love being able to see the buildings and think of all the Romans, and Vikings and Tudors and Victorians who lived here before us. It makes me feel safe. It makes me feel part of something bigger.

Our plan was to walk back home this afternoon. It's after five and neither of us has suggested moving. Claudio is straddling the bench so he can face me. His tall, dark, slightly stubbled proximity and his unexpectedly practical tone are starting to make me nervous.

'What conventions?'

He leans closer to me. 'Certain topics that must be discussed on any first date.'

Oh dear. I think he's going to ask about my ex-boyfriends, which is fine, I suppose, but there haven't really been any, well none worth mentioning anyway. And I'm twenty-three so that's really embarrassing; not that I'm still a virgin, because I'm not. I just feel that by my age I should have had at least one proper ex I could tell a sad story about.

Could I make one up I wonder? I bet he's had lots and lots of girlfriends. Do I really want to know? I look back at him.

'The topics are as follows: number one – first single ever bought, number two – favourite movie, and, of course, favourite kids' TV programme.'

The relief must show because he asks me what I thought he wanted to talk about. I pretend not to know what he means, but when I think about it this is worse. Now I have to come up with cool answers to his questions so he won't go off me. I need more time, 'You go first.'

'OK. Easy. First single Oasis, *Some Might Say*, I think. Favourite movie *Star Wars*, no *Empire Strikes Back*, no *Star Wars*.'

'Kids' TV programme?'

'*Fireman Sam*. Loved *Fireman Sam*. Your go.'

Oh no. His answers are not embarrassing, even *Star Wars*, he's a boy so I think that's basically compulsory – either that or *The Godfather*.

'OK. Favourite movie – probably *Dirty Dancing*.'

That's on the same principle as him picking *Star Wars*. I'm a girl so it has to be that or *Pretty Woman*. And I do love *Dirty Dancing*. I love it when he comes back at the end and saves her, well not exactly saves her, but you know what I mean. I take a deep breath. 'Can I say *Fireman Sam* too? I think they still make that.'

He nods. 'Quite right too. The Fireman rocks. First single you ever bought?'

I don't want to tell him, but I can't think of anything cool to say. I mutter the answer into my sleeve.

He looks at me. 'I'm sorry. Didn't quite catch that?'

I mutter it again.

'Once more for the people at the back?'

'*Don't Stop Moving*.'

'I'm not moving.'

'It was S Club 7.'

I can feel myself blushing.

He shakes his head 'Oh. That's bad. That's very bad indeed.'

'Really? I thought S Club was retro now. So bad it's good sort of thing?'

My tummy quivers. I knew I wasn't cool enough for him. A tremble edges across my bottom lip and waits there a moment.

Then he smiles. 'Really, no. We must obliterate all memories of this moment.'

'And how do we do that?'

'We replace them with new memories.'

The tremble subsides as he kisses me for the first time, and it's perfect, and I will keep hold of this memory forever.

Chapter Two

One Year Later

Trix

The doorbell rings again.

Henrietta is pulled up on tippy-toes on self-imposed lookout duty at the end of the bay window. With her tiny frame, sandy hair and lemon skinny jeans, she looks like an unusually perky pastel-coloured meerkat. 'It's them.'

'Well, answer the door then.'

She shakes her head.

'You're kidding?' She's leapt from the room every time the doorbell has rung in the last hour. The party guests who weren't an hour and a half late have been forbidden from touching the buffet until the guest of honour arrives, and now she won't answer the door.

I look at her again. She's peering out from under her fringe and she's actually blushing. I didn't honestly think women blushed any more. I thought it was phased out along with chastity belts and not having the vote.

'Well, is someone going to answer the door?' Our stand-off is interrupted by Danny Peters, my boss by day and drinking partner by night. The doorbell rings again. Danny points at me. 'It's your house.'

'But it's not my party,' I complain. 'Henrietta organised it.'

Even to myself I sound like a toddler. Danny shakes his head, and I trundle into the hallway, while Henri hides in the living room fussing over her vol-au-vents. I take an unhealthy swig of wine to lubricate my social graces and open the door. As expected, Claudio is looking perfect and chiselled on my doorstep. A year tour-guiding in Italy obviously agreed with him. He's tanned and toned and smiling. If I was five years younger ... well actually I still wouldn't go for him. He's a little too put-together for my tastes.

Also as expected, Benedict is lurking in his shadow apparently forgetting that you're supposed to do smiling and eye contact when you arrive at a party. Apart from their height, it's hard to believe they're brothers. Claudio got all the Italian colouring and sophistication of their parents' ancestral land. Benedict looks like the unfussiness of their adoptive Yorkshire home has seeped into his bloodstream. He seems, as always, slightly distracted.

I open, pointedly, with, 'You're late.'

'It was his fault.' Ben gestures at his little brother, who shakes his head.

'Well, if you'd told me you weren't going to drive ...'

'You could have driven.'

Claudio opens his mouth to respond, but doesn't actually get the words out because I grab him in a vigorous bear hug. I suspect I've reignited an argument that only finished when they arrived at the door. Perhaps pointing out the lateness wasn't the best welcome home anyway. I try again.

'It's lovely to have you home.' I direct the comment at Claudio, who politely hugs me back, although his apparent enthusiasm is somewhat undermined by the way he's looking over my shoulder for a better option.

I release him. 'You can go through.'

Claudio strides into the lounge and I'm left with Ben still on the doorstep. He nods at me, and steps inside. I watch him take his jacket off. He looks just the same. Hair still cropped short. Sideburns still there, probably because it's less face to shave, rather than to make a style statement. Eyes still dark chocolate brown, and, thankfully, not fully focused on me. Three months staying with Claudio in Naples doesn't seem to have affected him at all. You'd think he'd be tanned or have got fat on pizza and gelato. He could at least have had the good manners to get fat. I don't know why I thought he'd be any different. Every time I see him I peer for some sign of age or of the ravages of loss and broken dreams, or something, but he looks the same. I swallow. I probably ought to make conversation.

'Did you enjoy Venice?'

He frowns. 'We were in Naples.'

'Oh, were you?' I know he was.

We head through into the party. I can see Claudio standing with Henrietta by the window. Everyone else seems to be attacking the buffet like they've just come off hunger strike, rather than simply having been forced to stand staring at a table full of Marks and Spencer's party food for the last hour. Such is the lure of Marks and Spencer's party food - truly the highest form of food.

I'm about to join the throng when I feel a hand on my arm. I let Danny guide me into the kitchen.

'What's up?'

'Look.' He holds out his phone. I read a text message off the screen:

R u still there? Might come if it's not too lame.

It's from John, Danny's on and off again boyfriend.

'Oh. I thought you'd ...' I don't have to finish the sentence. He knows I thought they'd split up. I thought they'd split up, because he told me they'd split up.

'Well, we did, but then...' He waves an expansive hand in a way that signifies nothing in particular. I don't push the issue. Danny and I can say pretty much anything to each other. We've been friends since university, but all that seems to fade away where John's concerned.

I smile as brightly as I can manage.

'So it's OK if he comes round?'

'So long as it's not too lame for him.' My tone is light, but it's not hiding the edge in my voice.

'Oh, he didn't mean it like that.' There doesn't seem to be an obvious other way that he could mean 'lame' but I let Danny send his reply text while I open the fridge. I manage to dislodge a bottle of wine from the rammed-in alcohol options, and fill my glass.

I offer the bottle to Danny, who shakes his head. 'Find me something more interesting.'

I stick my head back into the fridge, and pull out a bottle of Pernod. I hold it up.

'Are you insane woman?'

I laugh. 'Henri brought it.'

'What on God's sweet earth can have possessed her?'

'She kept saying the party had to be perfect.'

He takes the bottle off me and holds it between his fingertips. 'And offering people bottled evil to drink helps how precisely?'

I shrug. 'You know what she's like.'

That doesn't get a reply. It doesn't need one. We both work with Henri every day. She's like a very nervous tornado. Sometimes you just have to go along with it.

'Very well then.' He opens the bottle and starts pouring.

'I thought that was bottled evil.'

'It is.' He looks slightly offended. 'But that doesn't mean I won't drink it.'

'You know it's basically absinthe?'

Danny shrugs and tops his glass of evil up with lemonade and, worryingly, rosé wine – 'For colour,' he says – and we wander back into the party. The throng has moved away from the buffet now, and Danny heads straight into the busiest part of the room, people moving to let him through without him having to push.

I head towards the decimated buffet table and grab myself a spring roll, which I manage to stuff into my mouth sideways. Happily there's still a good selection of cake left, all provided for free by Henri's Dad, who runs a bakery. I lever a big piece of cheesecake on to my plate, and step away from the table. Well, I step slightly away from the table. I stay close enough to keep an eye out for people snaffling the rest of the good stuff.

My focus on the food has meant that I've let my guard down so far as the company I keep is concerned. I find myself standing between Henri's Dad and Ben. I opt for Henri's Dad. His actual name is Tony. Part of me feels that a thirty-year-old woman should be able to call their friend's parents by their actual names. I can't quite do it though, even in my head.

'So, do you think Henrietta's enjoying the party?'

He looks over towards Henri and Claudio in the middle of the group, and smiles.

'I would say so.'

He keeps watching her. It's weird watching him, watching her. I can't imagine what it must be like to raise a child right from a baby and then see that baby all grown up. Henri's mum had a brain haemorrhage when she was about three or four. I've only known them since Henri started at work, but I suspect that he's always let her have whatever she wants. If Henri wants cake for the party, Daddy will provide. I wonder if he sees her as an adult or still as that little girl who lost her mum.

'It must be strange seeing her all grown up.' For a moment I actually wonder if I said it out loud, but then I realise that it's Ben talking. Typical Ben, just wading into other people's private thoughts. I am mature though; I shall rise above it.

'I'm very proud of my little girl. She's done very well.'

I smile at him. 'She's a credit to you.'

He's nodding but he looks like he's welling up, which is not a good thing. Old people crying puts a dampener on any party.

'You know what else is a credit to you?' I pull him towards the buffet to lighten the mood. 'Your cakes.'

I turn to Ben for support on this issue, and find him staring up at the ceiling. I prod him hard in the ribs. 'Aren't the cakes great?'

He glances at the buffet. 'Yes. Lovely, I'm sure.'

The man who has an opinion on everything can't provide one when it's needed. Henri's Dad doesn't seem to mind though. 'Don't mind him. Men don't feel the same as women about cake.'

'Except you?'

He nods. 'But I'm a rare and sensitive man. Don't get me wrong, pet; blokes'll eat cake but they don't have the love for it like girls do.'

'And I thought the way to a man's heart was through his stomach?'

'Oh it is, but you have to think savoury. Fry-ups, roast dinners, that sort of thing. Meat and potatoes.'

I smile at his clearly well-considered philosophy of love through food. 'So that's where I'm going wrong. My shepherd's pie isn't up to the job.'

I hear Ben snort behind me, but I ignore him, and talk to Henri's Dad. 'So did your cake win over the ladies?'

'Of course. It were the only reason Henrietta's mother married me. Bowled over by my éclairs.'

Ben must be sick of being ignored, because he takes the pause as an opportunity to interrupt. 'Well, cake is a better reason for choosing a partner than romance. At least there's some rationale behind it.'

Danny, John and Claudio come over as Ben is talking.

Danny laughs. 'Ben's views on romance. Never heard this before. Please go on.'

He adopts a posture of faux academic appreciation and gestures to Ben to continue.

Ben tries to protest. 'I don't go on about it.'

Danny looks at him. 'Really?'

'Really.' Everyone waits. No one speaks. Ben gives up. 'It's just that, well, love is like an illness, isn't it? That's been proven. Romantic love is the serotonin equivalent of having the flu. Deciding the direction of your life based on love is like deciding the course of your time on earth based on the unpleasant after-effects of a bad curry.'

Another silence. Danny looks at him. 'Are you done?'

'No. Actually ...' Ben tails off under Danny's unsympathetic glare, and nods. 'OK. You know I'm right though.'

The group starts to split off again but I can't let it go. I have no idea why I can't. Henri says that if I can't say anything nice to Ben, I shouldn't say anything at all, and I try. I really try. My brain orders my mouth to shut, but it doesn't; it won't. I step towards Ben. 'You don't like love because you can't explain it.'

He glances at me. 'And you can?'

'No one can. And that's what you can't stand.'

'I don't see what's wrong with basing your judgements on things that you can understand.'

'But you can't understand everything. What about beauty and love and art and literature and ...'

'Literature? How does literature help you understand the world?'

He's exasperating. 'That's not what we're talking about.' I point out.

'It is now. Come on. How do hobbits and the fires of Mordor help you interpret the world around you?'

We're toe-to-toe now and I'm very aware that the rest of the conversation in the room is dying away. We are in danger of becoming the main event.

'Hobbits? Is that the only book you can think of?'

I can see that he's fighting back a smile as he shrugs slightly and nods.

'Well, *The Lord of the Rings* teaches that co-operation is preferable to fighting ...'

'And?'

I take a breath to give thinking time. It doesn't help. 'And that it's important to look after your jewellery.'

'Important life lessons.'

I nod. I think I might be a little bit tipsy.

Ben tilts his head to one side. 'I thought you said we weren't talking about literature anyway.'

He's right. We weren't. What were we talking about though? I remember.

'We were talking about your inability to deal with love, because you can't explain it.' Yeah. That was it.

'I just think deciding who to spend your life with based on cake is far more sensible than basing it on chemicals misfiring in your brain.' I don't respond, which is a mistake, because he takes my silence as an invitation to continue. 'Anyway, when did you become a great fan of love and romance?'

This is more familiar ground. Dangerous, unstable ground, but more familiar. 'I can't be doing with men. They think they know it all.' I gesture around my living room. 'And they take up so much space.'

'Ok. Not a full grown man then. What about a boy?' He makes a great show of looking around for a boy under the table and behind the bookcase. 'Trix's secret toyboy, out you come!'

He looks silly. I'm not going to laugh. 'Boys are worse than men. They take too long to train.'

He calls off the search and moves to stand in front of me. 'Boys take too long to train? What about girls?'

The iPod has shuffled to a quieter track; the conversation around us has definitely lulled and I'm trapped in a conversation with this ridiculous, impossible man. He's had three months away for me to forget precisely how annoying he can be, and how unaware he is of personal space. He's close enough for me to hear his breathing. I force a smile from somewhere. 'Women are perfect already.'

He's looking straight at me, and that smile is still there lingering in the back of his dark brown eyes. I swallow and try not to think about eye colour. He cocks one eyebrow, which he knows infuriates me, because I can't do it however long I spend practising in front of the mirror. 'Perfect, really?'

I open my mouth to respond. Fortunately, for Ben, who was definitely, unquestionably going to lose this argument, Danny steps in. 'Thank you for the entertainment, but I think this party was supposed to be for Claudio.'

He turns towards the room and raises his voice. 'Chaps, Gentlewomen, Undecideds, if you could make sure you have a glass in your hand. This evening is to welcome home Claudio from his jaunt in La Bella Italia, so if you could all hold up your glasses and join me, on my mark ... one, two, wait for it, three ... To Claudio!'

'To Claudio!'

I turn away from Ben and join in enthusiastically. 'To Claudio!'

Someone has the good sense to turn the music up and the party slowly cranks back into life. Danny steers Ben away, and Claudio gravitates back into Henrietta's orbit, which leaves me standing apart from the group next to John. Danny's John. I didn't even see him arrive. He's like that. He has a face that you wouldn't really look twice at if you saw him in the street. He's neither grotesque nor beautiful, tall nor short, fat nor thin. His hair is bleached white blond, and it sits against his pale skin as if he's tried to whitewash his whole body. And he's quiet, as if he's deciding whether you're worth the effort of talking. You find him standing next to you, and you realise you have no idea whether he's been there three seconds, three minutes or three hours.

'You're right.'

So he's talking tonight. I wonder if I ought to feel honoured. I turn towards him, but he doesn't raise his eyes from the floor. 'Sorry?'

'You're right about men. They're not worth the trouble. You expend so much energy, invest so much time and in the end you don't get anything for it, do you?'

I swallow. 'Well you're lucky to have Danny then?'

He doesn't answer. We're silent for a few seconds and then he walks away – no 'excuse me', no 'goodbye' – he just walks away.

Charming.

Chapter Three

I can't help being a little bit cross with Trix for arguing with Ben. I don't say anything though. There's no need to upset anyone, and everyone else just treats them like it's a big joke when they fight. It doesn't matter though. They've stopped now, so everything can still be perfect.

Myfanwy from work is talking to Claudio about Italy. He's laughing at the way she says Amalfi with her Welsh accent and she's patting his arm as she laughs along. I've never been to Italy, and I'm not as tall as Myfanwy, and I don't have such a pretty accent. I put my smile back on. It's nice that Claudio's having a good time.

'The room looks good.'

I turn around. Ben is standing next to me. I think he's been standing next to me for a while. I look around. 'Well, it's Trix's room.'

He smiles. 'But it doesn't normally look like this. Normally there is more ... stuff, y'know like, where are all the takeaway boxes that live down here?' He gestures towards a space next to the sofa.

I have tidied quite a lot, and moved some of the furniture, and had the curtains dry-cleaned. Really it's all Trix's taste in décor and telling Ben about all the cleaning might sound like I'm being rude about how Trix keeps it, so I don't. Cleaning is one of my hobbies anyway. I do my own flat every Saturday, oven and bathroom and everything. It's nice to keep things nice.

Claudio is still engrossed by Myfanwy, and I don't want to interrupt or make a fuss, so I smile as brightly as I can at Ben. I'm not sure what to talk to him about. Ben is really Dr Messina, and he did his PhD in Maths at Cambridge, so his braininess is a bit scary. What do I know that I can talk to him about? He writes books. 'So, what's your new book about?'

And he tells me, and it all sounds very clever, but I only really understand about half of it. What I get is that the book is about Zero, which means it's a book about nothing, only not about nothing if you know what I mean. And that gives me an idea.

'You could come and talk at the library.'

'Why?'

'Well, writers talk at libraries, don't they? It promotes the book.'

He nods, but he doesn't look sure. 'What would I talk about?'

'About the book. About Nothing.'

The idea is really taking shape in my head now. I'm the city's Arts Development Officer, and I have to organise a big art project for all the schools, and we can do it about Nothing. It'll be brilliant. Ben's talk could launch the whole thing. I try to explain my idea to him, but he doesn't look very keen, so I go back to the start and try to explain it again. The babbling that I do when I'm nervous is still coming out of my mouth when Claudio comes over.

'Go on, mate. It'll be fun.' At least Claudio seems to have understood what I'm talking about.

'I don't know. I don't really know anything about art.'

'You don't need to. You talk about nothing and then I'll sort out the art bit.' I'm getting more and more confident that this is a good idea. Trix is always telling me I should use my initiative. This definitely feels like using my initiative.

Ben is still shaking his head. Next to me Claudio shrugs.

'Maybe you're right. Trix probably wouldn't want you turning up at her work anyway.'

His face changes immediately. The frown is replaced by a grin. 'Well, hold on. I didn't say I wouldn't do it. Actually, it sounds really interesting.'

My mouth has gone all dry and wrong-feeling. A talk at the library. The library is where Trix works. I know this. I share her office. It says *Beatrix Allen – Children's Librarian* on the door. Claudio's right. She won't like Ben being there too. And Trix has always been so nice to me, since we started working together. She completely took me under her wing. She introduced me to all her friends, so I wouldn't be lonely and she encouraged me to move into York. I was still living with my Dad out in the sticks when I first got the job. Trix rented me the flat downstairs. I probably pay loads less than she'd get if she went to an agent. I don't want Trix to be cross with me.

Now that my brain has identified what a horrible idea this was, it appears to be too late. Ben is marching across the party and explaining the whole plan to Danny, who is my, and Trix's, Big Boss, and he's nodding enthusiastically. Now he's turning towards me and giving a thumbs-up. It's going to happen and someone's going to have to tell Trix that it's happening, and that someone is going to be me.

Maybe it'll be all right. Maybe if I wait a few days she and Ben will be friends again. The way those two behave together makes no sense to me. Either you like someone and you're nice to them, or you don't like them and you're not.

A hand on the small of my back interrupts my thinking.

'Can I get you another drink?'

Claudio is leaning towards me. He has to bend down to get to my ear level. I've never had anyone so attractive pay attention to me before. He's tall, and dark and properly model handsome. He looks like one of the men on the front of the romance novels I hide under my bed so that Trix won't see them and laugh at me. I like them though. I like knowing there's going to be a happy ending.

I nod at the offer of a drink, and he heads into the kitchen.

As soon as he's gone I step out of the living room and run up the stairs to Trix's bathroom. A minute to think is all I need. Once I'm in the bathroom, I try to force myself to take deep breaths. Trix won't be cross with me. We're friends. I tell myself not to be silly.

There's a bit of dried toothpaste on the side of the washbasin. I pull some toilet paper off the roll and wipe it, but it doesn't come off. I run the tap and moisten the paper a little bit before I wipe again. This time the toothpaste comes off. I grab some more toilet paper and wipe all the way around the basin. There's a soap dish on the side of the basin. I lift it up and wipe underneath until I can't see any bits of soap stuck to the bowl at all.

I go back downstairs to the party, and see Claudio waiting clutching two drinks. Probably I should have brought him one, because he's supposed to be the guest of honour and I'm supposed to be the hostess. I try to hold on to the calm, clean feeling. It's working. Claudio spends the rest of the evening standing close to me and asking me questions and smiling right into my eyes. Myfanwy glares at me for a bit, but I don't care. Even if it only lasts for one night, right now I'm the popular girl that the perfect man wants to hang out with, and I laugh when he makes a joke and answer his questions without sounding stupid, and try to be perfect enough to carry on being that girl.

Chapter Four

'What colour are no tomatoes?'

There's a ripple of chat around the room, but nobody is risking an answer. At the front Ben grins. I remember that grin, all toothy and uneven and infuriating. He tries again.

'What colour are five tomatoes?'

No one answers. He spreads his hands. 'Oh, come on! Five tomatoes?'

Finally one of the younger kids at the front pipes up. 'Red?'

Ben keeps grinning. He always did like showing off.

'Thank you! Red, obviously. Let's stick with this. What colour are four tomatoes?'

The audience have got the idea now and five or six voices respond. Even if the kids are shy, the adults at the back are enjoying the opportunity to participate like children under the pretext of encouraging the little ones. Ben's practically bouncing with glee at the attention now. I'll kill Henrietta for this. I don't even know why she thought this was a good idea. Getting a mathematician to come and help with an art project? It's just stupid.

Although, the audience here this evening don't seem to agree. The library theatre is full, which is unusual. Normally the only time it's even close to full is for the amateur dramatics panto, and that's only because they give free tickets to all the schoolkids. I digress. Henri should never have invited him. That's the point, not that I gained anything trying to convince her of it. She just kept tidying her desk and saying that Danny thought it was a good idea.

'Ok. So what colour are three tomatoes?'

Ben has got people chorusing the answers. 'Red!'

'Two tomatoes?'

'Red!'

'One tomato?'

The audience are eating out of his hand. But he's talking maths to a room full of geeks; it's not exactly a hard sell.

'Red!'

'No tomatoes?'

Two or three kids, and worryingly rather more grownups, have got a little too caught up in the game and try 'Red' again. People laugh.

'Not so easy is it? And that's what I'm trying to explain. Zero isn't like other numbers. But without it none of the other numbers make sense.'

The talk is going well. Ben seems disappointingly determined not to fall over his own feet or conduct the whole evening with his flies undone. The point remains though, he has no business being here, and if it wasn't for Henrietta he wouldn't be. This is all her fault.

I feel bad for wishing it was going badly. I should be pleased that Henri is getting more confident. She is, slightly surprisingly, my best friend. I've never really done that well with close girlfriends before Henri. I'm not that good at girl things. I can't talk about diets and I only own one handbag. Henri doesn't seem to mind though; she sees me through the same rose-tinted glasses she views the rest of the world with, and it makes me want to be as nice as she thinks I am. I don't actually hate Ben either. I'm just calmer on the days that he's not where I am.

There are drinks upstairs after the talk. Henri will have all that in hand, but I pretend to myself that she might not and slip out to help organise things.

Ben

All in all everyone seemed happy enough with the talk – all that 'tomatoes' stuff went down brilliantly. Now I've been dragged up to the staff room for nibbles and warm wine with the staff. I'm trapped in small talk hell. I do try; but I can't do all this stuff about how it's turned colder lately, and maybe it will snow. People ask me about what I'm working on and so I tell them, and then it's fifteen minutes later and they're glazing over and I'm talking about equations. Apparently, they're not actually interested, and somehow I'm in the wrong for taking the fact that they asked the question as evidence that they are. Conversations end either with them developing a sudden need to take a leak or with someone who knows me better dragging me away.

I'm avoiding the embarrassment today and keeping myself to myself in a corner watching the rest of the room. Trix is holding the floor. Now, that woman can talk.

She has a curl that keeps dropping in front of her face. Every couple of minutes she flicks her head back to shift it and then it sort of half rolls, half bounces back across her eye, and then she starts the whole process again by flicking her head. She's done it four times now. What's the process, I wonder? Well, it must take account of the weight of the hair, the angle of the initial curl, the friction against the rest of her hair ... she flicks again. Five times.

'The look of love?' Danny is standing next to me.

'What?'

He nods towards Trix. 'You've been staring at her for about ten minutes straight.'

I shake my head. 'I'm not staring at her.'

'No. You really are.'

'Not at her. At that curl.'

Danny looks at me. 'What?'

He clearly thinks that I'm transfixed by every hair on her head. 'Not like that. It's purely scientific. I'm just considering the movement ... friction ...'

I peter out. Danny is just shaking his head at me. I shouldn't have tried to explain. Changing the subject is probably the safest approach now.

'When can I legitimately get out of here?'

Danny rolls his eyes. 'Anti-social git.'

'Thanks.'

'Give it another fifteen. We'll go to the pub. I'll just go and be managerly for a bit.'

I nod. That sounds like a plan. I watch Danny move around the room, patting backs and playing the big team leader. He's always had that social ease. We met on the first day of freshers' week at uni. I'd been in halls for two hours on that first afternoon trying to work up the courage to leave the room, and then he turned up – this huge black man with full afro, and, if memory serves, blue eye make-up. He had an entourage around him when he knocked on my door. I think he'd been wandering around the halls picking up first years. I assumed he must be a post-grad, a third year at least, but he turned out to be eighteen, just like the rest of us.

He dragged about eight of us off to find food. In the end we only found the bar, but some of the drinks towards the end had cherries in them, and Danny said that was food. I ended up sitting by him for most of the night. I think it was the first time I'd ever been at the centre of something, or at least right next to the centre.

We staggered back to our halls, and then. And then he tried to kiss me. I must have jumped about three feet backwards, but I managed to splutter something about how I didn't, or wouldn't. He just shrugged and said he'd see me in the morning. To be fair, a shrug is the standard response to being turned down by me. Well, I imagine it's the standard. I don't really do that much turning down. Danny was probably the most exotic person I'd ever met, and as of then he was basically my best mate.

Later he told me that coming on to straight men was a hazard of being gay and not having enough life in the bag to tune up your gaydar. He said I'd taken it pretty well, which was good. Even later, he said I was just equally scared by men and women, which might be less good.

'Thank you for the talk.' Henrietta interrupts my train of thought. Henrietta confuses me. It's not just that she's so damn perky and 'glass half full' about everything. She's beyond that; she's 'glass half full and my, what a pretty glass; you must be so pleased!' Claudio is what Danny would term a 'smitten kitten'.

'S'OK.'

She's shuffling her feet, and she's turned her toes inward. It makes her look like a socially awkward baby bird. It must be me. I must exude a sense of discomfort. 'Danny said we might go to the pub after?'

I nod. 'Yup.'

'Do you know if ...' She shuffles a bit more. 'Do you think Claudio might want to come?'

Here I was thinking it was me that was making her awkward. I should be kind. And if I don't ask him, and he finds out I was out with Henrietta all evening, I'll spend the rest of the week fielding questions about what she said and what she did. 'I'll text him and see.'

'Don't tell him I asked!'

I nod. She waits. I get the idea that I'm expected to take action right away. I pull out my phone and text a one line invite to Claudio while she watches. We stand in silence for a minute, before she breaks under the pressure and starts chattering.

'I do think the talk went really well. They all seemed really interested. And I've got loads of ideas for the project – you know pictures with repeat counted patterns, and huge black holes and tomatoes. Lots of tomatoes! And I think we might make it a competition, and …'

She's still talking. I wonder if I'm glazing over. Maybe it's not just what people do when I talk. Maybe everyone's boring if they go on long enough. She's stopped talking. From her expression, I'm guessing I ought to say something. I bet she just asked me a question. I smile.

'Yeah … sure.' I hazard. You can't go wrong with 'yeah sure'.

'Brilliant. I'll tell Danny.'

That sounds potentially bad. 'OK?'

'It won't be till the end of the school term probably, end of summer term. More chance of getting the secondary schools involved then, once exams are over. So maybe we should do different age groups? And then some sort of overall category?'

And now it's too late to admit I have no idea what she's talking about. 'Great.'

'Excellent.' She's waving at Danny and Trix now, beckoning them over. 'We were thinking …'

We were thinking? We were thinking? I have no idea what she's talking about and I'm getting half the blame. Why do I do this? Why do I not just say, 'I'm sorry Hen, I have no clue what you're talking about.' But I don't, do I?

Danny's nodding along now. She must have just explained to him, and I missed it again. If I believed in God I would offer up a prayer right now. Something along the lines of 'Please get me out of whatever the hell I just agreed to, and in return I resolve to listen intently to all conversations and not drift off into my own head at crucial moments.' God, sometimes I really wish I believed in You.

Danny's still nodding. 'I think that's great. The local press will love it, which means the Council will be beside themselves. Thanks Ben. Really appreciate you putting the time in.'

Local press? What the hell?

Trix looks unimpressed. 'I'm sure he doesn't mind Danny. Sitting in judgement will suit his personality.'

She turns to me. 'Just try not to make the children cry. It's just an art competition and you're not Simon Cowell.'

Judgement? Simon Cowell? Art competition? Arse.

Chapter Five

Claudio

They're twenty minutes later than Ben promised. They text me to meet them, and then they're late, and I'm stuck here on my own, the odd one out, waiting for everyone else. I can picture exactly what they're doing. Everyone is definitely ready to go and then Henri needs to go to the bog, and then Danny has to go back to his office for something, and then Trix decides she needs to pee too, and then ... and I'm left sitting in the pub eking out my pint, trying not to look like a proper Billy.

This'll be the second time I've seen Henri since I got back, and I need to arrange to see her on her own. I have to have secured a definite actual date before close of play tonight. If not, there's a danger that the moment will pass. It'll become one of those 'might have been ...' things that you only think about in wistful moments, when you're slightly drunk and recently split up from someone.

I feel like we're already together in a way. I have to remind myself that I've only kissed her once. We've e-mailed practically every day for the last year. I never meant to do that, but we just sort of fell into the habit. I've probably told her stuff about myself that no one else knows, but still, we've only had one actual physical date and that was over a year ago.

We've never even had sex. I don't have to remind myself of that. I am painfully and acutely aware of that one. Tonight is not a night for making assumptions. Tonight is the night for translating all the flirting and the virtual romance into a clear-cut opportunity to close the deal.

They eventually turn up, and we all squeeze into a booth in the Mucky Duck, which is our pub of choice in town. It doesn't work out well for me. I'm stuck in the corner between Ben and John, and then Danny is next to Henrietta, and Trix is on the other side of Ben. It means I'm as far away as possible from Henri and, even worse, trapped with John. I decide to give him a chance.

'So, how are things at work for you?'

He raises his head from his drink and looks past me. He shrugs. I realise I don't actually know what job he does, which limits what follow-on questions I can ask, so I just sort of nod and sip my pint like I'm thinking about his response.

Fortunately, Danny decides to go to the bar then and Henri slides along so John is sandwiched between the two of us. She leans round him and smiles. When she smiles she has the tiniest little dimple just in one cheek. I clench my fist to stop myself from reaching over and touching it. She grins and I grin. In between us John snorts and pushes the table away. Henri squirms as he pushes past her and goes over to the quiz machine. Now we're next to each other. She puts her hand down on the sofa between us, and I put mine alongside it, so that our fingertips are just touching.

I love this part of the game. I like her. I know that she likes me, and I know that something's going to happen, maybe even tonight. This is the best bit, when you know where it's leading but you don't know when. We spend the evening talking about nothing, because it's not the words that matter. It's the way she catches my eye and then looks away, and the way that she keeps twitching her little finger like she wants to move so she's touching my whole hand, but she doesn't. This is magic. This is my favourite bit. I'm good at this bit.

Just before the barman calls time, she excuses herself

to go to the ladies, and I lean over to Ben. 'I need you to distract Trix.'

He looks confused. 'Why?'

My brother is a clever man, but sometimes not very intelligent. 'It's late. It's cold. Trix is going to suggest that she and Henri share a cab home. That is not going to happen. I'm going to walk Henri home. Ok?'

'Then you can walk them both home, can't you?'

Maybe he's more intelligent than I give him credit for. You would really think he's trying to put a spanner in my works. I throw him a look for good measure, but Henri comes back and people start putting on coats and there's no time to discuss it further. We head out into the night. It really is cold out here. Ben's a plank – this would've been ideal walking a girl home weather. Lots of excuses to put my arms around her to keep her warm. Instead, I've got another night of re-reading some of the e-mails we sent while I was in Italy and getting friendly with a box of tissues.

'Kebab?'

It's Ben talking and we all turn. 'What?'

He pokes Trix in the ribs. 'I want a kebab.' He keeps jabbing her. 'Kebab, kebab, kebab, kebab.'

She's on the drunk end of tipsy and she nods. 'Kebab!'

Ben looks at me. 'Anyone else?'

John has already sloped off, and so Danny shakes his head and sets off after him. Ben keeps looking to me and Henri. 'Kebab, you guys?'

I shake my head. 'It's late.'

Henri nods. 'I should get home really.'

I turn to her. 'You can't walk on your own.'

I see Ben shake his head as Henri turns to set off. I mouth a 'Thank you' at him and follow her.

She's all bundled up in her huge duffle coat. It makes her look even littler than usual. Watching her walk I want to pick her up and carry her. She stops under a streetlight and turns towards me. As she turns the light catches in her eyes, and she looks like some sort of baby animal peering out of her hood.

'It's not on your way. Are you sure you don't mind walking with me?'

''Course not.' Like I said, I'm good at this bit.

Chapter Six

Trix

'I don't want a kebab.' Ben has stopped outside the kebab shop.

'Then why did you say you did?' I march past him into the takeaway. I really do want a kebab. I haven't eaten since lunchtime, and I need pitta bread, and unspecified meat, and salad, well not so much with the salad, but it's important to show willing.

'Claudio wanted us out of the way.'

'Aw, aren't they sweet?' I grin at him. I'm more a beer and takeaway than a hearts and flowers sort of girl myself, but anyone would have to admit that Henri and Claudio are cute as anything when they're together.

'It's not sweet. It's nauseating.' Well maybe not anyone.

'They're falling in love. Let them be.' I'm nicely warmed through with wine and looking forward to my kebab. I order and pay and take my lovely drippy supper over to one of the fixed plastic tables. Ben sits down opposite me. I can feel him watching me eat, but I don't care. At least spending time with an unfeeling toad like Ben means you don't have to make an effort to be ladylike. I wrap my jaws around the kebab, and feel the sauce run on to my chin. Ben pulls an exaggerated look of disgust, but I ignore him.

After a few mouthfuls I feel sufficiently satiated to restart the conversation. I much prefer to argue on a full stomach after all.

'I do think it's sweet.'

'You would.'

'What does that mean?'

'Well, women – it's all love and romance, isn't it?'

There's so much to object to in that sentence that I barely know where to start. I decide to kick off with the basics. 'Not all women are the same!'

'You say that, but then as soon as there's a bit of slushiness around you go as gooey as the rest of them.'

'Romance isn't just for women. In case you hadn't noticed, your little brother seems quite keen.'

'Temporary insanity.'

'You didn't used to think that.'

He pauses. This is dangerous territory. The topic around which we only ever skirt the conversational edges.

'People change,' he offers. He looks down at the table. 'We grow up.'

'And grow out of love?'

'And grow out of all sorts of childish things.'

'Again, anything you can't understand is dismissed? It's childish? It's just for weak-minded women? Just because you can't explain it!'

'Not at all. There are plenty of things that fascinate me that I can't fully explain.'

'Such as?'

'Slime mould.'

Slime mould? I shouldn't ask. It'll be some obscure bit of pub knowledge, and I'll just be giving him another excuse to hold the floor. I eat some more of my kebab while he watches me chew. Eventually I give in.

'What's slime mould?'

'Cellular Slime Mould, also known as Social Amoeba. They live quite happily as tiny individual amoeba so long as there's plenty of food around, but then if the food runs out they all mass together into a sort of slug thing and crawl away.'

'You made that up.'

'I didn't. It's a real thing. Go home and look it up.'

'Nope. You made it up.' I stab the table with my finger to emphasise the point. I'm starting to think I might be a little bit drunk.

He shakes his head and grins at me. I start to relax again. At least if we're talking about mould, we're not talking about the other thing. If we could get through life only talking about mould, we'd probably get on fine. It's only when we move on to other topics that it gets difficult. Unfortunately, Benedict does not share my exquisite sense of social restraint.

'I don't understand them but it's still fascinating, whereas falling in love is not fascinating. It's boring.'

'Claudio doesn't look bored.'

'It'll pass.'

'Not necessarily.'

'You say that, and yet you're hardly racing to skip off down the aisle with a well-turned-out young guy, are you?'

He's right, but that's different. I do believe in love. I absolutely do. I believe that sometimes you can meet someone and in that moment you can just know that they are going to utterly change the way that you see everything, as surely as if you'd been sitting in the dark for your whole life, and they'd strode right in and turned on the light. I do believe that. But, for some of us the light doesn't magically brighten our world; it just gives us a headache. So he's right about one thing. Love isn't for me. Not any more.

I look him in the eye. I can see the challenge of the fight there, and the beginnings of a laugh. I should turn away, but of course I don't. With hindsight, I can always identify the moment in our fights when a mature person would walk away. 'This isn't about me. You're the one with the problem.'

'What problem?'

'The running away thing. The hiding in your books and your silly little facts.' I try to emphasise my point by thrusting my hand towards him, but I'm still holding the kebab so all I achieve is a trail of sauce across my lap and on to the table.

'What do you mean "hiding"?'

'Oh come on. All that stuff, it's protection from feeling anything.'

He looks really angry now, which is weird for Ben. Normally, when we argue I feel like I've taken all the punishment.

'What about living in the house you bought when you were twenty-one and working for your best mate?'

'That's different.' This time I actually manage to bang the table with my kebab-free hand. The bang makes me look around. People are staring.

Maybe I have raised my voice a tiny bit, but now he's raising his back at me.

'It's not different. You're just ...'

I never get to hear what I'm just, because right then two community support officers walk in and tell us to calm down and step outside. It's humiliating. They're not even proper police.

I do as I'm told and head out into the street feeling sick and desperately hoping that no one I know will be around. There's a younger female not-a-police officer and she pulls me down the street a little way. She moves close to me and I can see her breath condensing in the air right in front of my face. Ben is outside the kebab shop still with the other not-police officer. I can see him shaking his head. The woman is talking to me.

'Was he having a go at you?' She's arranged her features into an understanding face. I guess she's been on a course. 'Is there anything you'd like to tell me?'

I look at her through the confusion. For a moment I'm tempted to make something up, and tell them that he's my brutally violent ex and he's just tracked me down. Maybe they'd take him away and I'd never have to see him again. I resist the urge and take a deep breath, trying to force my voice to come out calm and not shrill and angry.

'It was just an argument. I'm fine. I didn't think we were causing any trouble.'

I play it back in my head. It might a bit defensive, but hopefully I'll have come off rational enough for them to leave us to it.

The woman looks at me. 'Stay there.'

The two officers walk over to each other and I watch their conversation. Ben is still leaning on the wall outside the takeaway. He glances up at me and pulls an exaggerated 'Oh my God!' face. The older officer who had been talking to Ben is shrugging and shaking his head. I'm hoping that he's telling the girl not to take this too seriously and pointing out that there's a cup of tea waiting back at the station. She looks like the sort that'll want all her paperwork in order though. Eventually, she walks back towards me.

'Have you been drinking madam?'

Seriously, this cannot be happening. 'Just some wine.'

'You understand that you and the gentleman were causing a disturbance in the shop.'

'It was just an argument.' I glance at her face. She's not budging. I shrug. 'Sorry.'

I'm staring at my feet. I haven't felt like this since I got caught fighting in the school playground. That was when I was fourteen by the way. I hardly go around beating up adolescents at all any more.

The woman has brought out a pad of tickets. 'I'm going to issue you with a Penalty Notice for Disorder. The details are on the ticket, and there is a fine of £80. This will not lead to the creation of a formal criminal record. If you do not accept the Penalty Notice or do not pay the fine, further action may be taken. Do you understand?'

I'm numb. I nod. Further down the street, I hear Ben swear. With a bit of luck he'll get himself arrested if he keeps going like that. I can't stop myself grinning at the idea of him getting a night in the cells. The not-police lady glares at me. 'Do you think this is funny?'

I force myself to keep up my subservient face. 'No. Sorry.'

She takes my personal details and writes out the ticket. I can't believe this is happening. I have never been in trouble with the police in my life. This is Ben's fault. I concentrate on stopping the anger from showing on my face. My drunk brain is now losing the battle against my sober brain, and I manage to look suitably contrite whilst she talks about the dangers of drink and the unacceptability of this sort of anti-social behaviour. By the time she's finished her ticket writing and her lecture, Ben is standing on his own a few feet away. The guy dealing with him clearly adopted a brisker approach. The not-police lady looks at us both. 'Now, I don't want to get called back here because you two have kicked off again.'

We both shake our heads, and she turns away to catch up with her colleague. Ben lifts his hand up to show an identical ticket to mine. I mimic him and when I catch his eye he's laughing.

'This is so not funny, and it's your fault. Nothing like this has ever happened to me before. Never.'

Ben leans towards me and whispers. 'Shut up. Seriously, are you trying to get us both nicked?'

The not-police are still walking away from us, but within hearing distance. I wait a moment until they've rounded the corner. 'This is totally your fault.'

'How do you figure that?'

I open my mouth and close it again. 'It just is,' I hiss.

He steps away from me, running his fingers back through his hair. 'I'm going home.'

'You can't go now. We need to sort this out. This is your fault.' I can hear my tone getting harsher. He's got me into another mess. I can feel the rage pulsing through me. I'm a professional, intelligent woman, for goodness' sake. I do not get in trouble with the police.

Ben's lack of concern just feeds my anger. He stuffs the ticket in his pocket and shrugs. 'Seriously, it's late. I'm going home.'

'You haven't even apologised.'

He closes his eyes for a moment, and shrugs. 'Do you wanna share a cab?'

I cannot believe him. I suck my anger in deeply, and turn away. 'I don't want to spend a second more with you than I have to.'

'Fine.'

'Fine.'

I set off away from him. How could he possibly think I would want to get into a taxi with him after all of that? He should have been offering to pay my fine. This was all his fault after all. He's an impossible man, and he always has been. I set out to walk home. After about ten yards, I slow down so that he can catch me up and insist on getting me a taxi. After about twenty yards I turn round and see him rounding the corner at the other end of the street. Typical.

Chapter Seven

Ten Years Earlier

Trix

'My shoulder thing's falling off.'

Danny swings the hood on his academic gown theatrically and flops on to the bench beside me.

'Come here.' I lean over and start rearranging the hood. His is the same as mine, white trim, a grey gown and a grey mortar board.

'I don't like this grey either.' He gestures down at the robe. 'Black is so much more dramatic.'

'You're camp today.'

He grins. 'My Dad's coming. I don't want him to be short of things to disapprove of.'

'At least he's coming.'

Danny shrugs. 'Where's Benjamin?'

'Benedict.' I correct him automatically.

'Whatever. Where is he anyway?'

I shrug. I haven't seen him since lunchtime yesterday, which ought to be surprising because he was supposed to meet me last night. Danny is looking at me. If I don't change the subject pretty quickly he's going to ask more questions. He's like that. As soon as he sees a problem he wants to sort it out. It's lovely, usually. Today I don't think I want him to come in like a shining white knight. Today I don't want to think at all. I want to get across that stage, collect my degree and start off the rest of my life as quickly as I possibly can.

'Come on,' I stand up and grab Danny by the arm. 'Let's go graduate.'

The main hall at university has the definite look of an alien spaceship that just sort of touched down sometime in the sixties and hung around too long. So long, that some enterprising fellows came along and built a university campus around it. They were probably stoned – it was the sixties – so it would all have seemed like a marvellous idea at the time.

The hall is packed today with parents, academic staff and graduands –apparently we're not graduates till after the ceremony – who knew? That's good, because it means I'm less likely to see Ben. Danny and I file into our places. He's about three seats away and bullies the girl next to me into swapping so we can sit together.

'That'll mess the system up.'

'It'll be fine.'

'It won't. If you're not sat in the right place you won't go up in the right order. You'll get announced with that girl's name.'

'What is her name?'

I peer down the row at the innocent girl who should have been sitting there. She was in a couple of my tutorial groups in the last year. 'Cher, I think. It doesn't suit her. She'd be better as a Susan or a Mary.'

Danny nods respectfully. 'Poor thing. Probably for the best that we swapped then.'

'And you think you can carry "Cher" off?'

'You just watch me, girlfriend.'

'Girlfriend? You know your Dad can't hear you.'

He shrugs. 'I'm method, darling. Living the character.'

Once the ceremony gets started it's truly horrifically boring. There is an actual string quartet for entertainment. Given that the majority of the audience (sorry – congregation, again, who knew?) are twenty-one-year-olds who've only sobered up long enough to rent a gown and find a seat, I'm not quite sure why they thought chamber music was the way to go. One last attempt to educate us perhaps.

Then the actual graduating kicks off. Me and Danny are in the first group, and devastatingly for him, one of the staff on duty realises that he isn't Cher and makes him move back to the right place. Three years of your life are reduced to this – fifteen seconds walking across a stage and shaking the hand of someone you've never seen before and will probably never see again.

And then it's over. I am officially not a student any more. I no longer have this nice insulating buffer of university between me and the real world.

We file back to our seats, and Danny can't engineer another swap so I'm effectively on my own. Well, I'm sitting between two people I know slightly but not well enough to know whether they'll be amused by me making sarcastic comments about the whole event, and that is probably about as alone as it's possible to be. I'm clutching my degree certificate like it's the only solid thing in my life, which given that I have to move out of my room in halls tomorrow, and I don't have a job, and I guess now I'm hazy on a place to live, it pretty much is.

'Benedict Roberto Messina.'

Ben's name being read out cuts through my thoughts, and I look up to see him scowling as he walks across the stage. I know why he's scowling. They mispronounced Messina with a hard E, like egg or elbow or excrement. He hates it when people do that. Apart from that he looks fine. He's elected to take his maths degree as a BSc, rather than a BA, so he gets a slightly more attractive blue hood for his grey gown. He's wearing a suit underneath it. Most people here do just look like kids in fancy dress, but somehow Ben looks older than he did yesterday. I don't know whether it's the suit or the gown or just him, but he looks like a man who's already moved on. What he definitely doesn't look like is someone who has obviously been run over by a truck in the last twenty-four hours. So where was he last night? And where does wherever he was leave me?

As he comes off the stage he has to walk down the aisle past me. Despite myself I try to catch his eye, to give him the chance to grin or nod or something. I just think that he might do something to let me know that there's an explanation for last night. He might do something that makes me feel like the things we talked about, the things which constituted the totality of my life plans after today, might still be happening.

But he just walks past. He doesn't even turn his head towards us. And just for a moment I think I might be sick. I swallow hard and clench my fingers into a fist, digging my thumbnail hard into my palm to distract myself. It's a trick I learnt when I was a kid to help manage pain. It works, because your mind just concentrates on the pain you're causing yourself, rather than anything else that's happening. I force myself to breathe slowly, and I start to calm myself down. You see, I can do this. I can do this all on my own.

Chapter Eight

I practically skipped to the bathroom when I got out of bed this morning, and I am actually singing at the top of my voice in the shower. I adore this day. I lay awake most of the night waiting for it to be morning, because the sooner it's morning, then the sooner the day will pass and the sooner it will be this evening. And this evening is mine and Claudio's second official date, which given that the first date was over a year ago, is really effectively a second first date, rather than a first second date, if you see what I mean?

Anyway, it's a date, however you count it. It doesn't even feel like a second date though. It feels like I've known him forever. All the time he was in Italy I used to e-mail him. No one else knows that. It was our secret. Even if I had nothing to say I'd e-mail him as soon as I woke up, just so he'd have something from me when he got out of bed. That sounds silly. I hope he didn't think it was silly. Anyway, I know him so well, but we've only actually been on one date and kissed three incredible times.

He asked me last night. He walked me all the way home even though it was freezing cold, and he kept pulling me up against him to keep me warm. It was the loveliest thing. I was all wrapped up inside my coat and then wrapped up in him. I was close enough to hear his breath and I was pressed right up against him most of the way home.

I asked him in for coffee, of course, and then we sat on my sofa and drank coffee and for a bit I was sort of disappointed because he didn't seem that interested in stopping drinking coffee and maybe doing something else.

And I was trying to send him all these vibes that doing something else would be ok, but either I'm not very good at vibes or he was just not interested. But then, in the middle of the conversation, he leant over and took my coffee cup out of my hand and kissed me. Just kissed me, just like that, no preamble or build up, and it was amazing, even more amazing than I remember the first time. And then he just stopped. He pulled away really slowly and stood up, and said he had better go.

I followed him to the front door, probably looking very confused, but when we were in the hallway he pulled me right up against him and kissed me again. And then he looked me very seriously in the eye and asked if I would consent to join him for dinner this evening? And I did consent, and now here we are twelve hours away from date number two.

I keep skipping all the way to work. When I get there I realise how early I am, because I woke up so early, so, instead of going to the staff room, I head for the office I share with Trix. I love our office. It's got brilliant light, because it's a really old building with high ceilings and huge windows. Trix always moans that it's really impractical, and there's no storage, but I love it, especially in the mornings when there's only me there. Trix isn't a morning sort of person. When I first moved into her basement I used to wait for her so we could go into work together, but she gets up really late, and it used to make me stressed. It's easier if I just see her at work. That's why it's surprising this morning to find that the room smells of coffee when I walk in and Trix is leaning on the windowsill already.

'You're early.'

She shrugs. I try again.

'I didn't hear you go out.'

'I think you were in the shower.'

I get the impression she has something on her mind, but I'm bursting to tell her about the Big Date. I hate this. I know that the right thing to do would be to ask about her, but I just want to talk about me, even if it's only for a minute. She looks like she's in a really black mood though. 'A friend in need is a friend indeed' – that's one of my Dad's favourite sayings, and I do want to be a good friend.

'What's up?'

She shrugs again. 'Nothing.'

But even I can tell that there's something. 'Tell me.'

'It's humiliating.'

'What?'

'I got stopped for being drunk and disorderly last night.'

I try to stop the horrified look fixing itself on my face. 'What happened?'

Once she's started telling me, I start to worry that she won't stop. She doesn't really seem to need me to contribute to the conversation. I get that after me and Claudio left them to get a kebab last night, she and Ben had some sort of huge row and ended up getting cautioned or something by the police. Apparently, it was all Ben's fault, and she's absolutely had it with him this time and if she never sees him again it will be too soon. I decide not to remind her about him judging the art competition.

Eventually she subsides a bit. 'What were you so shiny and bouncy about, anyway?'

I smile just a little bit to myself, and decide that the moment has passed. In a way it's nicer to have it as my secret. It's a lovely warm feeling of anticipation that I can just hug to myself all day. I shake my head. 'Nothing in particular.'

She doesn't ask any more.

I don't really get a chance to talk to her, or anyone else, about my big date. I'm out visiting a community centre at lunchtime, and Trix's doing After School Storytime when I get back. I'm just getting ready to go home when Danny accosts me and asks for a word in his office. That makes me nervous. Danny is lovely, but he's still The Boss. I follow him into his office and watch as he sits down behind the desk.

'Shut the door'.

I do, and he gestures towards the chair. Once I've sat down his manager-face seems to melt away and he grins theatrically. 'So have you heard about Ben and Trix last night?'

This is tricky. I'm not quite sure if what Trix told me was in confidence, and he is her boss and I don't want her to get in more trouble. He takes my silence as evidence that I do know, and continues. 'It's OK. I already know.'

I hate this. I hate when people talk in half thoughts and riddles. Why can't they just say what they mean, and then I'd know, and I'd be able to answer the question. What if he doesn't mean the thing with the police anyway? What if there's something else and I don't know about it? And now I've been sitting in silence for far too long, and Danny probably thinks I'm either mute or stupid or both, so I nod, although I'm not sure what I'm agreeing too.

Danny is chuckling to himself now, big deep chuckles. 'It's typical of those two. They get under each other's skin and they just don't know when to stop.'

I nod again. That at least I can definitely agree with. Danny continues.

'And I've been thinking that maybe it's time that we, their friends, do something about it?'

This doesn't sound good. Trix definitely would not like us interfering in her life. 'Do what about it?'

He pauses. 'I'm not sure yet. Let me think about it.'

He grins, but somehow there's no joy in it. 'It'll be a nice distraction.'

I think I already know what he needs distracting from. I've heard Trix go on enough times about how bad John is for him. And even though I don't know him that well, you can't help but notice that Danny's good days and bad days seem to track John's moods. I decide that you don't get to be someone's friend without being a little bit brave, and so I ask him the question that's popped into my mind. 'How's John?'

The grin disappears, as absolutely as if someone had switched it off. 'Fine, you know. The same.'

Right. I don't really know what else to say, so I start to stand up, but he interrupts. 'How are you, anyway?'

'I'm OK.' It's the first time anyone's asked me that today. As soon as I start to think about how I am the big smile bubbles straight back to the surface. I am more than OK. I have my second date.

'You certainly look happy about something.'

I nod.

'Let me guess. Nice walk home last night?'

I nod again.

'Any more plans in that area?'

I nod again. 'He's taking me out tonight.'

'Fabulous.' He walks around the desk so he's perched on the front right by me. 'And what will you be wearing?'

Now this really is like a free rein to let the excitement run wild. 'I don't know. There are two main options, but I don't exactly know where he's taking me, so it's hard. I have a favourite *favourite* dress but I don't want to be overdressed, and so maybe jeans and a nice top.'

'The dress. Definitely the dress.'

'Are you sure?'

'Men like a woman in a beautiful dress. It's more feminine.'

'Really?'

He laughs. 'I have no idea. It's really not my area. I'm sure you will look fantastic in either though.'

He glances at his watch. 'You should probably get going. You don't want to rush the getting ready.'

I glance at my watch. It's quarter to five. I know that's not late, but on a Friday at work, it's the equivalent of about half past eight at night. I stand up properly. Danny puts his hand on my arm. 'Just one thing …'

I look at him.

'Make sure he takes good care of you, and if not, you send him to me.'

I giggle. It's weird him being all protective, but sort of nice, sort of like I thought Trix would be. 'I'm sure he'll be the perfect gentleman. Claudio would never do anything to hurt anyone.'

Danny doesn't reply. He gives a little nod and I feel the conversation is supposed to be over.

Chapter Nine

Claudio

'No.'

'Why not?'

'Because it's not my date.'

'You don't have dates.'

Ben doesn't seem amused. 'You're already chucking me out of my own home. I'm not cooking for you as well.'

This is a potential problem. Homemade is very much the vibe I'm aiming for tonight. And that means Dad's recipe tiramisu. Unfortunately the two times I've tried to make it I've ended up with sort of weird bitter tasting goo. Ben, on the other hand, has it down pat.

Tonight is my tried and tested first date. Now technically this is a second date, but I didn't use this one on her to start with, so it's fine to use it now. The plan goes like this. I pick Henrietta up at 7.30. She thinks we're going out for dinner, which in a sense we are, but I haven't told her where. Instead of taking her out though, I then whisk her back here. Ben has genuinely been chucked out for the evening, not to return this side of midnight. I make spaghetti carbonara – it has to be spaghetti; English girls just can't do the fork twirling, which makes them go all giggly and makes me look masterful and cosmopolitan. The carbonara is Delia's recipe, but I tell them it's my mum's, and I sound like a good dutiful boy which counteracts the slightly sleazy element in bringing them back to my place on a first date. In actual fact I don't think our mother has ever prepared any meal more advanced than cheesy beans on toast, but Henri doesn't know that.

The problem at the moment is with dessert, which Ben is refusing to make for me. At the moment he's leaning on the kitchen table waiting for the kettle to boil and staring out of the window. I decide to try appealing to his better nature.

'You'd be really helping me out.'

'No.'

Better nature isn't one of his more in-your-face qualities.

'It won't take long. I'll go buy all the stuff. You just have to make it.'

'No.'

I'm not getting anywhere here. And I'm not jeopardising this date because he's being a twat. I really do want Henri to have a good time tonight. I spent so much time e-mailing her while I was in Italy, it feels like we're already going out, but we're not so tonight has to be perfect. And by perfect, I mean that she has to still be here in the morning. Nothing less will do. With all this in mind, I have actually cleaned the flat. Hold on. That's an option.

'You could do it as payback for me cleaning up.'

'I never asked you to clean up.'

'But I did, and you're getting the benefit, so you could return the favour by making tiramisu.'

He looks at me, and for a moment I think he might cave. 'No.'

Ah well, was worth a try. Anyway I have proper cleaned up. Well, fairly proper. The living room, bathroom and my bedroom are absolutely pristine. I just have to make sure she doesn't have cause to go anywhere else. I've brought the plastic garden table inside, and put a tablecloth on it, and I've decorated the living room with fairy lights. It looks like some sort of magical grotto, if you squint and adopt a positive attitude. Henrietta is good at adopting a positive attitude.

Ben's kettle boils. He's grinning as he pours the water

into a mug. It's time to play my trump card. I give him one more chance.

'You know you're going to end up doing it.'

He shakes his head. 'Really, no.'

He picks his mug up and heads back towards his room. I do feel bad about this, just not bad enough to stop me doing it.

I raise my voice towards his retreating back. 'If you don't do it I'll tell The Parents you got arrested.'

He turns around. 'I did not get arrested. I accepted a fixed penalty notice, and it was all Trix's fault.'

I grin. 'Right. Not arrested, of course. I'm sure they'll totally understand the distinction.'

'You are a complete bastard.'

I'm laughing now. 'So you'll do it?'

'I didn't say that.'

'Fine. I'll call Mum, and then she'll be round here within the hour,' I pause. 'Actually, she'll probably be round Trix's first, because they get on so well, don't they? So that'll be fine. And then she'll come here.'

'All right.'

I might as well make the most of the win. 'Sorry, didn't quite catch that?'

'I'll make your sodding pudding.'

I clap him on the back. 'Thanks bro. You're a star.'

'But you're not allowed to use that one over me again.'

I shrug. I'm not promising.

He heads back into the kitchen. 'Off you go then. You said you'd buy the ingredients.'

'Yeah. Any chance you could lend me a tenner?'

Chapter Ten

Henrietta

I follow Danny's advice in the end and go for the dress. I mean last night being huddled up in my big coat and jumper was lovely, but Danny thought the dress and he seemed very sure about it. I put my make-up on and clean it off again about three times. I don't really wear make-up very often, and every time I put it on I feel like I look like a clown, a clown who's trying far too hard. So then I clean it all off again, and then I don't look like I've made any effort at all. In the end I settle for tinted moisturiser, mascara and lip gloss, in an attempt at the natural look. I think it might actually be the worst of both worlds, but then Claudio rings the doorbell, so it's too late to reconsider.

Claudio looks utterly beautiful. He's wearing a suit, which is so lovely. Most men wear jeans for everything, but he looks elegant and incredibly sexy. He is handsome, Claudio. I know I'm biased but I see how other women look at him too. He's tall and has olive skin and black hair and dark brown eyes. He really does look like my perfect romance novel hero.

And now I've just been standing looking at him for about two minutes, and I probably had my mouth open for most of that. Oh dear. I need to say something. 'Is what I'm wearing OK? I didn't know where we were going.'

He doesn't answer straight away. He sort of half coughs and half swallows before he says anything. 'It's perfect. You look perfect.'

I look perfect! I mean, obviously I know I don't look perfect really, but him saying it was kind. I run back inside and get my coat and handbag. He waits for me on the doorstep and we go out to his car. As we walk over to the car, his fingertips brush against my hand. I wish I was brave enough to just grab hold of it, or to just grab hold of him and kiss him right here, but I'm not sure if he'd like me being too forward, so I don't.

Chapter Eleven

Ben

Turfed out of my own flat, so that Claudio can get laid. Hardly fair, especially as I cooked half the bloody meal, but I'm passing it forward, as they say. Claudio tells me I can't eat in my own home; I tell Danny I'm eating at his. A problem shared, after all, is a problem two people have.

Danny's a better cook than me, and, therefore, about a million times better than Claudio, so it'll be a good change to be eating a meal that isn't toast. I knock on Danny's door. I hear voices inside and then footsteps in the hall.

Trix flings the door open.

'Don't you ever cook for yourself?' I get the opening jibe in first. Attack is the best form of defence, and all that.

She shrugs. 'Tried it once. It didn't work out.'

'No. I remember.'

She raises her eyebrows in a question.

'You tried to roast a frozen chicken.'

She grins. 'That wasn't actually the time I was thinking of.'

'The soufflés?'

'They were fine.'

'Only as paperweights.'

'Well, paperweights are always useful.'

'No. They're not. Where are paperweights useful?'

She pauses. 'If you're setting up an office.'

'A very windy office?'

'Yeah. If you're setting up an office on the deck of a ship.'

'A ship office?' I feel she's grasping slightly.

'Exactly.'

I'm still on the doorstep. 'Am I actually allowed to come in?'

'Did you bring wine?'

I hold up the bottle I brought with me.

'Only one? What are you drinking?'

She takes the bottle off me and heads down the hallway towards the kitchen. I follow her.

Danny is in the kitchen wearing a blue and white striped apron and a chef's hat. I don't question the hat. I've learnt, over time, that with Danny it's generally best not to ask too many questions about the outfits. It only leads to explanations, which usually start with something that happened to someone he met in a bar in 1997.

'No John?' I try to sound like I'm disappointed. I'm not sure I manage it.

Danny doesn't look at me. 'He'll be back for dinner.'

'Cool.' Now I'm trying to sound like I'm not disappointed. See - I've got this social skills lark down.

'What are you grinning at?' Trix is staring at me.

'I wasn't.'

'You were. You were smiling to yourself.'

So maybe the social skills aren't a hundred per cent yet. I'm working on it.

'He does that.' Danny's standing by the hob stirring a pan of very red looking sauce. 'If he's really engrossed his lips move.'

Trix laughs. 'I know. That means his brain's still operating.'

'I'm not going to be ganged up on.'

'I wouldn't bank on that.' Danny holds out a wooden spoon of the red sauce towards me. 'Taste.'

'Whoa!' I didn't realise red was actually a flavour.

'Too hot?'

'No. No.' I open a cupboard and find a glass to pour myself some wine. 'Just thought I'd get a drink anyway.'

My eyes are starting to water. 'What's in that?'

'Well it's chilli, so chilli mainly. It's not that bad.' He holds the spoon out to Trix. 'Your go.'

Trix takes a taste, and shrugs. 'It's fine.'

Danny grins. 'Told you. Lightweight.'

I shake my head at Danny. 'She has guts of steel. You can't trust her. She burnt her taste buds out years ago.'

Trix holds her glass out to me for a top-up. 'Well, if you can't take the heat ...'

'I don't mind a bit of heat. But that should have a licence from the International Atomic Energy Agency.'

'It's fine, Danny. He's just being a big girl.'

'Good. Good.' Danny looks at me. 'There's sour cream. You can just mix that in if you can't take it.'

'I can take it.'

Trix smiles. 'Sounds like a challenge.'

I resist the urge to square up to her. I suspect Danny would probably think it was amusing to call the old bill if we kicked off tonight.

'When are we eating?'

'When John gets back.'

'Ok.' I see Trix glance at the clock behind Danny. I wonder if she's thinking the same as me. *When John gets back* can lead to a very long wait.

Claudio has made the room look so pretty. It's all twinkly lights, and it smells of plug-in air freshener, which I think might be my favourite smell.

He takes my coat off me, like they do on dates in films, and he pours me a drink. It's a bigger glass of wine than I'm really used to. He tells me to make myself comfortable while he does kitchen things. I do try really hard to be comfortable. I can't be too comfortable though. If I don't sit up straight my tummy will stick out, and if I slouch I'll get a double chin. I decide sitting at the dining table would be better than the sofa, from a tummy-bulge point of view. The table looks lovely. There's a real tablecloth, and he's got chargers. I've got chargers at home. I think they're brilliant. They go under the plates, instead of a placemat. Mine are silver, and I've got white plates, so you get a little silver rim peeking out around the plate. Trix says that they're just big plastic plates, and she laughs at me when I tell her to get a proper plate and not eat off the charger. But that's right. When they came they had little stickers on the bottom that said 'Not for food,' so she shouldn't eat off them. She should keep them nice.

I can hear Claudio in the kitchen, moving around and banging pans. Does sitting at the dining table make it look like I'm waiting to be fed? I don't want him to feel like I'm impatient. Maybe I should have gone for the sofa after all, or just stood up. I stand up, but standing up doesn't look comfortable, does it? I should probably sit down. I try the arm of the settee but that's really awkward, so I stand up again.

I've never been beyond the stairwell to Ben's flat before. I've come with Danny and picked him up to go out before, but I've never been properly inside. It's a first floor flat, but it's got its own front door. Does that make it a maisonette, rather than a flat? Claudio and Ben both call it a flat. It's very different to my flat though. Everything's square and neat and fitting together. There aren't any nooks or crannies. It must be really easy to clean. There are shelves on one wall of the living room, three rows of books, and one each of DVDs and PlayStation games.

I look at the books; most of them have titles I don't understand. There's a laptop in a bag under the bottom shelf. And so far as personal items go, that's basically it. No ornaments, no postcards, no photographs. I wonder where all Claudio's stuff is.

I realise I'm now standing up inspecting his brother's possessions. If Claudio comes in now, he'll think I'm nosey and definitely not relaxed. I'm going to have to have another go at the sofa. It's leather and, by the looks of it, it saw its better days a long time ago. There is no way I'm going to be able to maintain a flattering level of tummy-pulled-in-ness sitting on that, and once I'm sitting on it, I'll probably need Claudio to pull me up to get out of it again. Not ladylike at all. I lower myself down and perch right on the very edge of the seat. Then I decide I should probably practise getting up and down, so that I can do it gracefully when Claudio comes back in. That means that when he does come back in I'm sort of half leaning backwards, trying to hold my wine aloft and level with one hand whilst pushing myself up from the armrest with the other hand. Not ladylike, not relaxed and definitely not comfortable.

I like it at Danny's house. There are always clean glasses, and you get real food without having to put grown-up clothes on and hand over money. It's brilliant here.

'So what happened last night?' Danny is pouring himself a drink and looking from me to Ben and back again.

'What do you mean?' I know what he means.

'You know what I mean.' Well, yes.

'I don't.' Ben is either severely short on memory or has picked denial as his getting nearly-arrested coping strategy.

Danny rolls his eyes. 'Your run-in with the fuzz.'

'I already told you about it.'

'Only the headlines. Come on. I need details. Let me enjoy the vicarious glow of dining with wanted criminals.'

'We're not wanted criminals.' Sometimes it's important to nip Danny's more expansive flights of fantasy in the bud.

'Speak for yourself. I am wanted across the globe for my daring criminal exploits.' Ben does a weird little karate chop hand gesture, apparently designed to demonstrate his awesome fighting prowess.

Danny stares at him. 'What on earth are you doing?'

Ben stops. 'It was cooler in my head.'

He shouldn't be joking about this anyway. I turn to Danny. 'The whole thing was his fault.'

'Excellent. This is exactly what I'm looking for. Gossip, blame and recriminations.'

Danny sits on a stool opposite me, and reaches his hand across to mine. He arranges his face into an expression of faux concern. 'It must have been very distressing. Now tell me all about it.'

'Well, I was quietly and innocently eating my kebab, when this madman ...' I gesture towards Ben, '... accosts me and starts shouting about slime mould.'

'Slime mould?' Danny sounds genuinely horrified.

Ben looks put out. 'It's interesting.'

I ignore him. 'Slime mould. I was simply trying to enjoy a late supper ...'

'You were inhaling a kebab.'

'... when I was yelled at, for absolutely no reason ...'

'There was a reason.'

This time I can't ignore him. 'What reason?'

Ben pauses. 'I don't remember, but ...'

'But?'

'But it was a really good reason.'

This is the moment again. The moment where it can go either way, and we'll either end up laughing or yelling. I'm not going to rise to the bait. I'm not. I'm not going to say anything.

Danny stands up and stirs the sauce on the hob. He glances at the clock. 'This is nearly ready.'

'What time were you expecting John?'

Danny shrugs. 'Said he'd be back for dinner.'

I don't know what to say. If Danny sounded angry I could work with that. I'm good with anger. Even if he were properly upset that would be something to talk about. But he sounds resigned. Not fine. He doesn't sound like he doesn't mind. He sounds like he really does mind, but doesn't have the energy to do anything about it.

Ben taps his fingers on the table.

I don't know what to say. 'We can wait.'

Ben nods. 'Sure. He'll probably be here soon.'

''Course he will.' Danny smiles, and turns back towards us. 'So what happened when the boys in blue turned up?'

'One boy and one girl.'

Danny shakes his head. 'I feel sorry for women police. Those uniforms are so unflattering.'

'I know. Have you seen the sort of weird tool belt thing they make them wear now?'

Danny nods. 'Horrendous.'

'I have no idea what you are talking about.' Ben is looking at us like we're speaking a foreign language.

'The belt? With all the stuff on it. Makes them look like they've got about a sixty inch waist?'

Ben looks at me. 'I know they were definitely both wearing clothes.'

'Great. What if we'd been victims of crime? What if you were having to describe your attacker?'

He grins. 'I'd definitely know whether they were naked.'

'Great.'

'Well that's useful, isn't it? They'd want to know if I'd been attacked by a naked person. That would probably be important. A naked man wandering down The Shambles. They'd be dead easy to find.'

I decide not to encourage this line of thought. 'Anyway, despite the whole incident being his fault, I still got a fine notice thingy.'

'How much?'

'Eighty quid.'

'And you're a convicted felon? Marked as a wrong 'un for all eternity?'

Ben laughs. I don't see why it's funny. 'It's not a conviction. It's not even an admission of guilt. It's just their way of going, we ought to do something, but we can't be arsed to go the whole hog.'

'It was humiliating.'

'It was hysterical.'

'They weren't even proper police.'

Danny looks at us. Ben explains. 'Community Support Officers.'

Danny shakes his head. 'This is very disappointing. I send you two out into the world, and you can't even manage to get nicked properly.'

Ben hangs his head. 'We're very sorry. We'll try harder next time.'

Danny pats him on the shoulder. 'That's my boy.'

'I still don't see why it's funny.'

'Oh come on. You get into an argument about ...' He pauses and looks at Ben.

'Cellular slime mould.'

'Right. You get into an argument about mould so heated that the police are called. That's funny.'

'When they first came, I think they thought Ben was some sort of abusive ex or something.'

'What?'

'She asked me all this stuff about whether you were hassling me.'

'Well, thank you for not throwing me to the wolves.' Ben actually sounds sincere.

'Don't think I wasn't tempted.'

Danny laughs. 'Eighty quid for a row about slime mould.'

Ben grins. 'Eighty each. A hundred and sixty all told.'

I can feel a giggle rising up. 'It's not funny.'

I let out a snort of laughter between the words 'not' and 'funny' which may undermine the sentiment.

Danny has started stirring the sauce again. It's quarter past nine. I think he was intending to serve food about an hour ago.

'Do you think we should maybe eat without him?' I ask.

Danny looks at me, but doesn't respond.

'We can put some to one side for John.'

Danny smiles, without it quite making it to his eyes. 'Of course we will. He can catch up when he gets back.'

Danny gets some plates out from the back of the cupboard and puts one down in front of me. It has a picture of Winnie-the-Pooh on it and a big chip in the corner.

'Nice plate.'

'Joke present from someone, I think.'

Ben holds up his plate, which has holly leaves all around the rim. 'Well that explains owning it. What's the excuse for using them?'

Danny shrugs. 'Your fault. If you had plates that weren't salvaged from a skip at your place, then little brother wouldn't have had to nick all my good stuff for his hot date, would he?'

'He didn't?'

Danny nods.

'What's wrong with my plates?'

Now that's one I can answer. 'Nothing at all, if you're studying the development and fossilisation of bacteria.'

'That's not fair. I wash up.'

'When?'

'When I run out of plates.'

'Exactly. I think Henrietta may have higher plate standards than your flat can really fulfil.'

'Well, I can't be blamed if Claudio wants to create some unrealistic romantic deception ...'

'Deception?'

'Deception. How's she going to feel when she finds out those aren't even his plates? Not his plates, she'll think, what else is he hiding?'

'That's ridiculous.'

'Romance is ridiculous.'

'And I'm going to stop you there.' Danny jumps in before I can respond, and starts to pile chilli on to the offending cartoon plates. Ben tops up everyone's glasses. We start to tuck in. Every now and then I take a glimpse at Ben and am very happy to see his face getting redder and his eyes start to glisten with the strength of the chilli.

Main course is spaghetti carbonara, which Claudio says is his mum's recipe. He brings it out in a big pasta bowl, and then dishes some into a smaller bowl for me. Then he dishes some more on top and grates a mountain of Parmesan over it, before he sits down and serves his own. It's one of the biggest portions of food I've ever seen. I have to eat it all, because he cooked it, but I don't want to look like horrible pig.

'You don't have to eat all that.'

'What?'

'I gave you quite a lot, didn't I? Don't worry. You don't have to eat it all if you don't want to.'

I feel like he can read my mind. I don't think I've ever felt like someone else was so in tune with me and what I'm thinking. I pick up my spoon and fork, and start to curl the spaghetti around my fork, trying to copy the way that Claudio holds the end of his fork against the spoon. I can feel him watching me.

'You're really good at that.'

'You sound like you're disappointed?'

'No.' He's still looking at me. 'Is it OK?'

I nod. He's still watching me. I can feel my cheeks getting pink.

'Good. You're very cute when you eat.'

I'm not. I'm all clumsy and uncoordinated. 'Thank you.'

I need to think of something to say to distract him from me eating. I can't think of anything clever. 'Did Ben tell you about last night?'

He nods. 'I can't believe those two. They need to get it on, and get over it.'

That makes me giggle. 'I'm not sure Trix wants to get it on with Ben.'

'Oh come on.' Claudio shakes his head. 'They're insane about each other.'

'Are you sure?'

'Absolutely. You don't spend that much time arguing with someone you hate.'

'But you wouldn't fight that much with someone you like.'

Claudio laughs.

'Don't laugh at me!' I know I don't understand things. I can feel myself going red again.

'Sorry. I'm not laughing at you. You're right.' He smiles. 'We shouldn't fight, because of them.'

I can feel my bottom lip starting to shake.

'Hey! Don't be sad. This isn't going well if I've made you sad.'

I shake my head. 'Not sad.'

He gets up from his chair and walks round the table and kneels alongside me, like someone about to propose. Obviously, he's not about to propose. You'd have to be mad to propose on a second date. 'So you're not sad?'

I shake my head again.

'That's a shame.'

'Why?'

He reaches out and takes hold of my hand. There are tingles running all the way up my arm. I can feel myself starting to smile, without my brain ever knowingly telling my muscles what to do. 'Well, if you were sad I'd have to find a way to make you happy.'

Oh.

'But you're not sad so I'll just go back over there then.' He nods his head towards the other side of the table. He starts to stand up.

'I might be a bit sad.'

He kneels back down. 'Really?'

I nod.

He lets go of my hand and touches my cheek, turning my face towards him. Time seems to slow down as he leans towards me. The closer he gets the faster I can feel myself breathing. Just as his lips are about to touch mine, I close my eyes, and then I feel his mouth over mine. His lips are so soft and so warm, and he's firm but gentle, and I feel like I'm melting away, and just for a second I'm not thinking about anything at all. Just for a second I'm not worried about being too fat, or too clumsy, or too stupid. I'm just quiet and still and living completely in this one moment. And then he slowly pulls away.

'Happier now?'

I nod.

He smiles his beautiful, sexy smile. 'Good.'

He glances down at the floor for a second. 'We should eat. It'll get cold, and the pasta will go all claggy.'

I pull my brain out of the kiss enough to make words. 'That sounds nasty.'

'It is. Very bad news indeed.'

'Claggy being the technical Italian term?'

'Nope. Claggy being the technical Yorkshire term. Still true though.'

He kisses me quickly on the forehead and lifts himself off the floor and back into his seat.

Kiss. Check.

This is going all right. She's eating the food, although she did look a bit horrified when I put it in front of her. Mental note - she's a tiny little English waif, not an Italian Mama. Adjust portion sizes accordingly.

And the kiss. The kiss was good. There's no mistaking that we're on the same page now. I didn't want to stop, but there's a plan for the evening, and I'm sticking to it. Tiramisu before anything else. Ben'll be well pissed off if he finds out he spent all afternoon making it, and we never even ate it.

Right. Time to roll out another conversation topic. 'So how are things at work?'

'Ok. We had a good start to the art competition when Ben came. Now I just have to try to get people to enter.'

'So what do they actually have to do?'

'A piece of art based on, or inspired by, the concept of Zero. To be judged in three age categories, by celebrity mathematician Dr Ben Messina.' She recites it, like a kid reading off a card.

'Celebrity mathematician?'

'Trix made me put that.' Her brow furrows like it always does when she's anxious. 'I don't think Ben was very happy about it.'

'He'll get over it. Can you even be a celebrity mathematician?'

'Well there's the book about the French guy with the theorem in the margin.'

'Fermat?' How do I even know that? I really need to stop living with my brother.

She nods. 'And then there's ...'

'Yes?'

'Well, there's a thing on Channel 5 with this FBI agent and his brother's a genius mathematician or something. And they solve crime together.'

'Without seeing it, I'm going to guess they're actors?'

She nods. 'Maybe.'

'So, Ben is the second best known mathematician out of a group of two, one of whom is a dead Frenchman.'

She giggles. 'I think so.'

'It doesn't look like the paparazzi are going to be hanging round outside the flat anytime soon.'

'What about you?'

'What?'

'What about your work?'

'Well, I'm not working at the moment.' Which I'm not going to pretend I couldn't get used to, especially as Ben isn't working much right now either, but still has enough cash to order takeaway and go to the pub. We've adapted quite well to a toast, takeaway and beer based lifestyle.

'I know but what next? You said you might go back to college, or are you going to work over here or …?'

She tails off. This probably means it's my turn to talk. I don't.

'Sorry. It's none of my business, is it? Sorry.'

'No. No. It's fine. I just haven't really … there are a few different …' I'm not explaining this well. 'Dessert.'

'What?'

'We should have dessert.'

She looks lost. 'Ok.'

'Wait there.' I try a smile before I grab the pasta bowls and head back into the kitchen. I need a minute. What am I planning to do? Well, I'm not totally sure. That's not true. I am totally sure. I'm going back to Naples. I've been offered a permanent job in Italy, and I love Naples, and I love the Amalfi Coast, and I did think about trying to get in as a mature student to do Geology at university, but if I did that it would be years of undergraduate study and then, if I was lucky, I might get on to a postgrad programme, that included vulcanology and I might possibly, if I was unbelievably lucky, get a research job that involved fieldwork out on a volcano. Doing tours I can be enjoying the Italian sun, earning decent money, and living in the shadow of the only active volcano on mainland Europe.

So why am I freaking out about telling this girl that? It's only a second date, really a first date if you think about it. We're not talking happy ever after. We're dealing with what happens between us tonight, or maybe for the next few weeks. After that isn't even on the agenda yet. So I'll just tell her I'm probably going back to Naples. No big deal.

I get the tiramisu out of the fridge, and head back into the living room. I put my smile back on.

'I hope you like tiramisu.'

She nods.

'Excellent.' I put one bowl down in front of her and sit down myself. 'Sorry about before ...'

'No. It's none of my business.'

'It's fine. It's just that ...'

She looks up at me. Her eyes are massive, probably the biggest eyes I've ever seen. She looks like a Disney character. She thinks I'm staying in Yorkshire. She thinks I've re-applied to Leeds to do Geology, and I did look at the website and I looked at the student finance website too. I did think about it.

'I don't think going to university is really for me.'

'So you're going to get a job then?'

'Yeah.'

'Cool.'

Well, it's true. I haven't lied. She didn't ask me where the job was, so it's all fine.

'Is the tiramisu good?'

She hasn't actually started it. She takes a quick spoonful and nods with her mouth full.

'Good. Do you want to hear a confession?'

'Ok.' She sounds uncertain.

'Ben made it.'

'He did a good job.'

'I know it's really easy, but mine always comes out as a big soggy mess.' It feels good to be telling her the truth, like lightening a weight.

'It's nice.'

We eat in silence for a few minutes. The stereo is playing Aretha Franklin in the background. *I Say a Little Prayer* comes on.

'Do you want to dance?'

She looks a bit surprised. 'Here?'

'Where else?'

'Ok.'

I stand up and take her hand. She stands up in front of me and for a second we just stand there, only touching with our fingers, before I snake my arm around her waist and lift her hand so it's resting against my chest. I start to move with the music. I love this anticipation. It's like going fishing and getting that very first bite. Only better. Much, much better. I pull her closer into my body, and then realise that, because I'm so much taller than her, I can't kiss her without stepping back. I can't step back straight away, cos I've only just pulled her close, so I keep dancing pressed against her for the rest of the song.

When the song ends I move so I can bend down to kiss her. I have to remind myself to keep it gentle, romantic. I've put a lot of energy into creating the right atmosphere tonight. We stand there kissing for a long time, until I put both my arms around her waist and lift her up, so her feet are off the ground and I'm holding her against me in my arms. She wraps both arms around my neck, and I can feel her fingers in my hair. Then I start to move very slowly towards the bedroom. Just before the door I pause, and pull my face away from hers.

'Is this OK?'

She nods.

I push the bedroom door open with my foot, and kick it closed behind us.

The bedroom door slams and the brakes are released. All at once I'm pulling at his shirt and he's dragging my skirt up and sliding his hand across my bum. I feel his hand slide under the elastic of my knickers and I'm glad I didn't wear my big tummy squashing pants in the end. I drag his jacket off, and he pulls his hand back to help me with his shirt buttons. His torso is amazing, tanned and muscular. I brush my lips over his chest and hear him groan before he pulls me back to my feet and presses his mouth against mine. One arm wraps tightly around my waist and the other is back on my behind, pulling my skirt out of the way and dragging at my knickers. I push them down my thighs and let them drop to the floor before reaching for his belt. I fumble with it, struggling to make my hands work with the distraction of his searching fingers reaching between my thighs. His erection is hard under the fabric, and I'm hungry to get his belt and fly undone, but he won't release me from the kiss. I'm not behaving like me. I like lights out, and foreplay and gentle, quiet men who take their time. But tonight I don't care about any of that. I'm inside this moment, frantic for more.

I push his trousers and boxers down. Straight away he wraps both arms around my waist and pulls me off my feet. Instinctively my legs wrap around him. I can feel him hard, already on the edge of being inside me. He carries me a couple of paces until I'm leant against the wall. Suddenly he pauses. He pulls back from the kiss and moves his lips against my ear. 'One second.'

I unhook my legs and he lowers me to the ground. He kicks his trousers and boxers from his ankles and steps to the chest of drawers. He grabs a condom from the top drawer, and hurriedly puts it on. I can hear myself breathing. Within seconds he's pressed against me again, lifting me off my feet, pinning my back against the wall. He enters me in one thrust and I gasp as he fills me, bending my head into his shoulder and breathing hard against his body. He angles me so I can rest one foot on a chair next to the wall and thrusts hard and fast into me. I feel every inch of him entering me and I let the waves of pleasure take over. I don't think or try to do or be anything. I just let him make me come. As I moan into his chest I feel his body tighten and then relax into one final thrust.

He holds me there for a second before pulling his head back to kiss my lips. For the first time I notice the sweat, wet on his chest, moistening the shirt that's still hanging undone from his shoulders. He pulls out of me, lowering me back to the floor. As he steps backwards my dress falls back over my hips.

After he's dealt with the condom he takes my hand and walks me over towards the bed. He stands in front of me and pulls his shirt off, so he's naked.

'Arms up.'

I let him pull my dress over my head, before he slides his arms around my back to undo my bra. Then he pulls me towards him so our naked bodies are pressed together, warm and sticky and familiar.

'You make some good noises.'

'I do not.' I'm mortified. I had my head buried against his shoulder the whole time.

'You do.' He pulls his head back and grins at me. 'Good noises.'

I shake my head. 'You're making it up.'

'Definitely not. I'll prove it.'

'How?'

The grin extends. 'By making you make them again.'

Chapter Twelve

Henrietta

Now it's twenty past seven on Saturday morning and I'm here in Claudio's bed in Claudio's bedroom in Claudio's flat. Actually I think it's probably Ben's flat, but I'm here. I'm actually here. I'm watching Claudio sleep. I can't stop myself so I lean over and kiss him very gently on the lips. He doesn't wake up, which is OK because it means I can just lie in bed looking at him, until I feel my eyes closing again.

The next time I look at the clock it's ten to ten and I'm on my own in the bed. I can hear Claudio and Ben in the kitchen. Ben's here. Of course. At some point I'm going to have to get out of Claudio's room and that is going to involve doing the walk of shame through the flat. Even worse, if I was really as noisy as Claudio said last night, Ben will have heard. Ben will have heard my sex noises.

I put my head under the duvet and try to imagine myself not there. Maybe if I stay here, quiet and still, I can just stay here forever. Maybe they'll forget that I'm here. My face starts to get all hot and sweaty, so I'm forced to come out again.

I'm definitely not ready to face going out there and seeing Ben so I take a look around the room. Claudio lived here before he went to Italy as well. He moved in when he came to York to go to college, so that's four years ago, but I've only known him for two. I met him about a year before he went to Italy. I remember thinking he was beautiful, properly artistically beautiful, like a renaissance sculpture. And I remember thinking he'd never notice me, because I'm not someone that beautiful people notice.

It's definitely a boy's room, but it has a kind of vaguely unloved feel to it. I guess that's because he's only been back here a couple of weeks. I mean, it's tidy enough, but there's stuff in boxes on top of the wardrobe and other stuff piled up in a corner. It feels more like Ben's spare room than Claudio's bedroom.

If I'm going to be coming around here more, it'll need some attention I think. Without meaning to I find I'm planning how I'd rearrange things. If you turned the bed around so it was on that wall it would get the morning light, and then you could put a mirror over by the door.

I'm still planning when Claudio comes back in, clutching two mugs. I scramble back under the duvet. Now he must think I'm a proper nutter. I was standing starkers in the middle of his room staring at the wall. I'm not even going to let myself think about the fact that he got a full frontal look at my body in daylight. I pull the duvet right up to my neck, while Claudio puts the mugs down on the table next to the bed. 'Hot chocolate, with marshmallows.'

'Thank you.'

I sit up and hold the duvet up over my chest with one hand, trying to pick up the mug, without exposing myself, with the other. 'I should probably go.'

Claudio sits on the bed opposite me. 'You can't.'

I giggle. 'You're going to keep me here?'

He shakes his head. 'No choice. You're not going to make it home in the shoes you had on last night.'

'Why not?'

He laughs. 'Look out the window sleepy girl.'

What's he talking about? Looking out of the window is going to involve me getting out of bed again, and now in the daytime, with him all relaxed and larger than life and, most importantly, fully clothed, I don't really want to walk naked across the room and give him a proper look at all my ugly bits. He stays sitting on the bed waiting for me to go and look out of the window. I put my mug down and tug the edge of the duvet out from under Claudio. I sit up, holding the duvet over my chest. Very carefully, I stand up, pulling the duvet off the bed and wrapping it around me as tightly as I can manage before I pad over to the window to peek around the curtain. It's beautiful. There's no one around outside and the street is covered in a layer of white.

'It's snowing.'

He comes up and stands behind me. 'And I can't let you walk home in the snow, so you'll just have to stay here.'

'Are you sure you don't mind?' I don't want to be in his way.

'Actually, I ordered the snow, so you'd have to stay. It was all part of the grand plan.'

I turn around and let him slide one arm inside my duvet wrapping. 'I've only got that dress with me. I can't even get dressed.'

He rolls his eyes. 'You have no idea how tempting that thought is.' He swallows. 'But we will have to find you something to wear.'

'We will?'

'It's a Snow Day. We have to go out and play. Wait there.'

Claudio disappears for a minute and comes back with a big man's coat and some Wellingtons. Combined with my dress and hold-ups from last night, a jumper from his wardrobe and about 4 pairs of socks, he eventually decides that I will do well enough. Dressed to Claudio's satisfaction I am dragged out through the house. Ben is still in the kitchen. He glances up when we come in. 'Good night?'

I can feel myself blushing and I nod mutely.

'What are you planning to do today?'

Claudio points out of the window. 'Snow Day!'

That's the second time he's said that. I look at them. 'Is a Snow Day something I should know about?'

Ben grins. 'When we were kids Mum and Dad would always let us off school if it snowed properly. It's a tradition. You're not allowed to achieve anything useful on Snow Days.'

Claudio nods. 'We are going to make a snowman.'

'I've never made a snowman.'

Both brothers look at me in absolute horror. Ben speaks first. 'How can you never have made a snowman?'

I try to shrug, but I can feel my cheeks getting flushed.

Claudio looks at me. 'She's a southern softie. That's why.'

Ben shakes his head. 'She's from Stamford Bridge.'

'Well, that's south from here.'

'No. It's not. It's sort of east. North-east really.'

They seem to be enjoying the argument, and it's stopped them looking aghast at me, so I don't interfere. Ben's right though. I'm not southern; I just didn't really play out much after Mum died.

I turn to Ben. 'You'll have to help then. It sounds like you're both experts.'

He shakes his head. 'I don't think you really want me hanging around.'

Claudio thwacks him on the back of the head. ''Course we do. It's a Snow Day. The more the merrier.'

And so all three of us end up standing in the communal garden behind Ben's flat rolling the snow up into a huge body-sized ball. It seems to take forever to build the snowman to Ben's satisfaction, mainly because Claudio seems more interested in putting snow down my neck than in building anything sensible. By the end of the morning I've learnt two things. The first is the ideal proportions of the ideal snowman, and the second is never to try to build one with a mathematician. It involves an awful lot more discussion and planning than actual building.

When we're finished Ben goes inside to make toast and more hot chocolate. Claudio wraps himself all around me again and plants a kiss on the side of my face.

'You're freezing.'

I nod, but I don't suggest going back inside, because I don't want the day to end. 'Ben's nice.'

Claudio presses his cold nose against my head. 'Should I be jealous?'

'I just mean, he's sweet. I was a bit scared of him before today.'

Now Claudio laughs. 'He's fine. Well, he's fine when he's not around Trix.'

I wonder about telling him about my conversation with Danny yesterday, but it seems a long time ago now. We stand in the garden admiring the snowman and resting our bodies against each other. Eventually Claudio pulls away. 'We should go in.'

The snow is starting to thaw off the roof of the building. I can hear it dripping from the corners of the dormer windows in the roof. It's probably nearly clear on the pavement by now. There's really no excuse for me to still be here, but, 'I don't want the date to be over.'

Claudio puts his arms back around me. 'Neither do I.'

Oh my God. I said I didn't want the date to be over out loud, didn't I? I can feel myself blushing bright pink again despite the cold. I always do this. Anytime anything is going well I manage to say something stupid and end up sounding needy or desperate or just wrong. I can't believe I did it again.

'So don't go.'

'What?'

Claudio turns me around to face him. 'Don't go. Stay here.'

I shrug. I need to sound nonchalant; I need to make up

for sounding needy a minute ago. 'I could stay a bit longer, but I need clean clothes, and I've got some work to do tomorrow, and ...'

'Stay.'

'I could probably stay tonight.'

'Just stay. I'll take you to get some clothes, but then stay.'

What's he saying?

'Stay forever.'

He's being silly, but he looks completely serious. I look at him. I've never heard a boy say the 'forever' word before, and you can't say it to them. It makes you sound desperate. Everyone knows that. Somehow it doesn't sound desperate at all when Claudio says it. He cannot mean what I think he means.

'Come and live here.'

I open my mouth, but I can't reply. I don't have the right words for this moment.

'No. Forget that,' he takes the deepest breath I've ever seen. 'Don't just live here. Marry me.'

'What?'

He's smiling right across his face and into his eyes. 'Henrietta, will you marry me?'

Henrietta is staring up at me with her little mouth wide open, but she's not saying a word. I replay the last few seconds in my head. What have I done? Did I just propose? I think I did. I did. I really did. So who can really blame her for the shocked goldfish impression? Inside my mind there's a tiny Claudio staring open-mouthed at me too. I realise my lips are still moving. 'I mean it. I love you. You love me. Let's get married. Say yes. Hen, come on. Say yes.'

'Yes.'

And that's that. A few minutes ago I was putting snow down her neck like an eleven-year-old with a crush on a girl in the playground, and now I have a fiancée, and I'm just a few more moments away from being a married man with a house and child-seats and trousers that I only wear for gardening. And it changed just like that, in a single moment, and I should be terrified. Right now, I know, that the muscles in my chest should be constricting and I should be feeling dizzy and there should be terror running through me, but there isn't. I'm not scared. I'm happy. Actually, it's stranger than that, I'm calm. I feel as though the world has jumped a frame around us, and me and Henri are standing perfectly peaceful and still while everything just rearranges around us.

I look at her. 'OK, then.'

And then I lean down and I notice that she's standing up on tip-toes to kiss me, and that might be the sweetest thing I've ever seen in my life.

'Are you two coming in or not?'

Trust Ben to wade into the moment. I wave my arm at him. 'In a minute.'

I grin at Henri. 'Shall we go in Mrs Messina?'

She laughs. 'Shall we tell him?'

I pause for a moment. I'm not that keen on telling Ben first. Might be better to ease in with someone who has a grasp of when they're supposed to smile in a conversation. We will have to tell him sooner or later though. He's gonna notice if I get married.

'We'll tell them all.' I say.

She nods. 'When?'

'Tonight. We'll go out. We'll get Ben and Trix, and Danny, if he can come, and your dad?'

'OK.'

Somehow the thought of telling them all in one go seems easier. The rest of them will give Ben a good strong hint that it's supposed to be good news.

'What about your mum and dad?'

Mum and Dad? Yeah. I guess we'll have to tell them as well. They could come. They already know Danny. OK, so Dad treats him like a visiting alien, but they'll be civil. Not sure whether they've seen Trix this decade though, which might be interesting, and they've never met Hen's dad. To be fair, I hadn't met him before this week.

'Maybe we'll go see them and tell them another day.'

'Tomorrow?'

I see no good reason why not, so I nod. I'm sensing that being engaged might involve a lot of nodding.

The rest of the afternoon is a bit of a blur. Ben just sort of grunts when I tell him we're going out for dinner. He doesn't object though, so I assume I can count him in. Danny is bringing John, who wasn't in my mental picture, but it'll put another body between Ben and Trix, so I'll take it.

It feels like ages after the proposal in the garden when I find Henri perched on the edge of my bed with a notebook and pencil in her hand.

'What you doing?'

She slams the notebook shut hard. 'Nothing.'

She looks like a little girl who's been caught taking sweeties.

'What were you writing?'

She shakes her head. 'Nothing.'

Unfortunately for her, she's tiny and a terrible liar. I lean over her and pick the notebook up from behind her back, and flick it open. She's planning the wedding. Already. There are notes about cakes, and dresses, and guest lists. But I'm still not scared. I think it's sweet, and I do really want to give her all this stuff she's written down.

I glance at her, and she starts talking straight away. 'I mean, I was just thinking about it, you know. It's not a big deal. We don't have to get married for ages, if you don't want. There's no hurry or anything ...'

'You don't think our wedding is a big deal?' I'm not really cross. Anyone can see that it's the hugest deal possible to her, but she's even more wonderful when she's all flustered.

'I didn't mean that. I just meant, that ...'

I take pity on her. 'I don't want to wait to get married.'

'Really?'

'Really. I want all this stuff.' I wave the notebook at her. 'Whatever you want, I want.'

She smiles the most perfect smile, and the dimple in her cheek appears. And now I don't have to stop myself. I can touch it whenever I want, and me and Henri can stay right here together. Well, possibly not right here. Actually, the 'right here' part could be a problem. Ah.

Chapter Thirteen

Ben

I've spent most of the day with these two lovebirds. To be honest, I'm not overjoyed about spending the evening with them as well. It'll be another night without cooking though, so I tag along. Trix, Danny, John and Tony are already at the restaurant, sitting around one half of a round table laid out for seven. The first clue that something more than just standard nauseating coupliness is happening is when Claudio orders champagne.

'I hope you're paying for that.'

Claudio baulks slightly. 'Of course.'

Of course. He's not paying rent; he's using my utilities and eating my food, but he can afford champagne. The waiter pours glasses for everyone, and then Claudio stands up.

'Ok. Right. Everyone ... well.'

Get to the point.

'OK, so the thing is, I, sorry, we ...' he takes hold of Henrietta's hand. 'We have a bit of an announcement.'

'She's up the duff?' Danny's suggestion is met with a bit of a funny look from Henri's dad who's sitting next to him.

'No. Claudio's up the duff?' Trix doesn't let it discourage her from having a go too.

Claudio taps his knife against his glass to restore order. 'No one's up the duff. We are, though, engaged.'

There's a silence. Everyone's mouths are open, but no one manages to say anything. I'm faced with an unexpected opportunity to demonstrate my social skills. I try to think what a normal person would say in this situation.

'Congratulations!'

As soon as I've spoken there's a murmur of similar sentiments, and people start pushing their chairs out to come and congratulate Claudio and Henri. I feel vaguely satisfied; this must be what it's like to say the right thing. I lean back in my chair and watch everyone else for a moment.

Tony is first to step up to the plate. He squeezes out past Trix to shake Claudio by the hand.

'She'll make a great little wife, this one.'

Did he just say 'little wife'? Why is Trix not yelling at him? She's standing right there. If I'd said that she'd have taken her dessert fork to my testicles by now.

'She looked after me and she looked after the house after her mum had gone. She always kept everything lovely.'

Tony moves on to hug his daughter. I do feel quite aggrieved that Trix isn't yelling at him. There really is no justice in the world.

Trix and Danny are queuing up to give their congratulations now. Trix is kissing everything that moves, and Danny is vigorously shaking hands and hugging people, including some people who aren't at our table. I think that means the 'congratulating' part of the evening has gone on long enough. I pick up my menu. The lamb sounds nice, or maybe the mackerel. It says whole mackerel. That might be bony. I wonder if we're having starters. No one else has sat down yet. Actually John is sitting down, but he never stood up, so that doesn't count. Claudio and Henri are still in a hug, congratulations, handshake cycle with Tony, Trix and Danny. I'm hungry. I think I probably have to wait for them before I order.

My little brother's getting married, and I'm happy for him. I am. I'm really happy. I think it's too soon. I think he's crazy to change his life because of an infatuation. It's like Harriet Brooks. Harriet Brooks was amazing. So far as radiation research went at the start of the twentieth century, it was basically all about Harriet Brooks and Marie Curie. Harriet Brooks did some incredible early research into radioactivity and thorium; she identified that thorium gives off radioactive emissions in the form of a gas which ... sorry. Anyway, she got married and gave up her research just because that's what married women did back then. Marie Curie married Pierre Curie, who was a scientist too, and kept going. Marie Curie won the Nobel Prize, twice, and no one's ever heard of Harriet Brooks. Well, you hadn't, had you? See. Getting married's OK, if you absolutely must, but you've got to find a way of making sure it doesn't interfere with the rest of your day.

I realise that Claudio's released himself from the hug-a-thon, and he's leaning towards me. 'Ben?'

I've already said Congratulations. Am I not off the hook now? I make an attempt to rearrange my face, and remind myself that this is Good News. 'Congratulations mate.'

'Really?'

Am I such a misery that my little brother can't believe that I'm happy for him? I shake his hand across the table. 'Really.'

'There's something else.'

I bet she is up the duff. That would explain the haste. He's done it this time, hasn't he? Although, that makes no sense. He was in Italy until three weeks ago, and I'm sure they didn't do anything at the party, so she can't be. Well, I guess she could be, but it'd be too soon to know, wouldn't it? How soon can women tell? I actually have no idea. I know they have a scan at twelve weeks, but they must already know by then, or else they'd have to scan all the women every twelve weeks, just in case. I guess it's when they miss a, you know, a menstrual, thing. But how late would it have to be? Days? Weeks? Not hours, surely? Interesting. I will have to look into it at some point.

'Well, will you?'

Claudio is looking expectant, and all eyes are on me. I think I did it again.

Trix snorts. 'You must have a fairly poor group of friends if Ben can be considered the best man.'

Thank you, Trix. Sometimes I almost wonder if she does that to help me out. Best man? I'd have to make a speech. It probably can't be a speech about maths. Maybe I could explain about Harriet Brooks and thorium emissions though. Claudio is still looking at me.

'Of course. Best man. Very excited.'

I stand up to shake his hand properly. He traps me in a bear hug, complete with cheek kissing. I really don't understand how he got all the Italian genes. I was fine with the handshaking.

At least the hugging puts us close enough to talk without everyone else listening in. 'This is a bit quick.'

He glances at me. 'I should have known you wouldn't approve.'

'No. It's just sudden.' As I say, I'm not great with the touchy-feely. 'I'm happy if you're happy.'

'Of course I'm happy.' He's absolutely emphatic. He hugs me again. 'It's gonna be great, mate.'

Danny has managed to find his way back to his own chair, and claps his hands. 'Food!'

Claudio nods. 'Yes. Yes. Order whatever you want. It's all on us.'

'No. No. It's your night. I'll get this.' Tony waves his hands.

'Not at all.' Danny interrupts. 'You'll have enough expense with the wedding.'

The three of them continue to try to out alpha male each other. I should join in, but it's probably my money that

Claudio's planning to pay with, and if last night's sleeping arrangements are anything to go by, I could end up playing unpaid landlord to Henrietta too. Financially, I've done my bit.

I order Brie and lamb. I decide the mackerel sounds high risk. Looking around the table, Claudio, Tony, Trix and Danny are engaged in a four-way conversation, which I'm just too far away to easily join in with. I'm between Henrietta and John. I decide Henrietta is the easier option. At least in a conversation you can generally just set her going, and then you don't need to do too much more work.

'So, was the talk on Zero OK for what you wanted?'

She nods, enthusiastically. She does everything enthusiastically. I'm not sure she has any other settings. 'It was brilliant. I loved all the stuff with tomatoes.'

'And the stuff after that? The Babylonians, and the imaginary numbers?'

'Yeah. That as well.'

'Brilliant. Sometimes I worry that people won't understand the more in-depth stuff. It can be hard to find a way into the detail.'

'And everyone's really excited about the competition.'

'Really?' Yes. The competition. I am judging an art competition. I know nothing about art. Seriously, how do I get myself into these things?

'Yeah.'

'Em, about the competition, I'm not really an expert on art ...'

'That's OK. You just have to pick the ones you like best.'

'Yeah. You'll be there too, won't you?'

'I won't be any help. I probably don't know any more than you do.'

'But you're Arts Development Officer?'

'Well, yeah ...'

'And you did a degree in Fine Art ...'

'Well not really Fine Art. It was Fine Art and History of Art, sort of combined, so ...'

'So you must know even more! So you can help me.'

She smiles. She actually seems a bit embarrassed that I want her help. I suppose that's sweet, if you have the emotional depth to cope with embarrassment. I don't, and now I can't think of anything else to say about the competition. I grasp at the most obvious straw.

'Are you excited about planning the wedding?' Get me. First I remembered to say congratulations and now I'm showing interest in a wedding. My social skills are on fire tonight. If I carry on like this, Trix won't have any excuses left to take the piss out of me at all.

'I haven't really thought about it.'

'Well, you should. There's lots to think about. Dresses, and cars, and ...' I tail off. That's actually all I can think of. What else do you need to get married? 'A big room. You'll need a big room.'

'Right.'

'Maybe two big rooms, if you get married in one and then have the party somewhere else. Yeah. Two big rooms.'

I've lost it, haven't I? I resign myself to eating the rest of my meal in silence. Predictably enough, Henrietta turns towards Claudio a few minutes later, and I'm out of the conversational loop again. At least I'm alone with my own thoughts now, which I really don't mind at all.

But I'm not alone. I'm sitting next to John. I can hear him breathing, and the more I try to tune it out the louder it sounds. He leans away from the table, and angles his face towards my ear.

'It won't last.'

His voice is quiet and uncomfortable, like he's out of practice at talking.

If it were Trix or Danny I know I'd come back at him and we'd be debating the merits of romance for the rest of the night. With John, I don't.

'I'm sure they'll be fine.'

'Nothing ever lasts.'

I glance around the table, expecting to see Trix or Claudio readying themselves to dive in, but everyone's engrossed in their own conversations.

'Some things do. Look at you and Danny.' As soon as I've said it, I wish I hadn't. An image flashes into my brain, and I feel like I need to physically shake my head to dislodge it.

'He's far too good for her.' It takes me a second to process that comment, because John offers it in an entirely pleasant voice, like the sort of tone normal people use to discuss the weather and the best variety of tomatoes to grow on a south-facing wall. I have to replay it in my head before I'm certain he is being unkind.

Well, maybe a couple of days ago I'd have said the same, but Henrietta seems to make Claudio happy, and she builds a decent snowman. And she's sweet and kind, and she's happy, and what do I know? If John doesn't like her that also counts hugely in her favour. I don't respond.

'Look at her.' He looks at Henri like he's inspecting a specimen in a laboratory, and then as abruptly as it started, the conversation is over. He leans away from me in his seat and says no more.

Chapter Fourteen

Ten years earlier

Claudio

'Why do I have to come?'

I see Mum raise an eyebrow. 'We've been through this.'

It's true. We went through it when the tickets were ordered. We went through it again when I heard about the party, and then again last night and at breakfast this morning. I still don't understand. 'S'not fair.'

She folds her hands on her lap. 'It's a big day for your brother.'

'It was supposed to be a big day for me.'

'Well, I'm sorry you're missing your little party, but it's your brother's graduation. We're all going.' She glances out of the window. 'Just as soon as your father gets back. We're all very proud, aren't we?'

She gives me a look when she says that. I'm not proud. It's just a stupid maths degree and all he's going to do with it is go to another university and do some more maths. You'd think he'd know enough maths by now. I know loads of maths and I've only done GCSE.

'It's just a party.' She's talking softer now, like she's trying to get around me. It won't work. It's not just a party. It's my school leavers' ball, and if I'm not there, well, I can't not be there.

'I was supposed to be taking Joanne.'

Mum likes Joanne. She thinks she's a nice girl. 'Well I'm sure she'll be perfectly fine going with someone else.'

I don't say anything. There's no point. Of course she'll be fine going with someone else. She's going with Patrick

Anderson. That's what happens if you're not there. She's going to dance with him, and go outside for a ciggie with him, and then she'll get off with him. It was supposed to be me.

'I don't want her going with someone else.'

Mum smiles that stupid smile she does when she thinks one of us is being cute. 'Well, if she's the sort of girl who just runs off with another boy, then maybe she's not the right girl for you.'

I give up. Mum really doesn't get anything.

Chapter Fifteen

Trix

Sunday and I have nothing planned. Nothing at all, which is fine, obviously. I can enjoy my own company. That's all part of living alone. You learn to love your independence. There's plenty I can do. With that in mind, I get out of bed, and make it as far as the kitchen. Breakfast. I can have breakfast. My mental image of a lazy Sunday breakfast includes fresh croissants and Sunday newspapers, probably with some classic Motown playing on the stereo and a cat lazily rubbing itself against my ankles. I don't have a cat. I don't have any croissants, and I don't have any newspapers. For this plan to work, I am going to have to get dressed and go to the shop. That's go to the shop to buy croissants and papers, not to buy a cat. That would be crazy.

I manage to stretch getting dressed out to about forty-five minutes. Don't ask how. I'm a bit slow-moving at weekends. Getting dressed involves a fair amount of wandering around the house looking for socks that match, and then I inadvertently start reading the letters page in the local free paper. The letters are the only thing I ever read in the local paper. I love that people see all these evils in the world and then believe that the Editor of the York Evening Press is the person to sort it out for them. This week he's being asked to sort out global warming, get the UK out of Europe and say thank you to all the nurses on Cherry Ward. He's a man of exceptional power and influence.

That all fills time, so it's nearly two o'clock by the time I set off to buy breakfast, by which time there are no croissants left and a choice between an Independent on

Sunday with half the bits missing and the Mail on Sunday. I take the Independent. There are limits.

On the way home I start to think about last night properly. Henri and Claudio are engaged. I can't wait to get Henri cornered over a bottle of wine and hear the full story, and I do love a good wedding. I mean, not enough to have one of my own, obviously, but still. I love all the stuff that goes on around them; the dresses and flowers and speeches and food. I've always been a sucker for a good buffet. Can you imagine what Ben would make of that? Further evidence for the belief that all women are romantic fools. There's a big difference between being foolish and being stupid. If he's scared of looking foolish, he'd better hope he never really falls in love.

I don't know why I'm thinking about Ben. I sat as far away from him as possible last night. When they made the big announcement, he looked like he'd just found something unpleasant in his soup. In fact, the only major fly in the ointment for this wedding is that Ben's going to be best man, and Henri asked me to be her best woman. Actually, she asked me to be her matron of honour, but I wasn't having that. Anyway, whatever my title is, it sounds like the sort of role that's going to end up with me dancing with Ben at the reception. Mental note: must buy bridesmaid shoes with especially pointy heels.

I turn the corner towards home just as Claudio and Henri are coming out of her flat. For a moment I almost turn back around the corner and wait for them to go. They look like an advert for John Lewis' Winter Collection. They're all duffle coats and scarves inside this little perfection bubble. I feel like an intruder. Henri sees me before I have chance to run away, and waves.

I walk over to them. Henri is still glowing like she was last night. She grabs me in a big hug. 'We're going to see Claudio's mum and dad, and then we're meeting my dad.'

She squeals this information at a frequency that is quite distressing for my human ears; it must be sending the neighbourhood's dog population insane. I nod politely, and hope she comes down an octave. She peers at me. 'What are you doing today?'

I feel bad about admitting that I'm still working towards breakfast, so just make a non-committal noise, which I hope demonstrates a nonchalant 'just chilling out' type of vibe. Clearly that's far more work than a shrug and an unvoiced sound can be expected to do, because Henri looks blank. I try again.

'Not much. Reading the papers, you know.'

'You can come with us.'

Claudio looks uncertain. Whilst Henri has reached the point where there's so much couply joy around that she wants to share it with her disadvantaged single friends, Claudio is presumably thinking through the realities of turning up to announce your engagement to your parents with your brother's ex-girlfriend in tow.

I shake my head. Given that an hour ago I'd have quite liked a social invite, I'm surprised to notice that I'm finding Claudio's reluctance to be a relief rather than a disappointment. Their happiness is bordering on suffocating.

'I ought to do some work, you know.'

Work? What work? I'm a librarian. It's Sunday. The books aren't going anywhere. What work could I possibly have to do?

Henri looks momentarily stricken. I'm guessing she's not really been thinking about work this weekend, and, unlike me obviously, she actually does do work at weekends. She always comes in with bags full of art materials she's found on her own time, and ideas for activities and stuff. Today, though, even the anxiety that I might be better prepared for the working week than her isn't enough to shake the perfection bubble. 'You do need to read Ben's book.'

'What?'

'For work. For the competition. If it's all about Zero, we need to get some ideas, don't we?'

'Well, I don't really know if I've got time.'

She glares pointedly at my carrier bag of newspapers and bread. I guess I'm not exactly giving the impression of being rushed off my feet. 'I bet you haven't even got a copy, have you?'

I shake my head. 'I'm not spending money on his book.'

Henri laughs. 'You don't have to. He left a whole pile of copies for us. There's one on my coffee table. Seriously, you should read it. It's really very interesting.'

They head off for their lunch and I go into the house. I start off by dealing with the important things, and preparing a plate of lovely hot buttered Marmite-y toast, and a big glass of milk. Later on I will dip the toast in the milk to make it all soft. Don't tell anyone that. On reflection, it is kind of gross.

I flick through the papers, but I can't really concentrate. The Mail would have made me cross, but would also have been easier to get into. Maybe I ought to do some work after all. Maybe, actually, Henri is right, and I should have a proper look at Ben's book. I am going to need some ideas about Nothing-based art to help the kids.

I head downstairs and let myself into Henri's flat with my landlady key. Now, legally, as her landlady I should only use my key for purposes of essential maintenance and pre-arranged inspection. Traditionally though, it's mainly used for borrowing T-shirts, which I then stretch out of shape pulling them over my size twelve, all right fourteen, frame, when I haven't done my laundry. It's a good job she's an understanding tenant.

When I first let the flat to her, it'd been empty for about two years, since I bought the house, so it was basically fine, but a bit musty. Now everything is pristine and fragrant. Coming down here always makes me feel like I ought to vacuum when I get back upstairs. I don't, but I become aware that I could. It actually smells of furniture polish right now. She can't have found time to dust this weekend, can she?

The book is right where it's supposed to be. It's shiny and hardback. Ben must be doing all right. His first book was only in paperback, but this looks all official and important. I flick straight away to the inside dust cover, and see Ben smiling out at me. I wonder how long it took the photographer to get him to smile. It would have been a whole new skill for him.

Benedict Messina was born in 1980 in Whitby, to Italian parents. He graduated with a BSc in Mathematics from the University of York in 2003, and completed his Dphil in the subject at Cambridge in 2007. Since then Ben has lectured at Universities and Schools across the UK, Australia and the USA. His first book, Counting Woes, was published in 2011.

Ben lives with his brother in York, and in his free time enjoys walking and cinema.

I laugh at the last line – walking and cinema – the go-to hobbies for people who don't actually have any interests. I make a mental note to take the piss out of him about that. I also like 'lives with his brother'. It's neater than the alternative; 'Ben is not married, doesn't live with a woman, but does not want to be considered a lonely old git, and is definitely not gay.'

I take the book back upstairs and put it down on the arm of the sofa, and then sit at the opposite end and turn the TV on. I spend twenty minutes flicking between repeats of minor celebrities who can't ice skate and repeats of total unknowns who can't sing. The book sits quietly and looks at me.

I take my toast plate into the kitchen and run it under the tap. When I come back the book is still looking at me. The annoying thing is that Henri is right. I do really need to read it. If I wasn't so angry with him about the whole police incident I'd probably have read it earlier.

I pause for a moment to let my anger simmer. And now he's going to be coming to work. That's even worse; at the moment work is pretty much my last remaining Ben-free zone. I take a deep breath, pick up the book, and attempt to begin, telling myself that it's only a book. It's not even like it's about him or anything. It's a maths book. There is no possible way that even Benedict Vittore Messina could annoy me whilst writing about maths. I pick up the book. I skip the introduction. That will just be Ben wittering on and trying to sound intellectual. I can live without that. I flick to the start of the real book and try to apply myself.

Chapter One: In The Beginning
Zero really did start its useful life as nothing. It wasn't a number, because numbers were for counting things, real things: beans, sheep, fingers and the like. Zero had no business amongst these real hard players of the counting world. The earliest form of Zero, invented by the ancient Babylonians, was simply there to tell the reader that there was, quite literally, nothing to see here.

What the Babylonians did was place their numbers in columns according to their value, and then they inserted a placeholder symbol, their fledgling prototype Zero, into the columns where there was no value. To modern mathematicians, indeed to modern nursery school children, this way of writing numbers is utterly self-evident. How could it ever have been different? But it was different. Before the Babylonians, sometime before 1000 BC, columns where no number was required were simply omitted, leaving the hapless shopkeeper to guess whether their order was for 12 eggs or 1000002 eggs.

Ben is, even I have to concede, not terrible at explaining this stuff. I've been reading about the history of maths and I haven't yet fallen asleep or been overcome by the desire to stick my head in the oven.

He always was best when he had some piece of burning knowledge that he wanted to impart. I remember when we were at uni. He took this elective course on avionics, which is all to do with aeroplane engineering. Anyway, after the first lecture he was all buzzing about aerodynamics. When he'd learnt something new he always had this need to get anyone else who'd listen enthused about it too.

I remember lying on my bed with him. He was using my teddy bear – yes, I had a teddy bear – to demonstrate the different sorts of roll aeroplanes can experience if they hit turbulence or if their aerodynamic design isn't right. He was holding the bear up above us and rolling it around. Somehow the conversation ended up with me hitting him with the bear, which ripped his leg. That's the bear's leg, not Ben's, obviously. Afterwards, I always told people Ben had torn it playing aeroplanes, and he'd always argue and say it was my fault for hitting him. I never admitted that he was right.

Chapter Sixteen

I'm wafting down the aisle on my dad's arm. It feels as though I don't even have to move my feet. I'm literally floating down the aisle, and I can see myself doing it. My hair is all big and flowing, and not like it is in everyday life at all. And my make-up looks just right, and my waist is tiny and my boobs might be just a little bit bigger than normal.

The congregation is a sea of colour and happy faces and my mum is there at the front of the church, looking just like she did in the pictures Dad's got from when I was a baby, with her flicky hair and her great big smile. But I don't walk to the front straight away. I stop and float above it all looking down on Claudio waiting, and looking down on my mum and my dad and Trix. And I float up above the church and I can see the beautiful white pony that pulled the carriage I arrived in. Are white ponies called white? I stop my floating for a moment to wonder. Aren't you supposed to call white ponies ...

'Grey.' Danny's voice interrupts my daydream.

'What?' I'm not floating any more. I'm sitting at a table in the pub near my dad's house. It's Sunday evening. Just forty-eight hours since Claudio picked me up for our date. Forty-eight hours and we're engaged, and we've announced our engagement to our friends and my dad and Claudio's parents, and now we're sitting with my dad and Danny and they're talking about our wedding.

I look around the pub. We used to come here for Sunday lunch when I was a little girl. Sometimes we still do. It's the same lady behind the bar. She still tries to give me twenty pence for sweets. My dad's doodling something on his napkin. It looks like a wedding cake. Claudio and Danny are staring at me.

'Grey suits, for me and the ushers?' Claudio clarifies.

I nod, and try to pretend I've been paying attention. I think I mainly was paying attention. Anyway, I'm the bride. Brides are supposed to be pre-occupied.

We definitely agreed that it would be OK to have the wedding in six weeks' time. Dad thinks he can find a venue through the hotels he does work for, and he's already phoned the vicar at the village church. Claudio says that finding a photographer is a best man job, and Ben's not here to complain, so that's dealt with. Claudio thinks finding cars is a best man job too. I do think carriages and ponies are so much prettier than cars. It's probably not as practical though. I don't say anything. I'm sure a car will be just as nice.

Ben and Trix should really be here for wedding planning, but Ben's going to Edinburgh next week and claimed he had to pack, and Trix isn't answering her phone. Danny's here; he seems to be enthusiastic enough for both of them. I only called him to check something for work tomorrow, and he practically insisted on coming along.

He and Claudio are talking about suits now, which Danny seems to think he should look after rather than Ben. He's probably right. I don't think Ben really thinks much about clothes.

That means that Trix and me just need to do dresses and flowers, and I can totally picture my dress already. It's happening. It really is going to be perfect just like I imagined it.

'So I think we've reached the point where, as their friends, we owe it to them to intervene.' Danny interrupts my thoughts a second time.

Claudio nods. 'What did you have in mind?'

'Just a little light deception and subterfuge.'

I must look confused, because Danny glares at me and starts to explain more.

'You see, the thing with Benjamin and Trixabelle is that neither of them will make the first move. They're too scared.'

'I don't understand.' Because I really don't.

'Well isn't it obvious?'

It's not.

'They're utterly in love with one another. You don't get that amount of hate unless it's really true love.'

I'm not sure about that, but Danny seems convinced. 'Maybe.'

'Definitely. So we just have to make each of them aware that the other is up for it.'

'Why?'

'So they'll feel confident enough to make a move.'

Claudio laughs. 'Genius. What's the plan?'

And Danny really does have a whole plan. I tried to get out of being part of it, but he said I was the glue that holds the whole scheme together. I think he has a grand vision of them declaring their great love for one another at the wedding. I'm not sure about that. It is my wedding after all. Everyone seems very excited about it though so I don't want to put them down.

Chapter Seventeen

Ben

The hotel room in Edinburgh is every bit as bad as I expected. The room is too hot, which hotel rooms always are, there's no way of turning the heating down, which there never is, and the windows only open about three millimetres, which is about three millimetres more than they normally open. Aside from anything else, it's a ridiculous waste of energy. It's about two degrees outside and I'm still struggling to open a window to make up for the central heating in here.

I don't even particularly want to be here. I blame my publisher, and my agent. I mean, I did do promotion with my last book, but it was all sixth form maths clubs and stuff like that. It was a slow burn success, and by success I mean that it was in fact the second highest selling maths-related title of 2011. I kid you not.

Only now, that level of success doesn't seem to be enough. Someone has decided that I'm going to be a great populariser, which means I end up sitting at these little tables with big piles of books and lines of people who want them signed. Half of them are fine, because half of them are the proper nerds – my people, if you like. All they want to talk about is an inconsistency that they found on page 173. It's the others I can't deal with, the ones who joined the line just because there was a line. They probably joined the line for Wincey Willis last week, and they'll be there for Bill Bryson next week. I'm just something to pass the time.

I lie down on the bed to rest for a few minutes before I set off to find food. I don't move again though until I'm jolted awake by my phone vibrating in my pocket. I contort on the bed and lift it to my ear without looking at the screen. 'Hello.'

There doesn't seem to be anyone there. It sounds like one of those calls where someone accidentally calls someone by sitting on their phone.

I glance at the screen – 'Claudio calling'. I lift the phone back to my ear. 'Hello?'

He answers it. Very slowly and carefully I put the phone down on the table between me and Danny. I can still hear Ben's voice at the other end. 'Hello?'

I nod at Danny, who makes a start. 'Well, I'm sorry Claudio but you know we can't tell him.'

Ben hasn't hung up. I can hear his muffled voice from the phone. 'Claudio, are you there? Hello?'

If we don't get his attention pretty fast he's going to hang up. I jab my finger pointedly at Danny, which I know Ben won't see, but it can't hurt to get into character. 'I have to tell him. He's my brother.'

Ben's gone quiet now, but he's still there. I guess he's interested.

Danny pulls a 'What the fuck?' face at the finger pointing, but does his bit. 'I know he's your brother. And he's my friend, but you know how he'll react.'

'I guess.' I nod at Danny to continue.

'He'll make her life hell.'

'You're probably right. If he had any idea how Trix felt about him though …'

I think I hear an intake of breath from the other end of the phone line. Danny grins.

'Well, he can't find out, and you're not to tell him. Henrietta shouldn't even have told you.'

'I won't tell him. I just wish Trix would.'

Danny is getting into his Laurence Olivier stride. 'Bare her heart, just to have it torn apart by his callous, unfeeling … er?' He looks over to me.

'Er… thoughtless?'

'Thoughtless. Yes definitely. Bare her heart just to have it torn apart by his callous, unfeeling, thoughtless jokes at her expense,' Danny shakes his head. I'm struggling to stop myself from laughing. 'Not Trix. She couldn't bear it if he rejected her.'

I'm still stifling a laugh. 'You're right,' I splutter. 'Ben's not exactly open to love and romance, is he?'

'Which is a shame, because they could both be so happy.'

'So happy,' I echo with my best rock ballad backing singer intonation.

Danny glances at the phone. 'So just to recap, Trix definitely told Henrietta that she's in love with Ben.'

'Definitely.'

'But he's not to be told.'

'Because of him being callous and unfeeling,' I confirm.

'And thoughtless.'

'And thoughtless. Of course.'

'Right.' Danny looks at me and then at the phone and nods.

'Ah, well. I'm sure she'll get over him. It's not like he's ever gonna find …' and I press the 'End Call' button.

I look up at Danny, who grins. 'Phase one complete. Another pint?'

'Don't mind if I do.'

Danny heads to the bar. He's left his own phone on the table. It rings just as he manages to attract the barman's attention. 'John' flashes up on the screen, and the options 'Answer' or 'Reject'. Danny is engrossed in conversation with the barman.

I pick up the phone and hit 'Answer.'

'Where are you?' The voice at the other end is slightly slurred.

'Hi John. It's Claudio. We're in the Duck.'

'Where's Danny?'

'He's here too. At the bar. Do you want me to get him to ring you?'

'Nah. I'm happy talking to you.'

'Ok.'

'Are you having a nice engagement, Claudio?'

'Yeah. It's fine. We're getting sorted for the wedding.'

'Oh. The wedding. Yeah. Gotta be all sorted for the wedding. Bet Danny's all hands on deck to help with that.'

'He's been great. Yeah.'

'Of course. Perfect Danny helping perfect Henrietta plan the perfect wedding. Bet you'd prefer to be having some real fun.'

'What do you mean?'

'You know what.' And he laughs, and then he hangs up.

Danny puts a pint down in front of me. 'Was that someone on my phone?'

'John.'

'Oh?'

'Just seeing where you were I think.'

Danny takes the phone off me. 'I'll just ring him back.'

He gestures towards the door. 'Quieter out there.'

He strides towards the door fiddling with his phone. I don't point out that we've just made two calls sitting right here, and could hear everything just fine.

Chapter Eighteen

Ben

I think my brain has decided that the best response to shock is to only process events occurring in the current thirty second period. Wider thought has been shut down, meaning that I sleepwalk through the rest of my trip to Edinburgh. I know I did a local radio interview, because I remember leaving the building. I have no idea what I said. I know I talked to my agent because her number is on my phone's call log. It was more than half a minute ago, so all other detail has been erased from my mind.

Once I get on the train to come home, all the activity stops. There are no more places to be, people to talk to, extracts to read, or books to sign. My brain is empty, and the thoughts I've been holding at arm's length fill the vacuum.

Normally train journeys are useful thinking time. They're like showers and buildings with noisy air conditioning; it's something to do with the constant background noise. My first thought is that Claudio and Danny have made a mistake. I mean, Trix and me? Me and Trix. I'm not one to dwell on the past, but if I were I might well conclude that that particular ship had well and truly sailed. I might conclude that that was no bad thing.

But that's not necessarily the best approach. You shouldn't reach any sort of conclusion without a proper evaluation of the evidence. I try to review the evidence. Trix has been single for a long time now. So far as I know, there hasn't been anyone serious since, well since me. That would make sense, wouldn't it? It would explain why she had never committed to anyone else if she was still in love with me.

In love? The whole notion feels erroneous. I mean, we're never going to get together. Trix is far too proud. She'll never tell me. And even if she would it's not as though I'm looking for someone, so it wouldn't make any difference.

The train pulls into Berwick, and I watch the people waiting to get on. It's fascinating this – you can see it in any busy doorway. People bunch up and then there's this moment where everyone sort of moves together. You can try to recreate the effect using marbles being channelled through a narrow opening, but it never quite gives the same results. To understand it properly you have to factor in the human combination of reserve and desperation to get a seat. And it's different in different countries, somehow culturally specific, you know.

The train moves away. The movement jolts my brain back to the point. You know, Trix might want to tell me, but she won't because she thinks I'll be callous, or unfeeling, or thoughtless, which I wouldn't. I have been known to make the odd joke about love and romance. And maybe I do have a bit of a go at Trix from time to time, but she knows it's all in fun. Unless she doesn't know that. She may have taken those things a bit more seriously than she ought to. Probably she's taken all those comments to heart, and coupled with her famous, and undeniable, pride, it's stopping her from being honest about how she truly feels.

Of course, she doesn't need to be honest now, because I already know. So, if I was interested, I could take the first step myself. I can imagine what Danny would say if I did. And Claudio. Claudio would be a total dick about the fact that I might have made some occasional somewhat negative comments about romance. But then, there's nothing wrong with changing your mind is there? And to stick to something just out of pride or fear of what people would say, that would be even more foolish.

It's like Eddington. Arthur Eddington – he was secretary of the Royal Astronomical Society during the First World War, and he started reading about this German, Albert Einstein, who suggested that gravity wasn't constant. That completely rejected the received wisdom. The problem was that Eddington was British and Britain was at war with Germany.

It didn't stop Eddington. He set out and made observations that supported the German's theory, because he realised that Einstein's ideas made sense. So right in the middle of World War I, Eddington planned an expedition across the world to make observations that could prove a German physicist's theory. And he did it. He took amazing pictures, which showed the light from distant stars bending slightly due to the Sun's gravity.

Einstein had the vision, but he needed Eddington to prove it. Once Eddington had proved that the evidence fit the theory, it would have been foolish to cling to Newton's ideas. Plenty of people did, especially in Britain. They clung to something that they knew was erroneous through pride or fear or sheer bloody-mindedness, and Eddington spent the rest of his career trying to explain Einstein's theory. He became a great evangelist, in fact, for something that he had previously believed to be a fantasy.

The train pulls into Newcastle, and I watch the people getting on again, squeezing through the doors like irritable marbles. Watching them gives me a moment to breathe, to send my brain somewhere safe for a few seconds. The train moves off again. Eddington's example is definitely to be admired, and if I were to embrace love, I could simply be following good scientific principles. It is good to be able to change your mind when new evidence presents itself. Not to do so would be ridiculous.

Of course, all of that only makes sense if I'm in love with Trix, and so, as a man of science, I have to ask myself that question. Am I in love with Trix? I did dream about her last night, but that doesn't prove anything. Most neuro-scientists now agree that dreams have a fairly direct correlation to real-life. If something is on your mind while you're awake, your brain continues to try to work it out while you're asleep. It turns out all that Freudian stuff about dreams being abstract and requiring interpretation is crap. So after we got stopped for being drunk and disorderly, I dreamt about Trix as well, but that doesn't mean I'm thinking about Trix. Well it does mean I'm thinking about Trix, but it doesn't mean I love her.

Last night, I didn't even dream about her in the here and now. I dreamt about her at uni. In the dream she was walking around the university campus, and I was trying to catch up with her, but she was never quite in reach. I kept spotting her just too far away for me to call out. Just before I woke up, the dream moved into a graduation ceremony. I knew I was supposed to make a speech, but I couldn't remember what I was meant to say. Then I was on the stage and when I looked out at the audience they were all Trix. That still doesn't mean I love her. It just means she's on my mind, which is understandable, after what I heard over the phone on Sunday.

At our real graduation, I closed my eyes when she walked across the stage, so I wouldn't see her. I was scared that if I saw her I'd change my mind. I thought that if I saw something in her face, wanting me to stay, then I'd end up staying. I would have changed my whole life because of something in her face. And that was it. I didn't look. I carried on like I'd decided I would. I'd made my choice. I didn't even think that it might be possible to go back. I certainly never thought about whether I'd want to. Everyone knows you can't go back.

And I'm not good at love. It is irrational. You can't measure it properly. I don't even think you can discern its inherent properties. There's no set of laws about how it behaves. But then, I'm not a scientist. I'm a mathematician. Irrationality is part of maths. Pythagoras was a great mathematician, but he didn't embrace irrationality, and he ended up dying because he refused to cross a field of beans. Really, if it's a choice between dying alone on the edge of a bean field and embracing the irrational, it shouldn't be a tricky decision. Choose life and all that.

Chapter Nineteen

Trix

Things have quietened down a bit since Henri and Claudio's big announcement, which is definitely a good thing. A whole week with no life changing announcements, no run-ins with the police, and no big dramas. That is mainly because I've not seen Ben this week, but that happy state comes to an end today.

Today is Wedding Dress Shopping Day. As Henri stayed with Claudio last night I said I would pick her up from Ben's flat, and Henri says I have to come in and say 'Hello' and be civil. She says that we have to show that we can be polite to each other reliably before the wedding. She was quite funny about it. She actually said that she wasn't having her big day spoiled by us going on at each other. The way she was talking, you would think that it was my fault.

Anyway, I will be civil to him, for Henri's sake, but he needn't think I've forgiven him. I still think he ought to have offered to pay my fine. I pull up and park outside Ben's flat, and brace myself to go in. I'm only halfway up the path when the man himself throws the front door open. 'Trix!'

Must be civil. I nod at him, perhaps a little curtly, but it's definitely not actively rude. 'Benedict.'

'You look ...' Ben peers at me, and I wait for the insult. Unusually, for him, he seems to be struggling for words. 'Lovely. You look lovely today.'

I run the comment back in my head looking for the double meaning. I can't see it. Either it's too well hidden for me to work out at this time in the morning, or Claudio's version of the 'be nice to each other' lecture was a whole lot scarier than Henrietta's. I nod again at Ben. Silence seems like the safest option. We're still standing on the front step. I don't want to push past him. I've already established that trying to speak to him takes us into a whole world of weirdness.

It turns out that the silence is no better. Ben is staring at me. I look at him, and he smiles a funny sort of half smile, half smirk thing. This is far more unnerving than the normal shouting. I take a step towards the door, aiming to be decisive enough to make it obvious that he should be inviting me in, but not so decisive that I end up sandwiched between the doorframe and Ben's torso. Ben, who has never been skilled at reading body language, doesn't move at all, and so now I'm just standing even closer to him, and he's still staring at me. If this is him trying to be nice, he's really not good at it.

I gesture towards the stairway. 'Shall we …?'

He physically jumps when I speak. 'Yes. Right. Of course. After you.'

He finally moves out of the doorway to let me go inside. Once I'm in the flat it doesn't get any less odd. He's all over me like an anxious hostess offering me drinks and biscuits, and even the chance to use the toilet. I'm not joking. After I've turned down the offer of tea and biscuits he actually said, 'You can use the bathroom? If you need to, or not, if you don't. Right.'

And then he just froze, as if freezing would somehow erase the moment and make him seem less odd. Unfortunately, this is Ben we're talking about, so there is really very little he can do now to make himself seem less odd. I actually take pity on him at this point and ask if he's feeling OK. He sits down right next to me on the sofa, and says, very seriously. 'I'm absolutely fine, Trix. How are you?'

'I'm fine.'

'That's good. Did I say that you look lovely today?'

'You did.' Clearly I have to get out of here as soon as possible. 'Is Henri nearly ready?'

'She was in the bathroom earlier. I'll go and see. I mean, not go into the bathroom. Obviously. I don't go to the bathroom with Henrietta. I'll just go and see if she's ready.'

He dashes out of the room. Maybe he's not well or something. Henrietta appears a few minutes later. 'Sorry. Sorry. Ben only just told me you were here.'

I stand up to hug her. 'Is he OK?'

She bites her bottom lip before she looks at me. 'He's fine. Why?'

I shake my head. 'I'll tell you on the way into town. Let's get out of here.'

She jumps up and claps her hands. 'Wedding dresses!'

It feels like today might be a long day. Henri is loving it though. In the car she says that today is going to be the best day of her life. I point out that traditionally the wedding is supposed to be the best day of her life. Apparently, it will be, but that doesn't mean that today isn't the best day so far. It's nice to see her so happy; whatever Claudio's doing for her, it's certainly put a smile on her face.

'So why were you asking about Ben?'

The question is delivered with the careful tone of someone trying to seem off-the-cuff, but there's more behind it. Clearly she knows something I don't. I hate being out of the loop. Lucky for me that Henri is completely incapable of keeping a secret then, isn't it?

'He just seemed a bit weird.'

'I'm sure he's fine.' She's turned away from me in the passenger seat so that she's looking out of the window.

Whatever it is she's not going to tell me straight away, but we have a whole day of girly enjoyment ahead of us. I will wheedle it out of her somehow.

I've booked us slots at two different wedding dress shops. That freaked me out to start with. Seriously, what sort of dress shopping do you have to book an appointment for? At least we've got time before the wedding though. The woman in the first shop very quickly puts us straight on that idea. When we tell her that the wedding is five weeks hence, she looks at us as though we've just announced that the wedding was on Mars, and the dress will need to be meteor-proof.

'Well, madam will have to have something we have in stock. There'll be no time to order anything. I don't know how on earth you expect us to have the alterations done.'

She's a tall, thin woman who, whilst wearing glasses, has disappointingly opted against a half-moon style over which she could peer schoolmistress-like at overly exuberant brides. It is a mystery; why do truly miserable, unhelpful people choose to make their living in jobs that are completely reliant on their ability to be friendly and provide a service? In this case, I can only guess that some past trauma has left her with some Miss Havisham-esque compulsion towards bridalwear. When the shop's closed she probably pops on a veil and sits weeping gently to herself behind the till point.

Right now though, the only person looking likely to weep is Henrietta. Clearly this is the moment to leap into bridesmaid action.

'Right then.' The shop lady might not have the schoolmistress thing quite down, but I definitely do. 'I'm sure there'll be plenty we can try off the rail.'

Fortunately Henri is a positively tiny size ten, so this turns out to be true. It's a good job she's not over a fourteen. From the range of dresses on sale here, I can only assume that curvy girls get married in their underwear and are just expected to count themselves lucky they've managed

to attract any man at all. We end up taking four dresses –
sorry – gowns, apparently – into the changing room. Henri,
I think, would have tried on every dress in the shop if she'd
been allowed to, but the Demon Shopkeeper started rolling
her eyes when we picked up the third one which sort of
spoiled the mood.

The first dress she tries on is big and white and wedding-y.
Looking at the three still on the hangers I sense that this is
going to get quite samey after a while. I'm trying to think
of something beyond 'It looks nice' to offer, when Miss
Havisham comes in and glares at Henrietta appraisingly.
'Well, how can you expect to look exquisite in a gown in
those things?'

She's staring at Henri's pink pumps which are peeping
out from under the dress.

'Off with them!' She produces a pair of four-inch heels
in white satin, with two interlocked diamante hearts on the
toes. They may be the most hideous shoes I've ever seen.
'What size are you?'

'Five,' Henri whispers.

'Well, these are a three and a half, so you'll have to
squeeze into them.' Henrietta obediently squishes her feet
into the too-small shoes, and turns back towards me. 'What
do you think?'

To be honest, the slightly-teary eyes aren't helping the
look. The dress itself is perfectly fine. People could shake
Henrietta's dad warmly by the hand and say, 'Doesn't she
look lovely,' without having to rehearse saying it with a
straight face for ten minutes in advance. But I can see that
she's not loving it. 'I like it, but I don't think you should get
the first one you try on.'

Henri nods. Miss Havisham has already started unzipping
her, and the dress falls to the floor. 'Step out.'

Henri steps over the heap of dress at her feet, and stands,

shivering, in the middle of the room in her underwear whilst Miss H rehangs the dress, and moves on to dress number two, pausing only to cast a critical eye over Henri's bra and knickers. 'Step in.'

Henri steps into the next dress and Miss H zips her up. She stands behind Henri facing into the mirror, and reaches a hand around Henri and across her, non-existent, belly. 'Of course, on the day with the proper girdle, you won't have this bulging.'

I knew she didn't think much of Henri's undies. I'm momentarily offended on behalf of my friend's knickers. They're decent knickers. They match the bra and everything. I try to focus myself on being offended on Hen's behalf instead.

'Not that she has any fat to bulge,' I interject pointedly. I prod my own, somewhat more generous, mid-section. 'I wish I had her figure!'

Miss H peers at my tummy. I suspect she comes firmly from the 'one can never be too rich or too thin' school of thought. As a philosophy it does not seem to have brought a lot of joy into her life. Henri's bottom lip is quivering though, so I decide the best thing is to power through as fast as possible and get out of the bridalwear store from hell.

'Shall we try the next one?'

Henri looks at me. I can see that she wants to say no and run away. I can't see Miss H permitting that though. 'Come on. This one might be the one.'

Henri is already being unzipped. Being a bride seems to involve quite a lot of people tugging and fiddling with you. It definitely looks like something I can live without. To be fair, the third dress is quite lovely. It's cream rather than white and somehow it makes Henri's cheeks look all pink and rosy. For the first time, she is starting to look like a blushing bride. Even Miss H is looking pleased; she kneels at Henri's feet and billows the skirt out around her. I grin at Henri. 'You look like a picture of a bride in a magazine.'

Miss H stands up. 'It is better isn't it? It doesn't cling so much.' She rubs a hand down Henri's hip to smooth out the fabric and reinforce her point. I think, 'It doesn't cling so much' might be the nearest she's ever come to a compliment. She pats Henri's hip again. 'But still ...'

But still? I'm getting the distinct impression that this woman doesn't actually want to sell things. Maybe she doesn't. The gowns are probably the nearest thing she has to actual friends. Henri is now turning her hips and bottom towards the mirror and staring at her reflection. The blushing bride look has been replaced by the forlorn face she was wearing earlier.

'Shall we try the last one?'

This time Henri actually shakes her head. Miss H rolls her eyes, as if she can't understand why all these women keep coming in, trying on her clothes and leaving in tears. Maybe it is us. Maybe it's not actually a shop, and she's just trying to be civil to all these random people who keep wanting to play with her stuff. That would explain why she insisted on us making an appointment, if nothing else.

I decide that Henri does need rescuing this time, and stand up briskly. 'Ok. If you don't like it there's no point trying it on.'

I turn to Miss H. 'Well, we'll think about it, then, and let you know.'

Miss Havisham is undoing the actually-quite-nice dress. 'Step out.'

Henri does so and stands on one leg to pull off the tiny shoes. She gets dressed with the sort of haste normally only employed when trying to leave a one-night stand without waking them up.

We practically run out of the shop. As soon as we're out of sight I stop. 'What a cow!'

'I'm never going to find a dress.'

'Of course you will. I'm sure the one this afternoon will be much nicer.'

'But I'll still be all bulgy.' Henri prods her belly.

'You're not bulgy!' I must be looking at her in disbelief. 'You don't actually think you're bulgy? You're about two sizes smaller than me. What does that make me?'

Henri looks up. 'You look lovely.'

'And so do you. Come on. We need lunch.'

We walk to one of our regular bars, The Graduate, and I buy us two glasses of wine. I order a burger, and let the barman pressure me into chips. I love the culture of up-selling. It's a brilliant system for getting chips whilst telling yourself you never intended to order them. Henri orders a chicken salad wrap, and eats it mournfully eyeballing my chips.

'She was just a mean lady. The next place will be better.'

Henri chews but doesn't answer.

'And that last dress was nice. You really liked it. You looked all princessy.'

She finally smiles. 'I did like it.'

'That's better.' Now that she's cheered up I feel completely justified in going back to this morning's efforts to find out what's weird with Ben, but I've already established that she's not going to tell me directly. I'm going to have to go for the indirect approach. 'So has Claudio sorted out the boys' outfits?'

'Sort of. He's picked what he wants, but they all have to go get measured.'

'*He's* picked what he wants?'

'I might have advised a bit.'

'I can't imagine Ben in top hat and tails.'

'Well, you'll have to imagine. He refused to wear a hat.'

'I think you should insist. It'd be funny.'

'I don't really like men in top hats. It makes me think of amateur dramatics doing songs from the shows.'

'It'd still be funny. Do you know how he's getting on promoting the book?'

She shrugs. 'Ok, I think. He moans about it, but I think he quite likes the attention really. Have you read it yet?'

Apart from the first chapter, I still haven't. I hid the copy Henri lent me under the coffee table. I swear it was looking at me. 'I've started it.'

'Well you need to finish it. I need ideas for this art project, and you said you'd help.'

Technically, I think Danny said I'd help, but I don't labour the point. 'I'm going to finish it.'

She looks at me dubiously. Sometimes I almost wish that Henri was actually as dumb as she appears. I avoid her look. 'Well, I am.'

She'd better read it. I'm starting to wish I'd never come up with the whole art competition idea. Of course, when I thought of it I didn't know I'd be planning my wedding at the same time, but still, she is supposed to be helping.

She has got Ben on the brain though. She talked about him all the way in the car this morning. Maybe Danny's on to something after all, but I'm not allowed to say anything to her about it today. Danny says he has a plan, and the more I seem like I'm covering something up, the more likely she is to go for it in the end. I wasn't sure about that, because it means that I have to not tell her anything whilst looking like I'm hiding something, and I'm not a great liar. Danny said that was for the best though. If she asks about Ben I just have to say he's fine and be generally non-committal about him. Danny says my naturally honest face will make it clear that I'm hiding something without me doing anything else.

She's still hot on the scent. 'So Ben's going to judge the competition then?'

'Yep.'

'And he's happy with that.'

I shrug. 'So far as I know.'

'And he's fine overall? He hasn't seemed odd to you.'

'No. He seems fine.'

'And he's not said anything to Claudio?'

'Why should he?'

Trix is trying to look non-committal too. I really hope I'm better at it than her. 'He just seemed a bit odd this morning.'

I can't manage this any longer. I look at my watch. 'Better get going to the next shop.'

'We've got loads of time.'

'Don't want to be late. We don't want to get in trouble again.'

The second shop is down a side street in the oldest part of the city, near the Shambles. I love this part of town. It's all higgledy-piggledy buildings, and different layers of history built on top of each other. Once, when I first moved here, I found the most incredible vintage shop in a tiny courtyard somewhere off Swinegate. Then it took me about three months to ever find it again. I've started thinking that maybe it's a magic shop that just appears when women really need it, providing perfect one-off outfits for any occasion.

The wedding shop is painted pink on the outside and the dress in the window is the hugest big white net meringue you could imagine, and someone has sprinkled glitter all over the floor and the mannequin. When I open the door I'm hit by a wave of warmth and flowery scent. The door hits an old fashioned bell and the tinkle brings a lady bustling through from the back of the shop.

'Hello, hello, hello. You must be Miss Leonard?'

I nod. 'I'm sorry we're early.'

She's a walking personification of effusiveness. She claps her hands when I confirm my identity. 'Excellent. Excellent. I'm Donna Berry, as in Berry's Brides obviously. Shall I call you Miss Leonard?'

'Henrietta.'

'Henrietta. How pretty. Marvellous. And you must be the bridesmaid?'

She extends a hand and a face-splitting smile to Trix, who nods.

'Wonderful. Now tell me dear, when is the big day?'

I wonder about lying, having learnt my lesson about wedding dress ladies and weddings that are only five weeks away, but Trix has already told her the date.

She claps her hands some more. 'How wonderful. So soon – you must be so excited.'

I nod again.

'And when did you get engaged?'

'A week ago.'

'Lovely. I do like a short engagement. So much more romantic. Don't you agree?'

I nod some more. It seems to make her happy. 'Are you sure there'll be time to get a dress, and, you know, alterations and things?'

'Oh, don't even worry for a moment about that. I'm sure we'll find the time. Anyway, look at you. A perfect ten, if my eyes don't deceive? I can't imagine I'll even have to open my sewing box.'

I start to look properly around the shop. It's small, but every available space has been filled with dresses, and veils, and shoes, and tiaras. It's like a little girl's dressing up dream. Donna turns and gestures towards the array of rails.

'Now ladies, you can try on anything you like, of course. So why don't you take a look around, and I shall find us a little something to whet the palate. Champagne all around?'

I nod again. I like it here. I start to wonder whether I could come here every Saturday, and just wear a different wedding dress every week for work.

Donna presses a handful of plastic tags into my hands. 'Anything at all you would like to try just pop a tag on the hanger, and we'll take them all through.'

She presents Trix with another handful. 'You as well, dear. There are bridesmaid dresses over to the left, or you can just pick out more things for darling Henrietta if you like.'

I've only been here five minutes and I'm already darling Henrietta. I start putting tags on dresses, wondering whether I'd be allowed to just try them all on. Trix has gone over to the bridesmaid dresses and is peering at them with a look of mild horror. I think she'd probably forgotten that she could be made to try things on as well.

I concentrate on the wedding dresses. They're so packed together on the rails that you basically have to climb inside the rack to look at them. I'm burrowing through the rack when I find it. It's a real princess dress; cream silk with long sheer sleeves that flare out to a point on the back of the hand and a beautiful cream bodice cut straight across the bust. At the end of the sleeves someone has embroidered tiny pink and blue flowers. The skirt flares softly in a way that doesn't say 1980s tight wedding dress or 1990s big meringue. It just hangs and flares. I reach up to feel the corset and the skirt moves gently as I touch the dress. At the side are two long loose pieces of fabric that look as though they are designed to wrap around the bodice and pull the dress tight under the bust. This is it. I know it.

I pick an armful of others, to show willing, and then I go and pick three for Trix as well. I don't see why I should be the only one getting my underwear inspected by strangers. And besides, she'll probably look lovely in them all. Trix is so striking to look at. For a moment I wonder whether I really want her standing next to me in photos. Maybe I should pick something awful; if I did she'd manage to make it look quirky and alternative anyway, so I might as well go for something beautiful to start with. At least then people might just think it's the dress doing the work.

I purposefully save the dress I fell in love with until last to try on. As I step into it I close my eyes, and keep them closed whilst Donna does the fastenings up my back. I feel her reach around the front, where two long wide pieces of silk are hanging loose. She pulls the fabric tight around my ribs where it sits snug to my torso to create a sort of fabric corset. She ties the ends of the fabric in a long bow at my back. I open my eyes. In the mirror I look like a medieval princess. I turn around to look at my back view. The tiny delicate flowers are embroidered around the ends of the long wide ties. Trix is grinning. 'You're Rapunzel.'

She's right. Just like always she's managed to explain it so much better than I could. I look like Rapunzel. I have actually managed to look not just like a fairytale princess, but a specific fairytale princess. Donna is still behind me looking directly into the mirror. She's squinting slightly.

'Oh my, dear.'

Trix is grinning. 'It's gorgeous.'

'Do you really think so?' I know I like it. I think I like it. I just want to know that it's ok.

She nods. 'It's beautiful.'

Donna shakes her head. 'Nearly. Wait there.'

She disappears back into the shop and leaves me and Trix staring at my fairytale-perfection. It feels like I've found exactly what I'm looking for, not just what I'm looking for today, but what I've been looking for every time I've ever been shopping in my whole life. All the times I've wandered around the shops in the belief that the perfect new pair of boots, or jeans, or knickers (yes, knickers – Trix refers to it as my 'foundation garments phase') would make me somehow better, were leading up to this moment. This is the dress that makes me look finished.

Donna bustles back in clutching a pair of shoes. She pops them down on the floor in front of me. 'What size are you my dear?'

'Five.'

'Just what I thought. I wondered about the six, but I thought no, no, she's a dainty one, and picked out the five.'

The shoes are beautiful. I just want to stand and look at them for a moment. They're cream silk, with a heel, and they fasten by tying a silk ribbon across your foot. They are the prettiest thing I've seen since, well since the dress, but, apart from the dress, they're the prettiest thing I've *ever* seen. Trix stands up and holds my hand as I step into the shoes, which Donna kneels to tie. She then produces a tiara from a box at the back of the changing room. It's decorated with tiny flowers again, and when she puts it on my head it glimmers in the light.

This is it. This is the dress I will become Mrs Messina in. It is the perfect dress. It makes me look like the perfect bride for the perfect wedding. Behind me Donna is chattering away about shortening and steaming and then she moves on to Trix and I hear her saying they have bridesmaid dresses that match the blue in the flowers. But it's like I can hear the words but they don't relate to me. All I can see is me, this dress and the wedding in five weeks' time. Just for a moment nothing else matters.

Chapter Twenty

Claudio

'I should go back to my place. I've got work tomorrow.'

Henri is sitting on the kitchen table. She can't go back to her place. It's Sunday now. She came over on Friday evening and stayed here last night after she'd been shopping with Trix as well. If she actually goes home then the weekend will be over, and I will definitely have failed to tell her what I meant to tell her on Friday night. So long as she's still here, it's like it's all part of the same date, so I haven't failed yet. And I do have to tell her. Not mentioning Italy felt ok to start with because nothing was certain. The e-mail that came last week changed that. If I don't tell her now, I'm actually lying, rather than kidding myself that there's nothing to tell.

She won't go back to hers anyway. She says she's going to two or three times every day. I think she sometimes worries that she's crowding me.

She probably read in a book once that men need space.

'Don't. You've got clothes here. Stay here.'

'Are you sure?'

'Oh yeah.' I move so that I'm standing between her knees and pull her closer to me, so her hips are tilted against my crotch. 'Stay here tonight.'

'OK.'

So we have sex, in my bedroom, not on the kitchen worktop – sadly dear brother gets all weird about being expected to squeeze past copulating couples on his way to make a cup of tea – but I know I can't put off telling her any longer. The fact that she hasn't been home since Friday doesn't really mean that it's still Friday night.

'Henri?'

'Yeah?'

'There's something I've got to tell you.'

She sits up and pulls the duvet up to cover her. 'It's all too quick, isn't it? I'm sorry. I've rushed you. I know. It's my fault. I've messed it up, haven't I?'

'Woah! It's not anything you've done.'

She's looking at me, biting her bottom lip. She always does that when she's scared. Most adults manage to stop themselves from doing those sorts of things. In real life you don't actually see people furrowing their brows, or wringing their hands that often. But with Henri all her emotions are right there on her face in the most upfront way. I kiss her forehead.

'It's about work. My work.'

She's still chewing her lip.

'You remember when I was in Napoli, I told you that another tour company had asked me to apply for a job with them?'

Now her eyes have got really big and wide. She's simple in her heart Hen, but contrary to what some people think, she's not stupid. She realises what I'm driving towards straight away.

'You're moving to Italy?'

I'm looking right at her. I'm hoping she can see how desperate I am. 'I was sort of hoping we might be moving to Italy.'

It really is a brilliant opportunity for me. Tour guides are regulated in Italy, but they've offered to pay for me to get my official license, so I'll be able to do tours of Pompeii and Herculaneum. Not a lot of Brits do that, so once I'm licensed I'll be raking it in.

This company know me and they want me, and to be honest, I basically told them I'd take it there and then, but of course, it was all provisional because I was still doing another job. And I didn't know that by the time they wanted me to start I'd be married.

'When?' Henri is still chewing her lip.

'Summer.' I shrug. I've thought about nothing but telling her, but how it would actually work has barely crossed my mind. 'I guess we could go earlier though.'

'What would I do in Italy?'

'Whatever you want. You could paint. You could teach English. You could work anywhere; there's always something for English speakers.'

'I don't speak Italian.'

'You'd learn. It's a beautiful language.'

'Where would we live?'

'If we moved out there, the company would probably put us in an apartment to start with. After that ... wherever you want. We could buy an apartment. If you were working, we could rent a villa even.'

I have no idea if any of this is true. I haven't even thought about where we would live. I just need her to agree. 'A villa with room for lots of little bambinos.'

For the first time she smiles. 'That means babies.'

'See. You're a natural. You'll be chatting like a local in no time.'

'How many bambinos are you planning?'

'Tens. Hundreds. As many as you want.'

'I've never been to Italy.'

'You'll love it. I promise.'

'What if I don't?'

'Then we'll come back.' Would we? Would I? If I really loved the work, and the place, but Henrietta was unhappy, would I really come back? It won't come to that. She'll love it. I know she'll love it. I can picture us living there, walking through the Piazza del Plebiscito, laughing at the tourists like proper locals. I'm thinking of all the places I would take her, and I'm thinking of the villa we'll have. I can see her padding barefoot over the tiles to kiss me when I come home. I risk a look at her face. She's stopped chewing her lip. She nods.

'Is that a yes?'

She nods again.

Chapter Twenty-One

Henrietta

I go to Danny's office as soon as I get into work. He's going to be the first person I've told. I'm planning to get them all out of the way today. I'll tell Danny this morning, and then I'll find Trix during the day. Claudio's coming with me to tell my dad this evening.

I knock on Danny's door, but there's no answer. I wait a moment and knock again. I've just about concluded that he's not in there, and I'm going to have to ball my courage up and try again at morning break, when he calls from inside the office.

'Just a minute.'

I wait outside the door, turning the envelope with my resignation letter round in my hand. It seems like ages before Danny opens the door, but time always seems slower when I'm nervous. I go in and sit down. I take a deep breath, but before I launch into my prepared speech I see Danny's face. He has a proper black eye, like in a film.

'What happened to your eye?'

He touches the bruising carefully with his fingertips. 'I tripped.'

'It looks nasty.'

He raises his eyebrows and then winces. 'Thanks.'

'No. I didn't mean. You look fine. It's just …' I stop talking. Claudio keeps telling me to shush. He says that when I'm nervous I talk too much. 'Sorry.'

'It's OK. And I'm OK. What can I do for you?'

My prepared speech has gone out of my head now, so I just push the envelope across the desk to him. 'Sorry.'

'More apologies.' He tears the envelope open and reads the contents over. 'I'm surprised.'

I don't really know what to say.

'You're a delight to work with. I didn't think Claudio would be the sort to want his bride tied to the kitchen sink.'

I can feel myself blushing with the compliment. Of course, I know he's just being kind, but it's still very sweet of him.

'I won't be tied to the sink.' I take a deep breath. I haven't explained why I'm leaving in the letter. I decided I needed to practise saying it out loud. 'We're going to live in Italy. Naples. Napoli.' I correct myself. I need to start trying to sound like a native.

Danny nods. 'It's a beautiful country.'

'That's what Claudio says.'

'Of course. He loves it there. I'm sure he will be as happy as a pig in muck.'

He will. He's already massively excited about the move.

Danny continues. 'It will be such a shame for the library to lose you though. You've done so much over the past couple of years. I guess I just assumed you would be working with us for years and years to come.'

'I would have liked that.'

Danny comes around the front of the desk. 'I would have liked that too.'

He pauses. I get the impression he's deciding whether to say more. 'But things change. You are young, and very much in love. Of course, you should go where your heart takes you.'

He smiles, and simultaneously winces as the muscles pull against his bruised eye. 'We'll miss you here though.'

'I'm still here till summer.'

'Good. I would hate you to leave before we had finished our little project with Ben.'

'The art project?'

He laughs. 'That as well.'

Chapter Twenty-Two

Five months earlier

Claudio

The bar's full tonight. It's early September so there are still plenty of summer visitors around. Somehow this place seems to be the designated drinking venue of choice for visitors and foreign residents in Naples. There's a load of tour reps and a smattering of foreign students from the university, including a couple of vulcanologists, which makes me sick. That's something I would really have loved to do. I actually had a place to do geology at college, but I didn't get the grades. Hardly surprising; Ben was the clever one in our family.

By the way, I never tell girls I'm interested in vulcanology. They either think you're some kind of sci-fi geek, or they know that it basically means you like rocks and that's so dull-sounding they almost wish you were a sci-fi nut. But saying you're a rep is tricky too. We do have kind of a reputation for drunkenness and never calling. It's not an unfair reputation, but still, it's one you have to manage quite carefully. I tend to claim to be enthralled by the culture, and just to be working as a rep to pay my way. Pulling's never about what you're selling. It's all about the pitch.

As soon as we arrive at the bar I look around for Theresa. Theresa has been my fallback girl for the last eight months, and I'm sort of feeling like cashing my chips before she loses interest all together. Always good to have one iron in the fire you know isn't going to say no.

She's a barmaid here, so I've seen her a couple of times most weeks since I got here, and she is definitely up for it. Drinks appear 'on the house' and she hangs about our table half the night. Seriously, I'm surprised no one else has complained about the lack of service. A couple of times when I've slunk off early the lads reckon she's asked for me when she got off shift. But it's never happened, for various reasons, including a number of other women who didn't suffer the distraction of having to leave to deal with paying customers mid-flirt.

Tonight I can't see her. I feel a sudden twinge of anxiety. What if she's gone off with someone else? So much for chip cashing. I get myself a beer and start scouting the alternatives, but then she walks in. I grin. 'Hi bella.'

'Hi.'

I ask her how she is, and she tells me, in Italian, that she's fine and not working tonight. That's a bonus. I'm guessing she must have got sick of getting left with the end-of-shift dregs. So here we are, not working, not committed to going home with anyone else, and practically popping out of our tube top in anticipation. That last one was just her, by the way, not me.

I buy her one drink as a nicety, and she pretty much necks it. We walk back to the apartment talking as little as possible, and then we have sex, which is good. Actually it's pretty run of the mill, but it scratches the itch and she goes to sleep fairly quickly afterwards, apparently satisfied, not that I check.

Now I can't sleep. Normally getting laid knocks me out like a light, but tonight I'm just lying here trying not to move too much so I don't wake her up. And I don't want to wake her because I don't want to have sex with her again. That thought is a bit of a shocker. Theresa is gorgeous, in an obvious sort of way. But I like obvious. Nothing at all wrong with obvious. I know I'm supposed to find true beauty in the imperfections, or whatever, but at the end of the day you know where you are with obvious. I'm scared of waking her up, because if she wakes up we're going to have to have sex again. We're naked. We're in bed together, and we have no conversational common ground. If she wakes up anytime soon more sex is inevitable. My skin feels clammy, and like I need to have a shower. I roll over as carefully as I can manage, but my body is refusing to be comfortable.

I get out of bed without waking her at about half past two. I go into the living room. Before I've had a chance to decide what to do, my body has sat itself down and switched the computer on. When the screen comes to life I click on e-mail. Part of me is watching myself from outside wondering why the hell I've got up and put the computer on in the middle of the night. The other part of me, the part that's winning, is fixated on the screen. The new mail alert flicks up and I click on it to see Henri's name in my inbox.

The outside part of me is catching up with the inside part. I have just left a very attractive, very available naked woman in my bed to get up at a ridiculous hour in the morning to see whether a virtual stranger thousands of miles away has sent me e-mail. And that's when I know that I am truly and properly fucked.

Chapter Twenty-Three

Claudio

'Get up! Get up! Get up!' Ben is banging what I have to assume is a frying pan and wooden spoon outside my bedroom door. 'Time to start drinking.'

I roll over and stick my head under the duvet. Ben takes my silence as an invitation and marches into the room still bashing the pan. 'Come on. I'm making fried food to line our stomachs.'

I stick my head out and nod at him. Cooked breakfast does sound good actually, although I am concerned that Ben thinks lining our stomachs is necessary. Tonight is my stag. Henri made me promise to behave. Then she made Ben promise to make me behave. Then Trix made Danny promise to make us both behave. The stomach-lining plan does seem to suggest that Ben has not really absorbed these warnings. I wonder if allowing Henri to schedule pre-wedding wine tasting for tomorrow was a good idea. Are you supposed to spit it out? Oh well, hair of the dog and all that.

The fry-up is good. While I eat Ben runs me through the plan for the day. If he was aiming for fool-proof simplicity I think he's pulled it off. It goes like this:

1. Arrive at pub around 12 noon.
2. Drink.
3. Re-convene here for further fried food around lunchtime tomorrow, before I get dragged off in the afternoon for official groom duties.

I like it. It's a good plan. This afternoon we will also be able to watch Italy play England in the six-nations rugby. I moan about the lack of football, but Ben reckons they weren't willing to re-arrange international sporting schedules just to accommodate my stag.

Honestly, I don't know why Italy play rugby. We're just wonderful at football. We make the best suits in the world. We have the most amazing women. The food is perfection on a plate. Why do we even bother with other stuff? Why not just sit back and accept our inherent superiority in all the areas that actually matter, and let people with malformed necks from other countries run around after a football that somebody's sat on? Whoever decided that Italy should play international rugby had no thought for the pain this would cause their countrymen living in the UK.

Even worse than that, not only will England win, but I will be the only Italian supporter in the pub, because my oh-so-unromantic brother supports England. This is a man with no sense of heritage or history whatsoever. When I was about fifteen I called him out on it, and he just sort of shrugged and said that he was English because he was born in England. When I pointed out that he was nearly born in Italy, his parents were Italian, and all his family were Italian he just looked at me like he was waiting for me to explain how that was relevant to him. So on my stag night, my team are going to get well and truly stuffed and even my best man won't be supporting me.

With that in mind, I shall skim over the details of the match. Suffice to say England won. Only 23-19, so it was nowhere near as bad as I was expecting. The piss-taking was actually pretty low key on account of how for most of the match it actually looked like England could plausibly lose. It's pathetic but only losing by four feels almost like winning.

There's ten of us in all: me; Ben, obviously; Danny; John, unfortunately; four guys from college; one guy, Deanó, who we know from years ago; and one guy, Gaery, an Irish bloke who was over in Naples with me last year. He's in the UK at the moment because of some girl, much to Ben's disgust. Fine by me though – he decided to support Italy over England, so I wasn't feeling like a Billy on my own stag.

Anyway, game over, we go to play some pool. Ben appears to have been collecting fifty pence pieces since the beginning of time, so it looks like we'll be playing 'winner stays on' until all but one of us passes out through hunger or alcohol consumption. Me and Ben start, and he thrashes me, which I think is unsporting given that it's my party. He's spouting forth about how the game is all about angles and applied maths, so I leave him to explain it to some other sucker and head for the bar with Deano.

Deano has been around and about me and Ben since we were kids. His mum lived up the road from us, until they moved when we were teenagers. I lost touch with him after that, but he found Ben on one of those pre-Facebook getting-in-touch-with-old-schoolfriends things online when Ben was at uni. He's a good mate to have around: he looks like a serious hardnut. He's one of those square blokes, who's big in every direction. He wouldn't know what to do with himself in a fight. That's how we ended up being mates. I saved him in the playground. Scrapping with Deano was the primary school version of the fairground strongman striker for ten-year-olds. I think that sort of stuff is supposed to toughen kids up, but it didn't work on Deano. He would always end up in the middle of crowds of kids shouting, 'Fight! Fight! Fight!', with some brat half his size pounding at his stomach, and he'd just be standing there like he didn't really get what was going on.

Hanging out with him now, he is exactly the same as when we were eleven. I wouldn't be at all surprised if he produced a 1995 copy of Playboy from his satchel and told me to keep it hidden from my mum. Ben says he's soft in the head. I mean, he says it in a nice way, but he does say it. It's only half true though. Deano's soft across the board. It's not specific to his head.

Anyway, we have a beer together at the bar. Compared with Ben and Danny he's quite restful company, quieter company anyway.

'She's pretty.'

'Who is?' I glance at the bar staff. There is a particularly hot girl that works here, generally known as 'hot girl behind the bar'. Ben coined that – descriptive but not exactly poetic. She doesn't seem to be around though, so I start scanning the room for alternative prettiness.

'Your girlfriend.'

'Oh. Yes. She is.' She is pretty. I swallow. It's just an observation, nothing to get wound up about, but somehow other men noticing how pretty she is doesn't feel cool. 'When did you meet her?'

Deano scrunches up his eyebrows. 'In town.'

'When?'

'Last week. She was with Trix.' He grins at me. 'Why?'

Something tightens in my stomach. 'She didn't mention it.'

Once Ben has beaten another eight people at pool, we're allowed to move on. The next part of the plan is our favourite curry house and some competitive spice eating. Walking through town John falls into step beside me. I still don't know what to say to him.

'Everyone seems to think Henrietta's a lovely girl.'

Seems to think?

'Danny says she's excited about the wedding.'

I agree.

'I hope she's as excited as she seems.'

I look at him. 'What?'

'Nothing that won't wait.'

I swallow hard. Of course Henri's excited about the wedding. She is, in fact, pretty much beside herself in crazy excited bride mode. Trix keeps having to reassure me that it's entirely normal and nothing to be scared about. 'What do you mean?

He shakes his head. 'It's probably nothing.'

'What's nothing?'

He doesn't answer straight away, just smiles a bit to himself.

'I think she's very lucky,' and he touches my arm, really gently, so as you'd hardly notice it, if you weren't a straight man and therefore naturally very aware of what the gay man you're talking to is doing with his hands. That sounded wrong. I'm not homophobic. Well, I probably am a bit, but no more than any other straight twenty-first century bloke. Danny is genuinely a friend, and I suppose he touches me, but not in a gay way. Actually, in a very gay way, but it's not weird. He's just big and camp and expressive and he's always grabbing people's arms, or slapping people's backs and doling out huge man-hugs. John's different. Everything he says, every movement that he makes is pre-meditated.

I'm aware that I need to say something. 'Oh no. I'm very lucky.'

He doesn't respond to that, but his hand rubs very definitely against my leg. I take an involuntary half step away to the side, and that's it.

He walks off and catches up with Danny.

'I think she's very lucky.' I must be imagining things. He probably just brushed his hand against me as we were walking. It was probably an accident. Twice. He probably thinks she's lucky because she's looking forward to the wedding so much. I'm telling myself this, but I don't believe it. You are very welcome to call me arrogant, but I think that my mate's boyfriend just made a pass at me on my stag night.

As soon as we get to the curry house, I grab Ben by the arm and drag him to the bogs.

'What the fuck are you doing?'

'We need to talk.'

'In here? We're not women. We do not talk in toilets.'

I scan the room, and kick the stall door so it swings open. There's no one else in here. 'I'm not quite sure how to say this.'

Ben closes his eyes. 'If you're having second thoughts, it's not too late.'

'I'm not having second thoughts.'

He opens his eyes. 'Good. I was lying. It is too late. You have to marry her now, even if she turns out to be Satan's special representative to the North of England.'

'Shut up.'

'Right.'

'I really don't know how to put this.'

'Get to the point. I want to eat.'

'Right. I think John made a pass at me.' As soon as I say it, it sounds insane. 'That sounds stupid. It probably is stupid. Ignore me.'

'What happened?'

'Nothing really.'

'What happened?'

I look at him. He doesn't look surprised. He looks concerned, which is scaring me; sympathetic, which is even weirder coming from Ben; but not surprised. Still, it does sound crazy said out loud. 'It was nothing. He just made some comment about Henri being a lucky girl, and then I thought he sort of stroked my arm, and there was something else he said about Henri being excited or not being excited.' I take a breath. 'It was probably nothing.'

'What are you two doing in here?'

Danny is standing in the doorway to the toilets. 'If you've finished fixing your lippy and talking about boys, we need to order food, and you're already half a beer behind the pace. What are you talking about anyway?'

I don't know what to say. I don't look at Ben. If Danny catches us exchanging a look he'll know something's up. I don't have an answer ready. I rule out 'We were just discussing your boyfriend coming on to me,' but don't get any further. Ben manages to say some words.

'Pre-wedding jitters.'

Danny looks at me. 'Having second thoughts?'

Ben laughs. 'Not him. Me. Have you any idea of the pressure on the best man on these occasions? Don't lose the ring. Don't forget your speech. Dance with the bridesmaid. Remember everyone's name. Make sure everyone has a lift from the church to the reception.'

Danny looks confused. 'Can't we get taxis to the reception?'

Ben pats him on the back. 'Good idea. Thank you. Well that solves that problem. Shall we eat?'

Ben ushers Danny back out into the restaurant and turns back to me. 'You're right. You're probably imagining things. Come on. It's your stag. Let's go enjoy it.'

I follow him back to the table, but there's something bothering me. Ben didn't look surprised. He should have looked surprised. I was certainly surprised.

Chapter Twenty-Four

Nine Years Ago

Ben

'What the fuck?'

I've tried to jump up from my seat but it's a stupid moulded plastic thing that's attached to the table so my jump has left me pinned to the back of the chair, half squatting, with my crotch pressed against the table edge. What my jump has singularly failed to do is dislodge Danny's new boyfriend's hand from my upper thigh.

I sit back down again, and physically lift his hand off my leg. 'I'm straight.'

He shrugs. 'I'm not trying to turn you. Just fun.'

He's slurring his words. When he leans towards me I can see the trail of spit hanging off his upper lip.

I point towards the dance floor, where Danny is shaking his thang with a gloriously tipsy gaggle of middle-aged teachers. This time I do manage to stand up. 'I'm straight. You're with Danny. End of.'

I walk away towards the bar. I'm actually pretty pleased with the 'End of' – I think it sounds kind of cool and street. I get into the queue huddle and try to look casually back towards the table. The new, apparent, love of Danny's life has disappeared. John. He seems to have turned up in Danny's life pretty much out of nowhere, and has gone from 'guy I'm sort of seeing' to permanent resident in Danny's home in about three weeks straight. They're already referring to it as 'our' house. It's not theirs; it's Danny's. So far as I can tell John's not working, so I assume he's not paying either.

It's taking forever to get served, which is a relief. It gives me an excuse not to fling myself back into circulation anytime soon.

By the time the crowd shifts me close enough to the bar to start the silent nightclub 'want to buy a drink' mime, I've calmed down a bit about John. I mean, Danny tried it on when we first met. Ok, so John's older, and living with my mate, but still. I'm probably overreacting, and on that basis, I conclude, I don't need to say anything to Danny about it. Just a misunderstanding. Better forgotten, I think.

I feel someone dragging on my T-shirt from behind. I turn my head and see Danny leaning past about eight other people to get my attention. He mimes raising a glass to his lips, and I nod. He holds up five fingers and gestures to the group behind him, who I'm fairly sure aren't people he knew when we arrived here tonight. I nod and get my wallet out.

I manage to drag Danny out of the club at about twenty past two, on the grounds that none of us have any money left. At first he's adamant that we're going to the cashpoint and then heading back to another club, but I tell him that it's time for bed. John sort of shambles along after us, walking four paces behind and never joining in the conversation.

Once we get back I head straight to bed on the fold-out sofa in Danny's spare room. The combination of the time and the alcohol sends me straight to sleep, which sounds much better than admitting that I all but pass out.

I wake up suddenly and for a moment I'm not sure why. There's a digital clock on the floor next to the bed which tells me it's now 4.12am. As I turn back over I see that I'm not alone in the room. John is standing very still over by the door, still wearing the clothes from last night. I register that that's weird, but he doesn't give me much time to think about it. As I sit up in bed he lunges across the room, so by the time I realise he's going to hit me I can't even get my arms out from the duvet to protect myself. He punches me, once, hard in the face, and I fall backwards slamming my cheek into the upright back of the sofa bed. I don't speak or shout or move or anything, and I have no idea why not. John is kneeling on the bed now. He slams his forearm hard across my chest and with his other hand he squashes my face against the sofa.

'I know why you dumped that stupid bint. I know why you keep coming around here. You think I don't see but I see everything. You're not welcome.'

He presses his arm harder across my chest.

'Do I make myself clear?'

I don't answer. I can't answer, but he seems satisfied that he's made his point. Without saying anything else, he just lets go of me and walks out of the room. He didn't raise his voice. He didn't actually seem that angry, as though beating up houseguests in the night is just a minor inconvenience of playing host, like having to make up the spare bed, or being expected to provide interminable cups of tea.

I don't sleep so well after that. I spend the whole night running it over and over in my head, trying to work out what I'm going to tell Danny, when I'm going to tell him. I realise it has to be straight away. I know that I have no choice. If I don't tell him the next morning, I never will.

I force myself to stay in bed until I hear Danny moving around. As soon as I do hear him I switch from being desperate to talk to him, to wanting to hide in bed for as long as I can. I know I have to get up but my body won't co-operate. I consciously make myself move.

I go downstairs, and they're both in the kitchen. I'd sort of expected that. During the night, I kept imagining me and Danny going off on our own and me being able to tell him in my own time, but, even in my imagination, I realised John wasn't going to let that happen. I hadn't expected to see them both looking so happy though. John's in a white towelling robe, with pyjama bottoms on underneath. His hair is still wet from the shower. Danny's dressed in jeans and a T-shirt and is whistling and frying bacon, whilst John sits on the worktop drinking tea. The radio's on. They look like a picture from a Sunday lifestyle supplement.

When I walk in, John jumps off the worktop smiling. 'Good morning. Tea? Coffee?'

'Coffee.' I reply before my brain has a chance to intervene. How am I drinking coffee with a man who attacked me in my bed?

Danny looks up. 'Bloody hell mate. What happened to your face?'

I haven't even looked in a mirror yet, but as soon as he says it I realise that I almost certainly have a fairly dramatic bruise across my cheekbone. John leans over to pass my coffee and peers at my face. 'That looks nasty. What happened?'

He's all innocence and concern. Maybe I misunderstood; even as I think that another part of my brain is screaming at my voice to say something.

Danny is still peering at my cheek. 'Don't tell me you can't remember.'

I move my fingertips to my cheek, and shrug. 'Guess I was more drunk than I thought.'

There should be a moment now. A moment where I grow a pair and say. 'Actually Danny...' but I don't. I didn't shout last night and I don't shout now. I guess it's already too late.

Danny laughs. 'Oh dear. Getting too old for the lifestyle, boy. Don't worry. Eat some breakfast. I've got antiseptic somewhere.'

John nods still all concern. 'I'll find it. Don't worry.'

He looks right at me. 'You're going to be fine. It's not far above your lip though. It's gonna hurt like fuck if you try to talk too much.'

Chapter Twenty-Five

Henrietta

One week from now, I will be Mrs Claudio Messina.
Henrietta Messina. Henrietta Leonard-Messina. No.
That might be too much. *'Messina? Yes, it is unusual. My
husband's Italian you see ...'* My husband? I haven't even
got used to calling him my boyfriend yet, and now I'm
going to have to remember to say husband. I bet I'll get it
wrong all the time. I hope people won't think we're having
an affair, or just pretending to be married or something.

Tonight is going to be my hen night. Claudio's probably
already out on his stag, but I insisted on having today to
myself. This will be my last Saturday on my own in the flat.
As soon as we get back from the honeymoon I'll be moving
into Ben and Claudio's. I suggested he could move here, but
Claudio's only just unpacked from the last time and it's only
for three months so I don't really mind. This morning it's
me, my flat, my duster, and a teach yourself Italian course
on my MP3 player.

When I told Claudio I was going to clean the flat today
he laughed at me. He can't understand why it matters when
I'm not going to be living there much longer, but it does
matter. If anything it matters even more. What if Trix rents
it to someone else and they think I didn't keep it nice? And
I'm going to be waking up here on my wedding day, so
every detail has to be perfect.

The wedding is actually going to be perfect. I know that
every bride probably thinks that, but this wedding really
will be. Since we found the dress, everything seems to have
come together. Trix has a perfect simple blue dress, which

even she agreed was 'tolerable.' My dad's making us the most amazing cake. We've hired a kind of souly-motowny band to play in the evening. Our first dance is going to be *I Say a Little Prayer*, which I didn't really know that well, but Claudio loves. It really is going to be perfect.

I start cleaning the kitchen. I love cleaning the kitchen. There's a corner behind the toaster where crumbs accumulate. You have to pull the toaster out to get at them, and then you have to brush them up with something dry. Once you've brushed the crumbs up then you can spray and wipe. I love cleaning that corner. After I've done the worktops, I clean the oven, and then the floor. I always do the floor last, because then you can sort of back out of the room as you clean and you don't have to walk over the wet floor. I don't like the idea of contaminating bits I've already cleaned. I'm the same in the shower; I always wash my hair first, and then my face and then go down my body, so that the dirt from bits I'm just washing doesn't run over the clean bits.

Cleaning gives me good thinking time, which I need today. I need to work through what I'm going to say when Danny calls tonight. He's decided that tonight is the night for putting part two of his grand Ben and Trix plan into action. To be honest I'm feeling a bit sick about the whole thing so I don't make much progress. I've reached the bedroom before I've really thought anything beyond the fact that I'm going to mess it up and make Danny cross.

I always start and finish cleaning in the bedroom. The first thing I do when I wake up is strip the sheets off the bed, and put them straight in the washing machine. Then I let the bed air while I clean the rest of the flat, and the last thing I do is put fresh sheets on the bed.

I must have been slow today because I'm still lying on the bed, enjoying the fresh sheet smell, when Trix bangs on the door.

'Just a minute!' I jump off the bed and wash my hands before I let her in. She's standing on the doorstep wearing jeans, a checked shirt, and a cowboy hat. She is dragging a holdall behind her with one hand and trying to manage two six-bottle wine holders with the other. She looks suspiciously around when she comes in.

'Have you been cleaning?'

I nod. She slams the wine down on the coffee table.

'It's your Henri Hen Party today! Why are you doing housework?'

I shrug. I don't want to tell her that I wouldn't enjoy the party if I knew the flat was messy.

'Anyway, I have wine. There is pizza coming in about an hour, and everyone else will be here in about half an hour, so you need to get changed.'

She practically manhandles me into the bedroom and thrusts the holdall she is carrying into my hand. 'Seriously, find yourself something pretty!'

Inside the holdall there is an Indian Squaw costume. I walk back into the living room.

'You said you wouldn't make me dress up.'

'I lied.'

'Ben isn't making Claudio dress up.'

'Well, Ben's a miserable bugger. You are going to be a Red Indian.'

'Native American.'

'Whatever. Just put the costume on.'

'Where did you get it?'

'Hire place in town. Now put it on, or I'll shoot.' She pulls a plastic gun out of a holster on her belt. I notice that her hat is accessorised with a Sheriff's badge.

'Can't I be a cowgirl?'

'No. You Indian Squaw. Go dress.'

I give in and go back to the bedroom. I give the dress a

little sniff. It smells clean but I don't like the idea of all the other people that might have worn it. It makes me feel itchy somehow. I know Trix will be cross if I don't wear it though so I do as I'm told and put it on.

I'm trying to arrange my feathered headband when Trix comes in. Apparently I'm still not in the full costume. She scrabbles around inside the bag and finds face paint which she uses to make red and black lines on my cheeks. She spins me towards the mirror. 'There you go Mini-haha!'

For fancy dress it's not too bad actually. The dress is loose, so I don't have so many bulges and sticky out bits, and the lines on my face distract from the pastiness of my skin. They also save me from having to try to put make-up on.

There's another bang at the door. 'That'll be everyone.'

Everyone in this case is mainly librarians, a couple of teachers from schools that I go into, and a few old friends of Trix's who sometimes come over at weekends. Some are just wearing normal Saturday night outfits with Stetsons added. They get properly told off by Trix for their crap costumes. Most seem to have gone for it though. There's a lot of double-denim and cowboy boots on display tonight. It's not very pretty.

The pizza arrives, and Trix has put some music on. With the combination of wine, music and junk food the place starts to feel quite lively. I'm hoping that if everyone looks like they're having enough fun here, Trix will forget that we're supposed to be going on a pub crawl, and permit us to stay here. No chance though. As soon as she's satisfied everyone is gathered she bashes her gun against her wine glass for quiet.

'Ladies, and ladies, thank you very much for joining us. We are here to send Henrietta off into coupledom with a good strong idea of the pleasures she will be missing as an old married woman.'

There are quite a lot of woops and yee-hahs while she's talking. I almost feel a bit intimidated. Trix continues. 'It is time, ladies, to launch ourselves into the night with our hostage.'

Hostage? I'm guessing that'll be me then. The party rolls out into the street. I'm relieved that none of them have actually tried to tie me up like a proper hostage. Worryingly, some of them do seem to have lassoes hanging from their belts. As we're walking down the street, my mobile rings.

Trix laughs. 'Probably Claudio checking up on you.'

It's not Claudio. It's Danny. Right. I guess this is it then. I slow down slightly. 'I'd better get this.'

I press the button to answer the call, and hear Danny on the other end. 'Is this a good moment?'

I let Trix get a little bit further in front of me. The rest of the group has walked on ahead, but she's half hanging back to wait for me. She's in the sort of halfway position where she's trying to wait for me without looking like she's listening in. 'Yeah. This is a perfect moment.'

'Good. Do you want me to talk you through it?'

'No. It's OK. I'm not going to say anything to her.'

'Perfect. I'll just wait here and prompt if you need it then.'

This is odd. I feel a bit like a performing monkey. I've got Danny on the phone checking that I'm doing it right, and I've got Trix in front of me, pretending not to listen. She'd better actually be listening. This is all for her benefit, and I don't think I'd cope if I had to do it all again.

'Seriously. I'm not going to tell her. It's up to Ben if he wants to say something.'

'Fabulous. Have you got her attention?'

'Uh-huh.' I pause trying to think of what to say next. I practically rehearsed the whole thing with Claudio last night, but it's different now.

Danny jumps in. 'Just to be clear. It's Trix you're not going to tell.'

'Of course, I won't say anything to Trix.' Now she's definitely listening. 'It's hard though. She's my best friend.'

'Good. Keep going.'

'I think he should just tell her.'

'You're a natural at this.'

I grin to myself, and turn slightly away from Trix, so she doesn't see me smiling; hopefully it'll make it look even more like I'm trying to have a conversation I don't want her to hear. I hope she is still listening. 'Ben's so proud. He should just tell her how he feels.'

'Ah, but he never will. That's why we have to help matters along a bit. Anyway it's not just him that's proud.'

'That's true actually.'

'Come on. Spell it out a bit. We're not dealing with the brightest people here, love life wise.'

I laugh. At least I know Danny is wrong about that. Trix and Ben are easily the cleverest people I know. Hearing them talk to each other always makes me feel like I should have done more revision. This is not the time for an argument though. 'Ok. You're right. Her pride's just as bad.'

'Nice. I can feel Cupid preparing his arrow as we speak!'

'You are sure that he likes her?' That was only half part of the charade to be honest. It was at least half a genuine question.

'Absolutely. I think he more than likes her. Go on!'

'Ben in love with Trix?' I lower my voice a little bit more. I'm sure she's listening now. I need to concentrate on making it look like I don't think she can hear.

'Nice. That's probably enough. Shall we wrap it up?'

'Well, look, I won't tell her. You don't need to worry about that.'

'Good. Good. Enjoy your night, sweetie.'

'You too. Where are you guys now?'

'Just arrived at the Indian.'

'Is Claudio there?' I know that calling your fiancé on your hen night is pathetic. Trix tried to stop me bringing my phone to make sure I couldn't, but this way I didn't ring him. And technically he didn't ring me, so neither of us would have broken any hen or stag rules.

'Um. I think he must have gone to take a slash. Ben's gone too.'

'Oh. OK. Well, have fun.' I hope he's OK. What if something's happened and Danny doesn't want me to know?

'I'm sure he's great though. I'll go make sure. Don't fret.'

'I'm not.'

Danny laughs. ''Course you're not. See you on Monday.'

Danny ends the call, and I turn back towards Trix. She's staring at me. She looks like she's just witnessed a car crash. 'The others are getting away. We'd better catch up.'

I skip past her without waiting. I think she's too shocked to ask anything, but I know I'd crumble under questioning. Best to get away and hide in amongst the group, which might be a bit awkward given that I'm wearing an Indian Squaw's costume with a feathered headdress.

Chapter Twenty-Six

Thirteen Years Earlier

Trix

I'm in the bar with Danny. Most of my university stories start in a bar with Danny. I do fundamentally believe that he is to blame for nearly all of my drink induced errors of judgement.

Anyway, I'm in the bar with Danny, when he sees someone he knows standing on their own. Danny can never stand to see anyone on their own. It seems to offend his sense of being self-appointed social leader for everyone who falls into his wake.

'Benjamin!'

I follow Danny around the bar and hang back while he pats the stranger enthusiastically on the back.

'Benjamin! You must meet Trix. She's fabulous.'

The guy half looks up, without ever moving his attention fully away from his beer. He has mousy hair that sticks out at the sides, like he's trying to cultivate some mad scientist eccentric side tufts. He's wearing worryingly stone washed jeans, and has tucked his T-shirt into them, in a deeply ill-advised way. He holds out his hand and I shake it feeling more like I've come to a job interview than out for a drink. His handshake is brisk and firm. Mine is probably limp and uncomfortable. Generally, eighteen-year-olds in bars don't do a lot of hand-shaking.

Danny seems satisfied that we are all now the best of friends though, and is ordering drinks. He has accosted the barman and demanded three jars of his finest mead. Ben steps in and asks for a beer, raises his eyebrow towards me, and takes my half nod as a request for beer. Then he looks at Danny who is grinning cheerfully, apparently waiting for his mead. The barman looks to Ben for guidance. Ben shrugs. 'Three beers, mate.'

Danny rolls his eyes. 'No mead?'

'No mead,' Ben confirms.

'Well what is the world coming to? We shall have to go back to that place with the mead, Benjamin.'

Ben shakes his head. 'I think that was a private party.'

'Really? Were we invited?'

'No.'

'Oh dear. Are you sure it wasn't a pub?'

'It was fancy dress.'

'Oh.' Danny throws his hands to the ceiling. 'And I thought they were real knights.'

The barman comes back with three beers and Ben pays. As the barman walks away Danny picks up his drink. 'Oh? I was going to get these.'

Ben laughs. 'No. You weren't.'

Danny shrugs. 'I'll owe you one.'

He takes a long look around the bar, and settles on a group of three guys looking nervous by the entrance.

'New people! Well, I shall leave you two to get to know one another.' And off he goes.

I pick my beer up and lean on the bar next to Ben. 'So, you're Benjamin?'

He shakes his head. 'Benedict.'

I'm confused. 'I thought Danny said ...'

'He did. He thinks Benedict's a silly name, so he's decided to stick with Benjamin.'

'Doesn't that piss you off?'

Benjamin/Benedict shrugs. 'Not really. Should it?'

I decide to try a different tack. 'Has he ever bought you a drink?'

Now he laughs. 'On the first two or three nights he bought hundreds. I think he might have spent all his money.'

'You're kidding?'

'No. He's a bit all or nothing is Danny.'

And so we chat a bit about how we met Danny, what courses we're doing, what A-levels we did. Me – English, History, and Art; Him – Physics, Chemistry, Maths and Further Maths. Apparently he feels that you can't have too much maths in your life.

I've got to the bottom of my bottle, and now so has he. There's a sort of uneasy silence. Technically, we don't really know each other, so offering to buy another drink might look a bit needy, but then he's bought me one so not doing so would be rude. Still, this is university. It is a whole new world, and I am a whole new mature independent woman. 'Can I get you another?'

I sort of half mumble it, hoping that if he is appalled by the idea I can pretend he's misheard somehow. My whole new woman thing is still a bit of a work in progress.

'Sorry?' He's leaning towards me to hear.

'Would you like another drink?'

'Sure.'

Sure? That's all. No applause for my bold taking of the initiative, not that there is any initiative to be taken. We're just two people having a chat and a drink. I secure two more beers, and we chat some more. I ask about his family. Parents – two; brother – one; family is Italian but live in Yorkshire.

'You didn't move far to come to uni then?'

'Well, my parents crossed a continent. I felt like that was probably enough jaunting about for the time being.'

'You don't live at home though?'

'No. In halls.'

Oh thank god. Obviously, this is still just a drink between

two people having a chat and nothing more. But it's good to know I've not been investing time and money in someone that still lives with his mum.

'What about your family?'

'They're dead.'

I really do need to work on some more socially graceful ways of dropping that into conversation. Maybe I could start off by saying that they're not well, and then kill them off at a later date. He looks a bit scared.

'I'm sorry.'

'It's OK. It was a long time ago. I don't really remember my parents. My nana brought me up.'

'Right. Ok. What's she like?'

'She's dead too.'

He closes his eyes. 'I'm sorry again.'

'Thank you. She died just after A-levels. It was like she'd decided her work was finished.'

'You must miss her.'

I nod.

'I'm not very good at this.'

I look at him. 'At what?'

'Chatting. I feel like I need to sympathise, but I'm not really sure how to go about it?'

'You're doing fine. Just say whatever is in your head.'

'So ... er ... do you have any living relatives?'

He looks at me, and I can't stop myself laughing. 'I take it back. You should keep whatever's in your head to yourself.'

He laughs too. We chat some more, and laugh a lot more, and drink some more.

I'm starting to wonder whether it would be OK to try and move things on a bit when the barman plonks four tequilas down in front of us. Ben tries to protest, but the barman just points across the bar. Danny is waving a £20 note at us.

'Where do you think he got that?'

Ben shrugs. 'I don't want to know.' He gestures at the drinks. 'Shall we?'

And so we do. And then Ben orders two more. And then I order four more. And then the bar closes, which is probably a good thing, because Ben is having trouble walking straight. I know this, because every time I move he bashes into me.

We get back to his halls and I follow him in. Outside his room he stops and looks at me. 'You don't live here.'

And I giggle a bit and kiss him, and he kisses me back. We go into his room and have some of the worst, most drunken, most uncomfortable, most fumbly sex imaginable. Afterwards he admits it was his first time, and I say I've done it lots of times before, and like a true gentleman he resists the urge to call me out on my, probably very obvious, lie.

Chapter Twenty-Seven

Trix

'What colour are no tomatoes?'

Henri is standing at the front of the community room repeating Ben's question from his talk about Zero. I'm sitting at the back wearing my Senior Librarian responsible, serious, 'Don't mess about for Miss Leonard' face, and trying to work out whether that really was less than six weeks ago.

'What colour is the void beyond the ends of the universe? How do you make a picture of nothing at all?'

This project was a good idea. I mean, I'll admit I was furious when Henri set it up, but that was understandable, knowing that that man would be coming into work. He is simply infuriating. Well, I thought he was simply infuriating, but maybe ...

I drag my attention back into the room. Henri is doing a great job. This is her regular primary art club, but there are about twice as many kids here as usual. She's got most of the local primary schools involved in the competition and one secondary as well. There's been stuff about it in the local paper. Guttingly, it does seem to be working out quite well.

Someone has raised their hand at the front. Henri nods at them. 'Does it have to be a picture, Miss?'

Henri shakes her head. 'No. You can make a model, or a painting, or a collage. If you want you can even make a video.'

I wince as she says this. They will now all want to make videos, which will be traumatic, because we'll have to borrow video equipment from one of the schools, and it'll be antique, and it'll take me and Henri weeks to work out how to make it work, when most of the kids probably have better cameras on their phones. Unfortunately, just letting them use those would kind of compromise our whole zero-tolerance of mobile phones policy.

Still, it is Henri's last couple of months here, so I probably shouldn't undermine her enthusiasm at this stage. I can't believe they're moving to Italy. I mean I knew that she was going to move into Ben and Claudio's after the wedding, so I sort of knew she wouldn't be living downstairs any more, but Italy? She says I have to go and stay every holiday and she'll be back loads to see her dad, but, you know, I worry about her.

She'll be off in a foreign country, and she's got used to having me just upstairs as well. I do pop down quite often to keep her company. At least if she had been at Ben's she'd have had him around, as well as Claudio. And I could have popped over there to see her.

Henri has started to hand out paper and pencils now so the kids can start sketching ideas for their projects. Ben's coming back to judge the competition in the summer, so they'll be working on this all term. Ben. Ben coming back here. The more I think about it the more Henri and Claudio leaving feels like the end of something. If Hen's not living at Ben's I won't have a reason to go around there. The art project will be over, so he won't have a reason to come into work. Danny seems to have given up on making us hang out together. Not that I'm bothered about not seeing Ben. I mean that's probably kinder, given how he feels about me. It must be painful for him to keep seeing me around. Some distance between us is probably all for the best.

I mean, if I am bothered, it's not about not seeing him. It's more like I feel cheated. I assumed any feelings Ben had were past tense. If they're not, surely I should know so we can talk it through like grown ups, but then I don't want to give him the impression I feel the same. Like I say, it's probably for the best.

Although, if he is having feelings for me, isn't it healthier that he has the chance to express that? I mean, where would Romeo have been, if Juliet had just shut the balcony window and told him to stop wittering on. Not that I'm comparing us to Romeo and Juliet, and actually that didn't work out that well anyway. Bad example. But still, sometimes feelings are better expressed honestly. Like Captain Wentworth in *Persuasion*. You see him and Anne were madly in love when they were young, and then they meet up again years later. Anne assumes his feelings have changed and they almost don't find each other again because they're scared of telling each other the truth. Not that me and Ben are going to find each other again. I'm just saying, probably for him all this emotion is better out than in, like a burp.

Henri is bustling around the classroom now, leaning over the table nearest to me. 'Oh that's really good. Just put down any ideas you have. Don't hold back. Just jot down whatever you feel.'

I'm not convinced of the wisdom of telling a group of ten-year-olds to jot down whatever they feel. Inevitably, it's going to involve violence.

'Whatever you feel.' That's a big idea. How do I feel? How did I feel when I heard Henri on the phone? Well, obviously I can't be in love with Ben. That's for sure. I've made that mistake before. Once is forgivable I think – twice would make me look foolish, and I'm not foolish.

Maybe that's what Henri meant though, when she said I was proud. If I were him, would I tell me how I feel? He's probably expecting to get laughed at, which I wouldn't do. In fact I'm quite cross with him for even thinking it.

Well, I shall prove him wrong. I shall prove that I can be understanding. For the next few weeks I shall be so nice and kind and understanding towards Ben that he will realise that he has no reason to be scared of telling me how he really feels. Then it will all be out in the open and we can talk about it like adults, which will be far healthier for Ben. Obviously, this is for his benefit, not mine. Well, I will be the more mature person. I will act with understanding and grace. That'll show him.

Chapter Twenty-Eight

Henrietta

It's half past nine. I've been up since six. I've dusted all my surfaces and wiped the kitchen, and later today, I'm getting married. Trix told me really firmly that I wasn't allowed to go up and wake her up before half past eight, so I thought I might as well make the place nice, as I was awake doing nothing. When I did go up at half past eight, like she said I could, she was still in bed anyway.

She says we don't need to start getting ready for ages, and she wouldn't get up, so I came back down to carry on cleaning. I've just finished vacuuming in the bedroom. My doorbell rings. It'll be either my dad or Trix. Probably my dad; I suspect Trix is hoping I'll keep myself occupied a bit longer. She's probably gone back to sleep.

It is my dad. He's wearing his normal checked shirt, jumper and corduroy trousers, but he's carrying one of those hire shop suit holders. I take it off him and hang it on the back of my bedroom door. My wedding dress is hanging off the front of the wardrobe, so between them it looks like we're going to have a sort of clothes wedding right here in my room.

'Would you like a cup of tea?'

'That'd be grand.'

I make the tea properly in my very pretty Art Deco teapot. It was a present from Trix, and is one of the loveliest things I've ever owned. I adore Art Deco. When I first got it I didn't use it, because I wanted to keep it nice, but Trix said she'd be hurt if I didn't use it, so now I make sure I do. I pour my dad a big mug of tea with lots of milk and two sugars, just how he likes it. Builder's tea, he used to call it.

'Are you not having one?'

I shake my head. My tummy's turning somersaults. A cup of tea would probably be a good idea. Trix's bound to try to make me drink champagne later, but at the moment I'm too excited to eat or drink anything.

My dad walks into the bedroom, so I follow him through. He sits down on the edge of the bed, and pats the space beside him.

'Now, pet,' he starts. 'Today is a big day.'

I nod. Today is a massive day. By the end of today I'm going to be Henrietta Messina. Mrs Claudio Messina.

'I just wanted to have a little chat with you, you know, before you head down the aisle.'

He says 'down the aisle' in a slightly jokey tone, as if he can't quite believe he's saying those words to his little girl.

'I just wanted to say that you've been a wonderful daughter.'

I've been a wonderful daughter?

'And I know you'll be a wonderful wife. I just wanted to say ...' His voice cracks slightly. I lean over and put my head on his shoulder. He pats the side of my face gently. 'Wonderful.'

'Thank you.' I don't know what else to say. I know I haven't been wonderful. I know that since Mum died I haven't done enough to make sure he's happy. But I am going to be a wonderful wife. I am going to make Claudio happy. I'm going to be the perfect wife.

'Right.' My dad pauses, and raises his mug of tea. 'Better get this down while it's hot.'

Chapter Twenty-Nine

Ben

My place is groom headquarters. From what I'd understood about being a best man, my role was getting Claudio to the church, and not forgetting the ring. It turns out there is more to it than that. This morning will mainly be spent giving lifts to flower arrangements.

I have to collect buttonholes, table decorations and bouquets from the florist and take the right bits to the right places. I'm not totally confident of my ability to tell the difference between a bouquet and a table decoration, but I'm trusting that the florist will recognise my uselessmanness and talk me through it.

Mum and Dad have arrived at my flat by the time I'm going out, so it's actually a relief to have stuff to do. Mum is fussing over Claudio like he's a photogenic eight-year-old with a terminal illness. I take the table decorations first. The woman at the hotel coos over them a bit, and then shows me the reception room. I seem to be expected to make some sort of comment. I hazard that the balloons are nice, and she seems happy with that. I don't know really. It's just a big room, which is good. I knew we'd be needing one of those.

I go to Trix's next. I'm still trying to decide whether to ring her bell or Henri's, and I haven't even started working out how to ring either bell without dropping the flowers, when Trix opens the door. She beams at me, and stands back to let me in.

'Hello. Come in. Come in. Bring them through.'

I follow her into her kitchen and put the flower box down on the worktop.

'It's quiet here.'

'Henri's downstairs with her dad. He wanted a fatherly chat. I think he might be telling her about the birds and the bees.'

I lean towards her and whisper. 'I think Claudio already told her.'

She laughs and then she keeps laughing. I sort of feel pressured to say something else funny, like I'm now in laughter credit and need to redress the situation.

'Actually, I know he told her. I have to sleep in the next room to the practical sessions.' I'm not sure that was funny enough.

'Ben!' She punches my arm, but she's smiling. I think she might be being playful. I'm not really sure.

She looks at the flowers. 'These are …' She pauses and looks at me. 'These are flowers.'

'That's exactly what I thought. Fortunately, the florist explained it to me.' I point at the bouquet. 'These blue ones, for example, are a particular sort of flower,that represents something.'

'Represents what?'

'You know, something. Something nice probably.'

She pokes me in the ribs. If this is playfulness, then it causes more bruises than the name suggests. 'I'm not convinced you really took in all the details.'

'I thought flowers were more your area. You know, romance and beauty and all that?'

I'm making a real effort to keep my tone light. I don't want to wind her up today, but I don't feel ready to leave yet either.

'Not hearts and flowers! Proper romance, with guts and tears and meaning to it.'

'Guts and tears? Really, I can't see why they don't get you writing Valentine's cards.'

'Very funny. Seriously though, romance should mean something. It shouldn't just be a pretty gesture.'

She's not looking at me any more, but sort of muttering to the floor. 'It should be deeper than that. You know what I mean?'

'Yeah. I know what you mean.'

Then neither of us says anything for a colossal period of time. At least it feels colossal, and I have no social skills. If it feels too long to me it's probably been about a year and a half. Henri and Claudio probably have twins by now. They probably named them after us in memory of how we mysteriously disappeared on their wedding day.

Stop thinking. Say something. And then we both speak at once, and then both stop again, and then both speak again. I stop. 'You go.'

She steps back. 'I was just going to say thank you for bringing the flowers.'

I nod. 'That's OK.'

She looks at the clock. 'Well, I suppose I'm going to have to interrupt Tony's little chat.'

'Right.'

'I mean she needs to start getting ready. Only …' She looks at the clock again. 'Only five hours to go.'

To me five hours sounds like enough time to redecorate the spare room and then start getting ready, but I will trust Trix's feminine judgement.

I start to leave. In the doorway I stop. 'Ok then. See you at the altar.' See you at the altar? 'I mean not at the altar exactly, just, you know, near it …'

She's laughing, so I laugh too. And then we stop laughing, and sort of look at each other, and she says. 'Right then.'

And I say, 'Yeah.'

I turn and walk too quickly back to the car. It's a good job I'm making allowances for the fact that she's hopelessly in love with me. Otherwise that would have been really awkward.

Chapter Thirty

Trix

Five hours to get ready? He must truly think I've lost it. He does think I've truly lost it. He practically ran back to his car. Was I always this bad at this sort of thing? Not that I'm planning any sort of thing, but if I was, you know, I just feel that I used to be more adept in that whole area. Yes. Right. Well, I'm glad that's clear.

I can't justify interrupting Tony for at least another two hours. In fact, I'm kind of grateful that his fatherly wisdom is keeping her occupied. She rang my doorbell at 8.30 this morning. 8.30am! On a Saturday! I was half surprised she wasn't already in her dress. If we run the day on Henri's schedule we'll be at the church several hours before Claudio. I did try to talk her through the notion that brides are expected to be fashionably late, but she screwed her face up at me and said, 'I'm getting married at three o'clock.'

I suggested that five past three would be perfectly fine, but apparently five past three would be perfectly terrible. The hairdresser is coming here at noon, and I really would like to keep Henri distracted from any 'getting-ready' activities until then. At least that will give us a chance of not being embarrassingly early.

All of that leaves me with some unexpected time to fill. That always happens on days like this. You mentally block out the whole weekend for The Wedding, but it actually only takes up about twelve hours. The rest of the time you're just kicking about wondering why you don't have anything to do.

Ben's book is lying on the coffee table, where it's been

165

being ignored for the last six weeks. Reading on Henri's Big Day feels slightly inappropriate but I don't have anything else to do, so I lie down on the sofa and pick up the book.

Chapter 2: What The Romans Did For Us

What did the Romans do for us? Well, in this case, actually nothing. Although, technically, that is quite wrong. The Romans failed utterly to do Nothing for us. They had no symbol for it, no number for it, no mathematical concept for it. So far as the idea of Zero goes the Romans had nothing.

It is, for many, one of the great mathematical mysteries of the past. The Romans were, in their time, almost unparalleled as practical engineers. They were great road and bridge builders, and designers of complex symmetric buildings, and even more complex systems to heat them. And, yet, they had a system of writing numbers that is unique only in the extent of its impracticality and ability to confuse.

After the mathematical inventions of the Babylonians, and their great breakthrough in recognising the value of the empty column, the Romans took maths on a giant trip backwards.

A giant trip backwards? How apposite. I turn to the cover page and inspect the picture of the author again. It's one of those black and white head and shoulders shots that only ever appear as author photos in the back of books. Black and white suits Ben though; it fits with his view of the world. This is ridiculous. I get angry just looking at his picture. Is it wrong to quite like getting angry?

'Trix!'

Henri is standing in the doorway in her bathrobe. I sit up to look at her.

'Trix, can I start getting ready yet?'

'Not until the hairdresser gets here.'

She crinkles her nose and comes and sits down next to me. 'That's ages.'

'Well getting ready now won't make the wedding happen quicker.'

She's swinging her feet and banging them against the settee. It doesn't seem possible that she's old enough to get married.

'Where's your dad?'

'He's taking the cake to the hotel. He'll be back about one.'

I nod.

'Is one early enough? We don't want to be rushing. Should I ring him and tell him to come earlier?'

'It's early enough. It's two whole hours before the wedding, and the church is only twenty minutes away.'

'Yeah, but we don't want to be late, do we?'

'We won't be late. Anyway, you're supposed to be late. You're the bride.'

She gives me her special 'I've decided not to understand' face, and so I drop the subject. Tradition or not, Henri is going to be one punctual bride.

'We could open the champagne.' Even as I say it I'm not convinced that it's my best idea. If we start drinking now, then I'll probably have to eat something later and will mess up my make-up and get crumbs down my dress, but champagne seems like a wedding morning sort of thing to do, and it might distract Henri for a few more minutes.

'You said not until the hairdresser arrives.'

'Well, you're the one that wanted to start getting ready.'

'Yes but, if there's a plan you can't just go changing the plan. Then there's just no system at all.'

She looks properly put out now. She's like this at work too. Everything she's involved in has a perfectly typed up plan, with targets and perfectly thought out SMART objectives. The first session she ever did for art club, she did this beautiful plan. When I read it I suggested to her that she might need to be more flexible. I asked her what happened if one of the children asked a question. She said that the plan allowed for 4.5 minutes of questions.

The doorbell rings. Henri dives off the sofa. 'The hairdresser!'

She's early. In the circumstances, I have no idea whether that's a good thing or not. 'Go answer it then. I'll get the champagne.'

I'm feeling like I need it.

The hairdresser is a special one who mainly does 'up-dos' for weddings. That must be odd for a hairdresser, to just decide you don't like cutting hair any more and you're just going to make a living out of posh ponytails. What she's doing is a lot more than a posh ponytail though really. I think it might be art.

She's managed to make all these little tiny curls and pile them all up on top, with more curls falling down around my face. I had no idea I had so much hair. When she's finished she starts on my make-up. Normally make-up makes my face feel all hot and too tight. Today I let her take over though. Hair and make-up are part of the schedule; they're part of making me the perfect bride for the perfect wedding.

Trix sits on the bed drinking her champagne while I'm being 'done'. I've conceded that she can wear her hair down. It took enough effort to get her to agree to the dress. And her hair is lovely anyway. She has all these thick beautiful red curls that just bounce around her. It's taking quite a lot of time and chemistry to get mine to create a similar effect.

After the hairdresser has finished Trix says I have to eat something before I put the dress on. I know she's right. We won't be eating the wedding breakfast until about 6 o'clock. I don't know why it's called breakfast, but it is. The lady at the hotel keeps calling it that, so it must be right.

When my dad gets back he makes us sandwiches, with white bread and real butter and proper ham. Trix says they're the sort of sandwiches they have in the Enid Blyton novels, all full of childhood and good intentions.

And then finally, after the sandwiches, and after I've brushed my teeth and Trix's redone my lipstick, it's time for the dress. Trix and I go upstairs to her room, which she has tidied especially for the occasion. I sit on the bed while Trix gets dressed. She says we have to do my dress last. I can't wait. I got it from the shop on Wednesday, and I've kept having to sneak little looks at it, to make sure it's just how I remember it. It is. It's going to make me perfect.

Eventually, at quarter past two, Trix agrees that I can put the dress on. She unzips it and holds it for me to step into, and then fastens the dress up my back, and ties the loose fabric around me. She walks around in front of me and grins before she turns me towards the mirror.

'Ta-dah! Rapunzel, ready for Prince Charming.'

I start to well up when I look in the mirror, but Trix tells me I can't cry because of my mascara. Actually, the hairdresser said the mascara was triple-waterproof because brides always get teary, so I can cry if I want to, but Trix tells me not to, so I'd better not.

We go downstairs to my dad, and he does cry. He keeps saying I'm his little princess, and he's so proud, which is lovely, and exactly what the father of the bride ought to say when he sees his little girl in her wedding dress.

He takes about fifty pictures of me, and then about another twenty of me and Trix, and then Trix takes some of me and my dad. I suspect that they're just trying to delay me, because Trix thinks the bride should be fashionably late. But I am walking down that aisle at 3pm, and no one is going to stop me.

I can picture it. The church is going to look beautiful. We've got flowers all over it. And I love looking at the congregation at weddings. There's always so much colour. Normally, everything's all black and grey and brown and navy and denim, but at weddings it looks as if everyone has blossomed. Whatever Trix says, I'm going to be bang on time; I am not going to be late for my perfect wedding.

Chapter Thirty-One

Trix

For some reason I get a car all to myself to the church. I'm not allowed to share with Henri and her dad because that's 'not traditional' apparently. I'm supposed to arrive before Henri to make sure everything's ready. I have no idea what I'll do if it's not.

Fortunately, Ben is standing on his own in the doorway at the back of the church, wearing a morning coat, waistcoat and cravat, so I can pass some time laughing at him. I open with, 'You look silly.'

He turns towards me. 'And you look,' he pauses. 'You look beautiful.'

I don't quite know what to say in response. Now I feel bad about saying he looks silly. 'You look OK really.'

He shakes his head. 'No. I look silly. I think women do better than men in terms of wedding outfits.'

'Not always. She was threatening me with peach.'

Ben grins. 'I'm going to assume that would be bad.'

'Very bad.'

'Well, I think that's the longest conversation I've ever had about clothes.'

'You coped admirably. Jolly well done you.'

He claps his hands together. 'Right then. Nearly time to get this show on the road.'

I nod. 'Henri should be here in a couple of minutes.'

'How is she?'

'Sort of perky but psychotic. How's the groom?'

'OK.' He pauses again. 'Quiet, but OK. I think.'

'You're not sure?'

He grins again. 'Pre-wedding jitters. It's a big day.'

'It certainly is. And then you get to share your home with newlyweds.'

'Thanks for reminding me.'

'They'll be fine.'

'They'll be nauseating. Maybe I could come and live with you.'

It's a joke. It's very clearly a joke. I should be laughing to show that I know it's a joke. I'm not. I'm just sort of gazing at him. Honestly, I really did used to be better at this.

Henri's car pulls up outside and saves me from popping his name on the answering machine right here and now. I gesture towards the car, 'Showtime.'

He nods. 'I'll let them know we're ready.'

He turns to walk away, and then turns back. 'At least tell me I can drop round and see you occasionally, you know, when they're particularly annoying.'

'Sure. Any time.' Any time? That's great. Don't try to sound like you have a life or anything. No. You just commit to sitting at home for the rest of your life on the off-chance that he pops in. Well done Trix. You're a walking talking masterclass in how not to play it cool.

I resist the urge to watch him walk away, and go and help Henri out of the car. In the church doorway I fiddle a bit with her skirt and loosen a curl that's got itself caught up in her earring. I'm feeling quite excited when the music starts and her dad leads her down the aisle in front of me.

The wedding service is beautiful. Danny reads that bit from Corinthians that they always have at weddings.

'Love keeps no record of wrongs,' he reads. I glance over at Ben, and I think I catch him looking and quickly looking away. I look away too. He was definitely looking at me. Probably. Or maybe he wasn't. Maybe he was just staring into space and now he thinks I was looking at him.

I force myself to concentrate on the actual ceremony. It gets to the bit where the vicar asks the congregation if they know of any reason why Henri and Claudio can't get married. In my opinion, the vicar milks it a bit. He does a lot of dramatic looking around and pauses for longer than I would think really necessary. I suppose he doesn't get that much other opportunity to ham it up. It's not really appropriate at funerals, is it?

Claudio is staring straight ahead with his face fixed on the vicar. Ben was right. He does look properly nervous. It's his turn first.

The vicar turns to him and asks him the questions. You know the drill; it goes something like this:

'Claudio, will you take Henrietta to be your wife? Will you love her, comfort her, honour and protect her, and, forsaking all others, be faithful to her as long as you both shall live?'

'No.'

Chapter Thirty-Two

Trix

Well, I didn't think he was that nervous. There's a sort of ripple of laughter through the congregation, because he must be joking. It's weird, and horrible, and not even a little bit funny, but clearly, it must be some sort of bad, bad joke.

Henri is just staring at him. She hasn't said a word, but her mouth is open with no sound coming out. The vicar leans forward, and pats Claudio on the arm. He looks towards the congregation and smiles. 'What a time to fluff your lines? We'll try that again.'

There's another ripple of half-laughter. I look over at Ben and I can see him whispering to Danny who seems to be shrugging in response. It seems to take an age for the vicar to speak again, but it's probably no more than a few seconds.

Very quietly and very slowly he repeats the question, just the same as before. Love, comfort, honour, protect, forsake others; it's all there. Everyone is staring at Claudio, waiting for his answer.

'No.'

Chapter Thirty-Three

Ben

I collect two bottles of beer from the bar and go and put one down in front of Trix.

'Want some company?'

She shrugs, which isn't 'No,' so I sit down. She might want company or not, but she's stuck with me. We're in the bar at the hotel. I figured telling them the reception was off might be a best man duty, although it wasn't on the list that Henri wrote out for me. Trix came with me. I think she wanted something to do.

'Do you know how Henri is?'

Trix shakes her head. 'How do you think?'

'Did Tony take her home?'

'Back to his house.'

I nod.

'Do you know where Claudio is?'

'Not answering his phone.'

'Have you tried your landline?'

I nod.

'Did you know what he was going to do?'

I shake my head.

'And you really haven't talked to him?'

I shake my head. I don't think she believes me. She thinks there's something I'm not telling her, but I really don't know what happened with him. I could guess, but a guess is all it would be; I have nothing to base it on. I've been trying to ring him ever since he walked out of the church and drove away. Drove away in my car, as it goes. Something tells me that it's not really the time to moan about that.

I take a hefty swig of beer. I keep replaying what happened in my head after Claudio said, 'No.'

Tony went mental. He was yelling at Claudio, and pushing and trying to hit him, and Claudio just kept saying, 'She knows why. She knows.'

That must have been going on for a minute or more before anyone else reacted. Then Danny pushed past me and pulled Tony back, and I tried to put myself in between Tony and Claudio.

And then Trix grabbed my shoulder and turned me towards Henri. That was the worst bit. Henri was just standing there exactly the same as she had been before. Staring straight ahead at the altar, clutching her bouquet. Trix went over to her and touched her shoulder and said, 'Henri? Hen? Are you OK?'

She didn't react at all. She didn't even turn around, and Claudio was still saying, 'She knows. She knows why.'

I think that was when the vicar tried to intervene, and said something about calming down and discussing things in the vestry. And Claudio walked out. I went after him, but by the time I got into the car park he was slamming the door to my car and then he was gone.

When I went back in Tony was trying to lead Henri away. In the car, coming here, Trix said it looked like someone trying to teach a mannequin to walk. I know exactly what she meant. Henrietta was stiff and set fast to her spot on the floor. Eventually, Tony managed to turn her around to face him, and said something about going home and having some cake. And she just sort of nodded and followed him out. She never said anything.

So now we're at the reception that never happened. We still have to pay for the food, which is fair enough, I suppose. The hotel woman said she'd try to contact the band. If she can get hold of them before they set off, we might not have to pay them the full amount.

'I hate Claudio.'

I know where she's coming from, but he is my brother. I feel some attempt to defend him is in order. It's a tough one. He's not given me a lot to work with. 'We don't know the full story.'

'We know enough.'

'He must have had a reason.'

'Nothing justifies that. Did you see Henri?' I've never seen Trix this angry with anyone, well, not with anyone who wasn't me. 'He's destroyed her life.'

'Give her time.' I'm trying to rationalise the situation. 'People break up. People get over it.'

'Not like this. What he did was just ...' she tails off. She doesn't need to finish. I saw what he did.

'Are you OK?'

'Not really.'

'Is there anything I can do?'

She doesn't answer. Or at least, she doesn't answer before Danny comes in. John is trailing behind him.

'I think we know what's going on.'

'What? How? Have you talked to Claudio?'

Danny shakes his head, and puts his arm around John. 'Tell them.'

John shakes his head. 'They won't believe me.'

Danny rests his head against John's face. 'They will if you tell them. Come on. Sit down.'

They pull chairs up at our table. Danny is holding John's hand. 'Go on. It's not your fault.'

John takes a breath. He seems like he's building up to actually talking, as if spontaneous speech might be too much for him. 'Henri was having an affair.'

Trix doesn't say anything, but I can feel her tensing

beside me. She's breathing more heavily, and the hand that was resting on her leg has started to tap repeatedly against her thigh.

I can't imagine Henri cheating. I don't see her as someone naturally suited to intrigue and deception. Everything that's on her mind comes out of her mouth. And besides, they only got together eight weeks ago, and they've only spent about fifteen minutes apart since then. Unless she's having an affair with someone at work, I don't see how it would physically be possible.

'How do you know?'

'I saw them together.'

'Who? When? Where?' Getting John to give information takes too long. I decide to ask all the pertinent questions in one burst and see if that works.

'I saw her with Deano last week, the morning after the stag.'

'Deano?' It turns out John was right about one thing. I don't believe him.

Trix has stopped tapping. I have a sudden acute understanding of the idea of the calm before the storm. She speaks very slowly and very quietly. 'You saw them together?'

'Yeah.'

'Where?'

'He was coming out of her flat.'

'And you just happened to be passing?'

John grins at her. 'Yeah. Me and Claudio.'

'You were with Claudio?'

'Yeah. We were just hanging out. What's weird about that?'

'Bastard.' Trix hasn't raised her voice. She's still sitting with her hands on her lap. I want her to shout. It would be less scary.

Danny stands up. 'Come on Trix. This isn't John's fault.'

'Yes. It is.'

She's crying. Without thinking about it, I put my hand out towards hers. She pushes it away, and stands up leaning across the table to Danny. 'It is his fault. He's lying.'

She's sobbing harder and harder now. 'He's lying.'

Danny swallows hard. 'Why would he lie?'

Trix clambers round the table to stand right in front of Danny. Her whole body is shaking with the tears. 'Because he always lies. He always lies, and you always believe him.'

It's one of those moments that you can't step away from. Things are being said that won't easily be taken back. It's the sort of situation that I usually try to arrange my life to ensure I never find myself in the middle of.

Now the shouting starts. Apparently she's never liked John (true), and never given him a chance (not true). In return, Danny is being a fool not to realise John is making things up (true), and is as much to blame as Claudio for what happened today (definitely not true).

John is still sitting down. He's impassive. He's tossed his grenade into the middle of all these lives, and now he looks a bit bored with the fallout.

'Tell her she's being ridiculous, Ben.' Danny and Trix have both turned towards me.

'It's not really Danny's fault, Trix.' I know that from Danny's point of view I've not gone far enough, but I seem to have found myself on a very narrow tightrope indeed.

'You don't believe Henri was screwing Deano though, do you?'

'Well, no.'

Danny is focused on me now. 'So you agree that John's lying? And Claudio's lying too?'

'Maybe they could be mistaken.'

Trix snorts and turns away. I continue. 'Maybe it wasn't what it looked like?'

Trix isn't going to accept that either. 'Or maybe he's just making it up?'

'And why would he do that?'

And straight away I know why. I've known why since the moment I realised John was involved. I feel like I've been here before. I'm back in that kitchen with a bruise across my face and John laughing at me, because he doesn't think I'll say a word. I take a very deep breath, which isn't as effective at calming me down as I hoped it would be. This time I am going to say something.

'He did it because Claudio turned him down.'

There's a silence after I've said it. No one reacts. For a second I wonder if I did actually say it out loud, or just inside my head. But then I see their faces. John looks interested again. He's leaning towards me, waiting for the next move. Danny's nostrils are flaring in and out as he breathes. 'Don't be ridiculous.'

I look straight at him, hoping that somehow the whole looking in his eye man-to-man thing will make him believe me. 'It's true. He made a pass at Claudio on the stag. Claudio brushed him off.'

Danny looks at John, who shrugs. 'He's lying.'

'I'm not.'

John stands up. 'Come on, babe.'

He starts to walk away. Danny doesn't follow him. He's still looking at me. 'I thought we were friends.'

I stand up. 'We are.'

John is standing over in the doorway. He's enjoying this. 'Come on. We've told them what I saw. We're wasting our time.'

Danny nods and follows him out of the bar. Trix just looks at me and walks away. I'm wondering why she's cross with me when she reappears with two more bottles of beer.

'Is what you said about John coming on to Claudio true?'

'Yeah.'

'And he'd do all this just because of one brush-off?'

I'm remembering standing in Danny's kitchen with a bloody lip too many years ago. I shrug. 'Guess he doesn't handle rejection that well.'

'Why didn't you say anything at the time?'

It takes me a moment to realise that she can't read my mind, and is still talking about Claudio and John. 'Wanted to be wrong I guess.'

'Benedict Messina, admitting that he can be wrong? I should be recording this moment.'

'Don't.'

'Sorry.'

I can't resist it. 'Trix Allen apologising? Now I should be recording.'

We fall silent and sip our beer for a minute. Trix breaks the silence. 'I can't stop thinking about Henri.'

'I know.'

'She looked broken.'

'I know.' When Tony led her away she looked as though she didn't even know what was happening. 'I ought to try to call Claudio I suppose.'

'Why bother?'

'He's my brother.'

'She's my best friend.'

'But that stuff John must have told him. He must be gutted.'

Trix shakes her head. 'This is his fault. People like John will always be like that. Claudio didn't have to believe him. Would you have?'

'What?'

'If it was someone you really loved, would you have believed him?'

'No.'

'See.'

'That's different.'

'How?'

How is it different? Well, because I've only ever really loved one person, and she is full of massive great flaws, but always truthful. I don't say anything, so Trix continues.

'You asked if you could do something for me.'

'What?'

'Before Danny came in, you asked if you could do something for me.'

I take her hand. I want to do something. 'What do you need?'

'Kill Claudio.'

Ben is looking quite concerned about me now. I run what I've just said back over in my head. I can still taste the words in my mouth. 'Kill Claudio.'

And, honestly, just for a second, I really mean it. He broke my friend, and I never want to see him again. When he said No, in the church, Henri didn't cry and shout; she seemed to shut down. I've seen people who were upset or angry before, but she just stopped. It was horrible.

I take a swig of my beer. 'I mean it. The thought of him being out there having a nice life, meeting other women, sleeping with other women. It gives me rage.'

Ben is looking at me. 'He's my brother.'

'So you won't kill him?'

He's sort of half laughing, like he's hoping it's a joke but isn't totally convinced. 'No. I won't murder my brother for you.'

And when he puts it like that it does sound a tiny bit insane. I do understand that actually killing Claudio is out of the question, but I do still want to hurt him, even if it's just a little bit. I want to see it. I turn back towards Ben, and try to focus on what's in front of me, rather than what's going on inside my head.

'So what will you do for me?'

'I'll buy you another beer.'

'Ok.' He stands up to go to the bar and I stop him. 'Beer's not helping. Something stronger.'

He nods. I need a real drink. If I can't annihilate Claudio, maybe I can annihilate my memory of Henri's face instead.

Ben comes back with two more beers and two tequilas.

'Tequila?'

He nods.

'I am not drinking tequila with you.'

'You said you wanted something stronger.'

'I remember the last time I drank tequila with you.'

He grins. 'And that didn't end so badly, did it?'

I didn't think he'd remember, but I push the glass away anyway. 'I am not drinking tequila with you.'

He pushes the glass back towards me. 'Go on. For old time's sake.'

And so we down the tequila and drink the beer, and then I go back to the bar, and we start all over again. Every slug of tequila makes me want to hurl, but feeling sick gives me something to focus on that isn't feeling sad or angry or vengeful, so we keep going. We talk in fits and starts, but there's no pretending now that we're not drinking with the express purpose of getting mind-clearingly, stomach-emptyingly drunk.

'How are you getting home?'

Mr Benedict does ask a good question. We've just downed our third tequilas, and we're starting on our sixth beers. We made one of the wedding drivers bring us here, and now I've spent all my cash on drinks. I suspect Ben has done the same.

'Have you got any money left?'

He pulls out a tenner and a handful of change. That won't be enough to get us both home. 'I've got plastic. We'll have to get the cab to stop at a cashpoint.'

'I don't want to go home yet.' I pull the tenner out of his hand and head to the bar.

We eke two more rounds, sans tequila, out of his £13.21. I announce that I want to burn out Claudio's eyeballs in retribution. I'm sort of taken with the idea of him being humbled like Mr Rochester at the end of Jane Eyre, only without the bit where he wins the girl back and it's all ok really.

Ben explains how this might be possible, and explains

how Archimedes used mirrors to focus the sun's light to set fire to warships. I say that I just want to stick a hot poker in Claudio's eyes. Ben says that lacks finesse.

Ben is about to go and find out whether the bar takes credit cards, when a woman with a name badge comes over to us.

'Mr Messina?'

Ben nods, and she hands him a room key. 'The key to the bridal suite, sir. I've just come on duty and I noticed you hadn't collected it yet.'

Ben opens his mouth, but the woman keeps talking. 'I'd hate to think of you being locked out. It's such a lovely suite, four-poster bed, double-ended spa bath, complimentary champagne.'

When she says complimentary champagne Ben closes his mouth abruptly. The woman smiles. 'Enjoy the rest of your stay.'

I turn to him. 'What just happened?'

He's looking at the room key. 'She must think I'm Claudio.'

'But she must have noticed there's no wedding going on.'

'Apparently not.' He looks at me. 'It's just a mistake though. I'll go and explain, and ask them to call us a cab.'

I really do not want to go home. I know Henri's at her dad's, but if I go home I'll be picturing her downstairs all alone. I can't quite face it just yet. I put my hand on his arm. 'She did say complimentary champagne.'

He looks at me and I can hear the wariness in his voice. 'She also said four poster bed and double-ended spa bath.'

I lean forward and take the key out of his hand, and start, with some wobbling, to walk towards the lift. I don't look back to see if he's following, because I want to look cool and confident and like I don't need to look back.

He catches up with me just as I'm getting into the lift. As soon as the doors close, I kiss him. I know that if I wait, I'll lose my nerve. When he kisses me back I could cry with relief.

Chapter Thirty-Four

Henrietta

There are one hundred and forty-three flowers across the row on the wallpaper in this room. I think there should be one hundred and forty-four but there's one bit where the wallpaper doesn't line up properly, and at the top one sheet is slightly stuck over the top of the other. I'm wondering about standing on a chair and seeing if I can peel the top bit back to see the hidden flower.

I don't think I shall, just at the moment. At the moment I'm concentrating on lying as still as I can. My dad looked in a few minutes ago. I closed my eyes so he'd think I was asleep. I think it might worry him if he saw I was lying awake.

It's OK really though. I'm just not sleepy. My phone is lying on the chest next to the bed. I think Claudio's probably been trying to phone me. I shan't look yet though. I'm just going to keep still. He might not have phoned. He might have e-mailed. He used to e-mail me every day when he was in Italy.

Yes. Probably he's e-mailed. I can't check that though. My phone's antique and Dad doesn't have the internet. My dad's house hasn't really changed since I was a little girl, apart from this room. I was staying here before I moved into Trix's flat, but it was too far away from work really. When I moved out he redecorated my room. The first time I came back here I cried. That's the only thing that has changed though. He doesn't have the internet. He doesn't have Sky. He doesn't have a DVD player. He's never really watched much telly. Even when Mum was alive he preferred the radio. In the evenings she'd watch her soaps, *Emmerdale* and *Coronation Street*, but my dad always preferred Radio 3 and 4.

I wonder what time it is. I know I went to bed early. Dad tried to get me to have something to eat, but I wasn't hungry. I'm still not. I'm not hungry. I'm not sleepy. I'm perfectly all right just lying still and counting the flowers on the wallpaper.

Every time I finish counting them, I wonder whether I should stop and do something else, like look at my phone, but then I start counting the flowers again instead. Maybe I should try to think about what happened today. I do know what happened today. I think my wedding dress is hanging up on the door, but I'm occupied keeping very still so I'm not able to look at it at the moment. I do know that Claudio decided not to get married, and so I came back to Dad's house rather than staying in the hotel with Claudio.

It feels a bit odd. It was a bit surprising when he said he didn't want to get married, but then it is a question that they ask, so I suppose he can give whatever answer he wants. He's probably phoned or e-mailed lots of times. I shan't look yet. I think I'll count the flowers one more time.

I suppose it's different from when he was in Italy. Then I'd check my e-mails lots and lots to see if he'd sent me one. I'd sit in front of the screen hitting refresh again and again until the new message thingy popped up.

There are still one hundred and forty-three flowers. There always are. I had flowers yesterday. I had bride flowers, and I had the flowers that one of Claudio's friends brought around. They weren't from him. They were from Danny and John, a sort of good luck pre-wedding present. He said John had asked him to bring them around, which was sweet. I don't think John is normally very good at things like presents. Now I have wallpaper flowers. If I keep very still, it will all be the same.

Chapter Thirty-Five

Ben

I haven't been to sleep yet. Trix is out for the count, which given how much tequila I threw down her before we got here, is hardly surprising. I'm lying very still, so I don't wake her up. When she wakes up we are going to have to have the talk. After we've had the talk I'll either be committed to something that yesterday was still pretty much unimaginable, or we'll definitely never be doing this again.

People kid themselves that they can have some clever modern middle way. Fuck buddies maybe? Friends with benefits? The people who say, 'Oh yeah, we're sort of seeing each other but it's not that serious,' or who claim that they're 'not exclusive.' Maybe you can get away with that for a few days, three weeks absolute tops, but really the whole relationship thing, it's kind of binary isn't it? It's a one or a zero. You are or you aren't. Anything else is just delaying tactics. It's time for a one or a zero. So really I've only got the time between now, which is 3.46am, and whenever she wakes up, which given the tequila might actually be a while, to enjoy this fluid state.

Enjoy probably isn't the word. I should be applying myself to deciding what I want before she wakes up and tells me. The problem is that I don't know. I've been single for a long time. I'm used to it. I have friends. I go out, but essentially it's just me. If I want to watch bad Westerns at 3am I can. If I want to write until two in the morning and then stay in bed until two in the afternoon I can, and I like that. I clean the bathroom once a decade. I change my sheets when they start to crunch. I keep jam in the cupboard, not in the fridge. It annoys me when Claudio moves things. And with him I know it's temporary.

Trix rolls over next to me and flings her arm across my torso. Specifically she flings her arm across my bladder, which is not great, because we drank a lot last night. I am going to need to move and go to the bathroom, which is going to mean rolling her back over, which will almost certainly wake her up. There's nothing for it though. It's either that or peeing in the bed. As gently as I can, I lift her arm up and slide myself out from underneath her, holding on to her wrist with one hand. I put her arm back down on to the empty bed and she sort of wriggles and murmurs, but she doesn't open her eyes.

I take a slash without turning the light on, and don't get back into bed afterwards. I stick one of the hotel robes on and sit down on a chair. Does watching a woman sleep have a bit of a serial killer vibe to it? I decide it's probably OK, if the woman already knows that you're in the room.

Her hair is all over the pillow and Trix has spread out to occupy the whole bed. I don't think I could get back in even if I wanted to. I might not be the only one that's a bit too used to living alone. She's lying on her tummy and the covers have pulled down so I can see down into the curve of her back. It's been so long. I was surprised by the sex. Not surprised that the sex happened. Once the receptionist had handed over the room key I think that was pretty much inevitable. I was surprised how well we fit. It was a bit fumbly and a bit drunken, but it wasn't awkward. There was one moment where I was on top of her and everything was getting sweaty and sticky, as it should, and I went to lift myself up on my arms and as our bodies pulled apart it made this horrible squelchy ripping noise, like the worst fart you've ever heard. She just laughed and laughed. I'd forgotten how much we laughed. I've never been with anyone else where laughing during sex was acceptable behaviour, when really, sex is ridiculous. And then we stopped laughing and the sex didn't feel ridiculous at all. It felt ... I don't have the words to finish the thought. It felt like there was no reason, no argument in the world strong enough to stop us having sex again and again and again.

I don't want to get last night out of context though. Trix, especially, was really upset by what happened at the wedding. We were both very drunk. And the room was already paid for. I would hate to think that just because there's history, just because we feel good together in one way, Trix automatically assumes that there's more to it than that.

I conclude that yesterday was a day that requires further analysis, in all sorts of ways. So far as I know, nobody's actually spoken to Claudio since he walked out of the church. To be honest, I'm struggling to care. I mean, I hope he's not in intensive care or anything, but, beyond that, I don't know.

I walk across the room and find the trousers I was wearing yesterday. I pull my phone out of the pocket. *6 missed calls*. I look at the call list. Five from Mum, and one from Danny. Neither of them have left messages. I look at the time. One from Danny after he left us last night. I hope he's come to his senses over John, but, realistically, I'm more likely to be getting another earful of abuse when he does get hold of me. I feel guilty about Mum. I didn't even talk to her and Dad before I left the church. I look at the clock. Still before five am. They'll have to wait until morning now.

'What are you doing?'

I turn around. Trix is sitting up on the bed with the sheet pulled up to cover her breasts.

'Just looking to see if Claudio had rung.'

'Has he?'

I shake my head.

'Good. I hope he's lying in a gutter somewhere.'

'Trix ...'

'Well I do. How long have you been awake?'

I shrug. 'Not long. You?'

'I remember you going to the toilet.'

'Sorry. I tried not to wake you.'

'That's OK.'

I move over and sit on the edge of the bed. 'So ...'

She puts her hand out and touches my arm. 'Yeah.'

'This was all a bit unexpected.'

She pulls her hand away. 'Is that a complaint?'

'No. No. I just don't quite know what to make of this. You. Me, you know.'

She's closed her eyes. She looks exhausted. When she opens her eyes again she shrugs. 'I don't know ...'

'Sssh.' I put my finger against her lips. Even to me it feels like a bit of a cheesy move, but I don't know how else to stop her talking. 'We can worry about it later. You look like you need to sleep.'

'Oh, thanks.'

'You just look tired.' I take a breath. 'I'm trying to be nice. Help me out.'

She leans forward and rests her head against me. I put my arms around her back and hold her like that for a moment.

'Ben.'

'Yeah?'

'I think I'm going to be sick.'

Chapter Thirty-Six

Trix

It must be the sound of my phone ringing that finally wakes me. It's lying on the floor next to the bed. As I lean off the bed to pick it up I feel my stomach contract.

'Hello.'

It's Tony. He says Henri won't get out of bed. Well, of course she won't. It's the middle of the night.

'That's OK. It's only ...' There's a clock on the bedside table. 'It's only ... oh.' It's eleven o'clock, which is not late for me, but is about four hours late for Henrietta. But she did have a horrid day yesterday. You can't really blame her for wanting to hide out for a while.

'Isn't it better to let her sleep?'

'She's not asleep. She's just lying there. She won't move.'

I sit up on the bed very carefully. 'OK. I'll come over. Give me an hour.'

As soon as I hang up I regret promising to go round. I don't want to get out of bed myself. It's at least forty-five minutes to drive to Tony's house, and my car's still at home. I'm probably still over the limit anyway. I can't say no though. If she wasn't my friend, Henri would never have met Claudio, would she? It was me that encouraged her to move out of her dad's house. It was me that encouraged her to meet all my friends.

I lie back down, not through choice. My body just decides it needs to be horizontal for a bit longer. Lying down takes enough pressure off my head for my brain to start to work, and as soon as it starts to work, it starts to wonder where the hell Ben is.

I let my mind jump through the events of last night. There was tequila. There was, I am aware, some sex. I decide to skim over the details of that. There will, I'm sure, be more than enough time spent worrying about that later. Then we went to sleep, and now I'm awake.

Something is nagging at my brain, telling me that that isn't quite it. There's more. I swallow. It tastes of … well it doesn't taste good. We went to sleep and then we woke up, and then I was sick. I definitely remember being sick in the en suite bathroom. I pull the covers back over my head as I realise that someone was holding my hair out of the way when I threw up. Logically, that can only have been Ben. So I ended our night of unbridled passion crouching naked over the toilet bowl.

I hear the room door opening, and pull the covers tighter around me.

'Are you awake?'

It's Ben. I'm not sure whether I'm relieved that it's not a cleaner trying to chuck me out of a room I clearly have no legitimate right to be in, or horrified that it's Ben.

'Uh-huh.'

'Shall I take that as a yes?'

I stick my head out from the covers and look at him. He's wearing the dress trousers and shirt from yesterday, and carrying a shopping bag.

'Where've you been?'

He tips the bag out on top of me. 'Supplies.'

There's paracetamol, Alka-Seltzer, two bottles of water, two toothbrushes, toothpaste, deodorant, two pairs of knickers. 'Two pairs?'

'Small and medium.' He shrugs.'Well, I didn't know.'

'You didn't risk getting large?'

He grins. 'I'm crap with women. I'm not suicidal.'

I sit up and help myself to two paracetamol and some water. 'Thank you.'

He sits down on the bed. 'How are you feeling?'

'Like death.'

'Like death that needs to sleep some more, or death that needs to eat.'

'Not sure. What time do we have to be out of the room?'

'Three, I think. Claudio had booked a late check-out.'

Ben mentioning Claudio reminds me that we are staying in what was supposed to have been Hen's bridal suite. My stomach contracts again with the thought. 'It feels wrong being here.'

Something flickers across his face. 'Right. Well, you'd better get dressed then.'

He picks one of the toothbrushes and the toothpaste off the bed and heads into the bathroom. I don't feel like moving, but I'm not liking having the disadvantage of nudity while Ben strides about like he lives here. I pull on the knickers (medium) that Ben bought and pick my bridesmaid dress up off the floor. With me in this and Ben in half a tuxedo it's not exactly hard to work out what happened to us last night. I clamber into the dress anyway. It's either brazen out a cab ride of shame in yesterday's clothes or brazen it out naked, and I'm not really feeling particularly brazen this morning.

Ben strides back out of the bathroom. 'Are you ready to go then?'

I'm confused. A minute ago he was bringing me paracetamol and talking about getting something to eat. Now he clearly wants out of here faster than a super speedy fast thing which I would definitely be able to think of if I hadn't drunk all the tequila in the hotel bar last night. Well, fine. He can be like that. This is exactly why I'm better off without him anyway. 'I'm just going to use the bathroom.'

I pick the second toothbrush up and shuffle past him with as much dignity as my hangover and bridesmaid shoes combination will permit. I pee and brush my teeth as quickly as I can manage and stalk out into the bedroom. Ben is sitting on the bed. 'I don't get it.'

I can do without this now. 'What?'

'Well now being here feels wrong. What about last night?'

I really don't want to get into this. I mean, if he wasn't so proud then he could be honest about his feelings, and we might be able to have an adult conversation. 'Last night was last night.'

'Look Trix.' He's closed his eyes. He always does that when he's uncomfortable. It's like he's trying to separate himself from the conversation somehow. 'I know how you feel.'

'What?'

'I heard Claudio and Danny talking. I know you still have feelings for me.'

This is ridiculous. 'I have feelings for you? You're the one that's still in love with me.'

'What?'

'I heard Danny telling Henri.'

There's a silence. Ben is looking right at me. You can almost see the cogs spinning behind his eyes. I won't admit it to him, but he does actually get there a second before me, well quite few seconds before me. To be blunt, I'm none the wiser until he spells it out. 'You heard Danny telling Henri I was in love with you, and I coincidentally overheard Claudio talking about you being in love with me.'

He shakes his head and starts to laugh.

'So you think this is funny?'

'Don't you?'

'No. We've been deceived by our friends. We were tricked into all this.'

'Tricked into sleeping together?'

'Yes.' I can't believe Henri was involved in this. She's a terrible liar. It's like being tricked by Snow White. It shouldn't be possible.

'Trix, if anything we were alcoholed into sleeping together.'

'Alcoholed isn't a word.'

'All right then. Tequila'd. We have no one to blame but ourselves.'

'So you don't think we were tricked?'

'Well not into what happened last night.'

'So you didn't do it because you thought I ...' I can't say 'loved' ... 'was fond of you.'

He doesn't answer, so I continue. 'I don't think Danny and Henri were far off the mark about you though. I think it was pretty clear how you felt last night.'

'And what about you? If anyone has feelings, it's you for me!'

'Hardly. I took pity on you.'

'And I was drunk. Clearly, my judgement was impaired.'

'So you're not in love?'

'Of course not.'

'Good. Me neither.'

Ben stuffs his hands in his pocket. 'Fine.'

'Right. Fine.'

If this was a soap opera we'd have yelled those last few lines at one another and ended up nose to nose, before jumping on each other with passionate kisses and ripping each other's clothes off. It's not a soap opera though, so we mutter at each other from opposite sides of the room, and end up in an awkward silence. At least we're clear about where we stand though. Ripping each other's clothes off, again, could have been seen as a mixed message.

We share a cab back into town without talking. I get my phone out and ring Tony to explain that I'm running late, and then busy myself deleting old texts and not looking at Ben. When the taxi pulls up at my house I get out without even making eye contact. I fling a 'See you then' over my shoulder and bolt indoors.

Chapter Thirty-Seven

Henrietta

Dad comes back into the room. He tells me that Trix is here. Would I like to get up to see her? Would I? Maybe I would, but I don't think I shall. Would I like Trix to come up here and see me? I don't answer. I don't really mind one way or the other.

I hear Dad go back downstairs. There are thirteen stairs. I can hear voices. He's probably telling Trix that I won't get out of bed. It's not that I won't though. I just don't want to yet. I just feel like being very still. Someone is coming upstairs now. It's not Dad. The steps are too quick. It must be Trix. She knocks very gently on the door, and when I don't reply she puts her head around the door.

'Can I come in?'

I don't say anything, so she comes in and sits on the edge of the bed. It turns out people don't really need me to do anything very much. They just do exactly what they wanted anyway. Maybe I can be quiet and still forever. I wouldn't be surprised if no one really noticed.

'How are you feeling?'

How am I feeling? I'm not really feeling anything. It's not unpleasant in its way.

'Your dad said you didn't want to get up.'

I don't deny the fact.

'You know that you'll have to get up at some point, don't you? You'll need to go to the toilet at least, and maybe eat something.'

I have thought about that. I will need to go to the toilet. I'll probably need to go quite soon. I've sort of planned it though. If I get out of bed very slowly and walk very carefully I think I can hold my head level and still while I go. That way it won't really feel like I've moved at all, and I can come straight back to bed and carry on.

'I could bring you some food.'

I do wish that people would stop trying to feed me. My dad tried to make me eat last night, and then again this morning. I really don't feel like it. I don't see the need. I'm just being still. It's not really using any energy at all.

Trix seems annoyed at my unresponsiveness. I am sorry about that. I don't want to make people angry, but I'm not asking them to come in and see me. I'd be perfectly content if they just left me all alone here. She reaches out and puts her hand on my cheek. I let her. I hope she doesn't go any further. If I have to move to stop her touching me I shall be very cross I think.

My lack of reaction must be off-putting. She withdraws the hand.

'Do you want to talk about yesterday?'

Do I want to talk about yesterday? I don't really know what I would say. I will have to talk about it to people who weren't there I suppose, but Trix was there, so she knows what happened. I don't really know what I would tell her. Trix pats my face again.

'I'll leave you for a little bit then, shall I?'

She stands up and walks over to the doorway.

'I'll just be downstairs. Let us know if you need anything.'

There is one thing. I haven't asked Dad because I know he's just been here, but Trix has been out there in the world. I swallow. My mouth feels clammy and sort of clogged up.

'Have you talked to Claudio?'

She shakes her head. I do hope he's OK. Maybe when I go to the toilet I shall check to see if he's phoned. I definitely shall. I'll just be still here for a few more minutes first.

Chapter Thirty-Eight

Claudio

I reckon they're gonna try to chuck me out of here soon. Ok, so I haven't shaved, or showered, and I probably smell like someone who slept in their car, but that wouldn't be a fair assumption at all. In fact, I slept in Ben's car, so that's completely different. Having said that, I am still wearing a full morning suit, so I think I'm pretty much raising the tone.

It's quite a nice pub. I brought Henri here once, about a year ago, just before I went to Italy. We sat outside all afternoon. It's about a five-mile walk back into town, and we ended up staggering in the dark. I drink some more beer.

The bar staff are giving me dirty looks, so I move away from the bar and into the beer garden. The inside is full of families enjoying Sunday lunch. They're kind of oppressive anyway. Outside there's a small gaggle of smokers around the porch but no one else. It's not warm, so at least I should be left alone out here to drink my beer.

There's two girls smoking a bit away from anyone else. I decide to have a crack. Gotta get back on the horse, as they say. I wander over to them. I don't bother trying to look casual. You see people tying themselves in knots trying not to look too interested, and then tying themselves even further up in knots wondering how to let the other person know they are interested. Nothing wrong with making your intentions clear. Attracted, attractive and not too sleazy. A bit of humour usually takes care of the last one. I flash my best Italian stallion smile at them. 'All right, ladies.'

They nod and turn their bodies away from me. Playing

hard to get, huh? This is where you use humour to avoid coming off as sleazy. 'Don't worry. I won't bite.'

They look at me. One of them, the prettier one, actually wrinkles her nose. I mean, OK, as I said, I could probably use a shower, but it can't be that bad.

I shrug. 'Just being friendly.'

Maybe this time, discretion is the better part of whatever. As I walk off towards the tables in the garden I can hear them giggling. I tell myself it's probably at something else.

I sit down and sip my beer. I suppose I will have to go home eventually. Apparently the need to shower is more urgent than I thought. I didn't go back last night. I didn't want to see anyone. I didn't want to have to answer any questions. I didn't want to have to tell the story again. I feel like I've been a fool. I can't believe I was sucked in by the idea of her being so sweet and pure and naïve. I feel like I've been sold a right lemon.

I finish my beer and head inside to get another. I have to scrape all my change together to pay for it, after the barmaid informs me that they only take cards if Sir is ordering food. Well Sir doesn't want food. Sir wants beer. I manage to pay for my pint and head back outside.

My phone's ringing. It's been ringing on and off since yesterday. Mum, Danny, Deano, who's got a nerve to be ringing me at all, and now Ben. He called yesterday a couple of times right after, but this is the first time today. I haven't talked to anyone since I walked out of the church, but all my clothes are at his flat, and I've got his car. At some point I am going to have to talk to Ben, even if I never talk to anyone else. I answer it.

'Where the hell are you?'

I tell him.

'Have you still got my car?'

'Yes.'

'How pissed are you?'

'A bit.'

'How pissed?'

I remember the girl wrinkling her nose, and am vaguely aware that I'd thought that 'Don't worry. I won't bite,' could be classed as humour. Ben takes my silence as not having heard, and asks again.

'Seriously, how pissed?'

I mumble the answer. 'Very.'

I can hear him sighing on the other end of the phone. I don't have to listen to know what he's going to say next.

'Stay there. I'll find a cab and come get you.'

He is my brother, after all.

Chapter Thirty-Nine

Sixteen years ago

Claudio

'I don't have to listen to you.'

'No. You don't, but I think you should.'

'Don't have to.'

Ben is holding his hand up in front of his eyes to shield them against the sun, and squinting as he stares up at me in the tree. 'You don't have to, but I'm telling you that if you crawl further out on that branch it will snap and you will land on the concrete and probably smash your face on the floor.'

My big brother is the dullest, nerdiest sixteen-year-old you've ever heard of. I'm stuck with him all summer because Mum and Dad are dead busy with tourists at work. At least I don't have to do what he says.

I swing my legs around and sit on the branch. Then I shuffle my weight back a bit towards the trunk. Ben's not right about it snapping though; I just want to be nearer the trunk.

'We did about birth certificates at school yesterday.'

Ben doesn't hear. He's sat down on the steps near the bottom of the tree, and is pulling a book out of his bag.

'What you reading?'

'A book.'

'Looks boring.'

'It's not.'

'I'm bored.'

He doesn't react. He seems to have gone off into the book. I kick my leg against the tree. It hurts.

'I can see Mum and Dad's restaurant from up here.'

Ben glances behind him. 'I can see Mum and Vittore's restaurant from down here.'

'Why d'you call him Vittore?'

Ben shrugs.

'Sometimes you call him Dad.'

He shrugs again.

'We did about birth certificates at school.'

Ben puts his book down. 'And?'

'And nuffin'.'

'Really?'

I nod. 'I don't have to do what you tell me though.'

Ben lays down on his back, and pulls his sunglasses down over his eyes, so I can't see where he's looking.

'Tell me what you learnt about birth certificates, short stuff.'

'I'm nearly as tall as you.' It's true. I've had new school trousers twice this year.

'Yeah. You're tall like Dad.'

'They said that everyone has to have a birth certificate, and on it it says your mum's name, and if your mum's married to your dad, it says his name too.'

'That's right.'

'So Deano's just has his mum on it?'

Ben shrugs. 'I guess.'

'So I asked Mum if I could see my birth certificate.'

'And?'

'Was boring.' Well, it was. It just said where and when I was born and that Mum and Dad were my mum and dad.

'Right.' Ben sits up and pushes his sunglasses back. 'Anything else?'

I shake my head. Ben's staring up at me again. 'I'm guessing you asked to see my birth certificate.'

'Might've.'

'And did Mum show you it?'

I shake my head. She wouldn't. She said she didn't know where it was, but it was right there in the envelope with mine. I saw Ben's name on the top when she took mine out. Then she put the envelope back in the drawer and said it was time for her to go to work and that I should go and make sure Ben was up before she went out. When I went back to look again the whole envelope had gone.

Ben shrugs. 'Maybe she couldn't find it.'

'Maybe.'

I don't want to talk about this any more, so I decide to try and get a bit further out along the branch. I reckon if I get a bit further along I'll be able to get a view of the sea.

'Claudio!'

I pause and twist around to have a look at Ben. As I twist I feel my knee slip off the branch; without thinking about it I sense my foot scrabbling at the air trying to get a hold back on the branch, but it's too late. I know I'm going to fall before I do. My own weight pulls me sideways and I'm heading for the ground.

I can make out voices a long way away. One of them is Ben, and it sounds like he's shouting. Then it goes quiet.

When I wake up I'm in bed. Mum and Dad are sitting by the bed. I can hear them before I work out how to make my eyes open.

'Well, Ben was supposed to be watching him.' That was my dad.

'It was an accident.'

'Well, that's what he says.'

'Don't be ridiculous.'

'I just mean that if that boy spent a little bit less time trying to build some sort of super-computer in his bedroom, then maybe my son wouldn't be lying in a hospital bed.'

I concentrate on making my eyes open, and then blink a few times. It feels scratchy.

'Darling!' My mum is leaning over me. 'Vittore, find a nurse.'

My dad goes running from the room, while Mum talks at me. 'Do you remember what happened?'

I nod. Talking still seems a bit of a challenge.

'You fell from a tree. Ben had to call an ambulance.'

I nod again, and manage to look around. Where is Ben anyway?

'They had to put a pin in your knee.' For the first time I notice that my left leg is kind of numb. A pin sounds cool though. 'You've been asleep since then, but the doctors say you're going to be fine.'

I nod again, and try to form a word. 'Ben?'

Mum nods. 'He's outside.'

A woman in a white coat comes in with Dad, and so I can't see Ben till after she's finished prodding me. When I've wiggled my toes and told her what year it is about three times I'm allowed to have visitors.

Ben comes in still carrying the book he was reading in the park. There's a dark red mark across the cover. I lift my finger to point at it. 'Blood?'

Ben nods. 'Yup. Came out of you,that did.'

'Cool. Ben?'

'Yeah.'

'What we were talking about before …'

I see Ben look over at Mum and Dad. 'We can talk about that later.'

'No.'

Ben looks really uncomfortable. 'Really. Not now.'

'No. Not ever. I just think …' I'm not quite sure how to explain this, but I'm absolutely sure that I'm right. 'I just don't think it matters, does it?'

Ben swallows. 'No. I don't think so.'

'Right.'

Ben turns his back on the bed, and Mum starts talking. When I look back at Ben his face looks kind of blotchy, like with girls when they've been crying.

Chapter Forty

Ben

I opt for just wandering around hoping I can spot him. It seems somehow less embarrassing than accosting a barman and asking if they've seen a guy in full morning dress crying into his beer. He's not in the bar, so I check the car park, where I find my car. Claudio isn't with it. Eventually, I locate him in the beer garden, still, as expected, wearing yesterday's suit. He's got his head down on the table next to a stack of glasses. He looks up as I sit down opposite him.

'Ben!'

'Hello.'

'How did you get here?'

'Taxi.' They actually sent the same taxi driver who picked us up this morning. He's not getting a representative picture of my social life. A hotel pick-up still in last night's clothes, followed by a mercy run to an out-of-the-way pub, is not my usual Sunday. It's normally much more PlayStation oriented than this.

'Do you want a beer?'

'No, thank you.' I don't quite know what to say to him. He's not dead, and not obviously bleeding. I sort of feel I've done my brotherly duty. I suspect Mum won't agree until he's actually at home, cleaned and fed, and ideally sobered-up. 'Have you been here all night?'

He shrugs. From the state of him, I'm guessing that's a yes. This isn't the sort of situation I'm good for. I should probably be asking him how he feels, trying get him to open up or something. If Trix had her way I'd be punching him but I'm not well equipped for that either. Claudio works out. He actually goes to the gym four times a week all year round, not just three times in January and then never again. If Trix had really wanted me to kill him it would have to have been a slow poisoning. I tell myself to stop thinking about Trix. If punching isn't an option, I realise, it has to be talking. 'So why here?'

'Didn't want to come back to the flat.'

'Why not?'

'Didn't want to talk to anyone.'

'There wasn't anyone there.' Didn't mean to tell him that. I think last night's events are best neatly compartmentalised with the mental equivalent of 'Police – do not cross' tape across the entrance to that part of my brain.

Claudio looks at me. 'Where were you?'

'Mum and Dad's.' It's not a great lie. If he mentions it to them he'll find out that it's a lie. Hopefully, he's too preoccupied to remember.

He puts his head back down on the table and mutters something.

'What?'

'Is Mum freaked?'

'Just a bit.'

'I can't believe this is happening.'

'Well, it is sort of your fault.' See; I'm a total natural at this sympathy lark.

He sticks his head back up. 'It's not my fault.'

'So it's Henri's?'

The head is back straight on the table. 'How is she?'

'Not seen her. Tony took her home.'

'I bet she's really milking the sympathy. Poor little Henrietta. Daddy's little princess can do no wrong.'

'She was really upset, like in shock.' So I can't actually kill him. That doesn't mean he gets a free ride.

'She was the one that was screwing around.'

'With Deano?' Even though I knew this was where we were going, I still can't believe it.

'So even you knew? My own brother, and you didn't think to tell me? You didn't say anything!'

'Woah! I heard it from John last night. You don't believe it?'

'I know what I saw.'

'And what did you see?'

'Her, precious little Henrietta with Deano. He was at her flat.'

'And from that you get that she's shagging around?'

'Yes.' He really is certain. I don't know how, but I'm convinced that John did this. Somehow the pieces are starting to fit. There are still some big gaps, but John looked so pleased with himself last night. There's definitely something there.

'So, Deano was leaving Henri's flat, at a time when you just happened to be passing, with John, who you don't even like and don't really socialise with.'

'He called me. At least he thought I should know the truth.'

'Right. So he called you and took you to stand outside your fiancée's flat, and you didn't ask him how he knew Deano was there? You didn't ask Deano, who's been your mate since childhood, what was going on? You didn't ask the woman you were planning to marry what was going on?'

'I saw it. I didn't need to ask anyone.'

'You twat.' It's not a well-formulated point in my argument, but I think it is one that needed making. Henrietta may actually be better off without him.

'So you saw what John took you to see, and you're now convinced that Henrietta was having an affair with Deano?'

'Yeah.'

I can tell Ben's not impressed, but I don't care. I'm not about to start taking advice on my love life from him. The man has no soul. He doesn't feel like a normal human being would. And I know what I saw. John had taken a picture on his phone of Deano going into her flat, and then we both saw him coming out. She cuddled him on the doorstep, and he'd brought her flowers. Straight men do not bring flowers for no reason, and I already know he thinks she's fit.

Ben closes his eyes and tilts his head back away from me. He always does that when he's stressed. Trix says it's a way of him screening out inconvenient human interference. She's probably right. She usually is about Ben.

Eventually he starts talking. 'Walk me through it again.'

I don't want to talk about it any more, so I shake my head, which he doesn't notice. He's still screening.

'So you just happened to run into John.'

I can't be doing with him now. 'No. He phoned me.'

'And you didn't think that was weird?'

'No. Well he didn't phone. Danny did. No. I did.'

Ben opens his eyes. 'So Danny phoned you?'

'No. Danny texted, and so I phoned him back.'

'So what's John got to do with it?'

I've explained all of this to him once already. Sometimes I wish my brother could accept that sometimes the obvious explanation is obvious because it's just right. 'John answered the phone.'

'Danny's phone?'

'Yes.'

'Danny's mobile?'

'Yes.'

'Why?'

'I don't know. They live together. It's like me answering your phone.'

'Do you answer my phone?'

'Well, no.' I'm not letting him win the point though. 'But I might, you know, if people called you.'

'People call me.'

'Who?'

He opens his mouth a couple of times, before he comes up with an answer. 'Mum rings.'

'Mum rings the landline because she doesn't trust these new-fangled ways. And if you're trying to sell your mother ringing you as a sign of a healthy and active social life, you've already lost.'

'Don't change the subject.'

I smile. It feels weird. 'Was worth a try.'

'So, Danny texts you.'

'Yeah.'

'Saying what?'

'Just that he needs to talk to me.'

'So you ring him.'

I nod.

'And John answers.'

'Yes.'

'And then what?'

I really don't want to talk about it. 'You know what. I meet him near Henri's and Deano's been there giving her flowers and then they're all lovey-dovey on the doorstep.'

'Lovey-dovey?'

'Yeah. All kisses and hugs.'

'And flowers?'

'Yeah.' I can still see them in my head, and I can hear John in my ear. He was good about it actually. He said he hadn't been sure whether to tell me, and he stopped me confronting her right then and there. That was good of him.

He could have just left me to it, but he stayed with me until he was sure I'd calmed down enough not to storm round there and do something I might have regretted.

Ben has done the eyes closed thing again. When he opens them he's speaking slowly, like you would to a naughty child.

'And were these kisses, hugs and flowers, in the visiting aged aunt in the care home sense, or in the post-coital best-I've-ever-had sense?'

'That's disgusting.'

'That's not an answer.'

'I know what I saw.'

'Still not technically an answer.'

'Fuck off.'

He mutters it, but I can still hear. 'Still not an answer, actually.'

'Leave it.'

Ben grins, and does his best Mitchell brother mockney accent. 'Leave it.'

It's something he used to do years ago to cheer me up. I'm not going to smile. Ben carries on. 'Just leave it. I'm gonna sort it.'

I cave. 'Good. I want it sorted.'

'I thought you wanted me to leave it.'

'Nah. Sort it.'

'Sort it. Leave it. Sort it. Leave it.'

'Oh God.'

'What?'

'I jilted someone at the altar.'

Ben nods. 'Yep.'

'It's as if someone had announced it was going to be the best wedding Albert Square had ever seen.'

'It's not funny.'

'I know.'

Chapter Forty-One

Four weeks later

Henrietta

'Are you all right, Miss?'

'I'm fine.' I am fine. Everyone keeps telling me I'm fine. I'm coping ever so well, apparently. So, yes, I am fine. I'm in the big meeting room that we use for Art Club and all the children are looking at me. I can't quite remember what I was talking about, but I am definitely fine.

'Just look in your books and ...' I look out at the room. No one has a book in front of them. There is paper and chalk and charcoal set out on the tables. 'Right, not your books. Silly me. Why don't you all just draw something with these things?'

I pick up some of the chalks from the nearest table. 'Yes. You can draw whatever you like. Carry on.'

Normally the kids will take any hint that I'm not completely on top of things as permission to start throwing things at each other, especially at an arts workshop; there is an awful lot of cool stuff to throw. Today I seem to be making them uneasy.

'Miss, can we work on our projects for the competition?'

I nod. 'Why not?'

I sit down at the front of the room and just let them do whatever it is that they're doing. Some of them probably will work on their projects. The rest can do whatever they like. I can see now that I do actually have a session plan on the desk in front of me. You see, last night I must have printed this out and when I got here today I must have got the charcoals and chalk out. I look at the plan. It says that we're supposed to be making repeating patterns in black charcoal, and then again using colour. I imagine there was some point to it.

It's not that I don't remember doing any of those things. I do. It's just that they feel like someone else did them, and now getting up and explaining things and talking to the children just feels like something that somebody else would do. It feels like there's a big puffy layer of bubble wrap between me and everyone else. It means that everything feels a bit muffled and distant. I quite like it, I think.

There's a knock on the door. I look through the window and recognise the knocker as the mum of one of the kids. They're here early, I think. Then I look around and see that most of the kids are sort of staring at me, and there are quite a lot of parents waiting outside. I look at the clock. It's nearly ten minutes after finishing time. That makes me giggle. I sort of wave my hand towards the door and sit and enjoy the giggling while the kids file out. Some of them are pushing. I'm probably supposed to tell them not to do that.

There's a lot to clear up after the kids have gone. I don't quite feel like it though. Actually I feel like going for a little walk. I head out of the room and down the stairs. I pass by Trix in the main library, but I don't stop to talk to her. I think she asks me something, but I just need to get outside. I want to be able to see the sky. That would make things better, I think.

It's cold outside. I giggle again as I realise my coat is still in the staffroom. It takes about an hour to walk home. It's normally quicker than that, but today I walk in and out of all the little side streets around the housing estates on the way. I like looking into other people's houses. It's better than television. There's one house that I stop outside where there's a little girl playing in the living room. It's a pretty room, a bit old-fashioned, but pretty. Trix would say it was chintzy, but I like it. The little girl is clambering up on the furniture. She's got little blond ringlets and she's just wearing a vest and pants. I hope she isn't cold. She seems happy, so I think that it must be warm inside the house. There doesn't seem to be anyone else with her. She climbs on to a chair in the bay window and looks out at me. For a minute I watch her watching me watching her. Then she waves, and I wave back. Then her mummy comes into the room, so I turn and walk away quickly before she can see me.

At home I decide to clean the kitchen. It's not Saturday, but somehow things seem to be getting dirty so quickly at the moment. I decide to do a proper job and empty the cupboards out and defrost the freezer. I start by taking all the frozen food out and putting it in on the worktop. Then I re-arrange the food on the worktop into piles by type of food. Then I re-arrange it into neat towers according to size. Then I get a spoon and sit on the kitchen floor eating the ice cream. While I'm eating a puddle of water starts to form on the floor underneath the freezer. I get four tea towels and build a sort of tea-towel wall around the bit of floor I'm sitting on so I can watch the water without getting wet. I'm quite proud of my ingenuity.

It means that when the phone rings I can't answer it though, because I can't get off my little island. I hear the phone go on to the answer machine, and someone, it sounds like Trix, leaves a message. I stay sitting on my little island. It's nice to be still again. It's like it was before my dad and Trix made me get up at Dad's house, and before Trix brought me back here.

The water is starting to soak through my tea towel wall by the time I hear the banging at the door. I know it's Trix this time, because she says. 'It's Trix. I'm going to come in. Is that OK?'

I don't answer.

'I'm going to come in now.'

I hear her unlock the door and come through into the flat. 'Shit.'

She disappears into the bathroom and returns with an armful of towels, which she uses to start soaking up the water off the floor. They're my nice towels. She shouldn't really be using them on the floor.

'What were you doing?'

I point at the freezer, but she's still looking blank. Trix is a lovely woman, but not the most domestic. 'I was defrosting.'

'Well I think it's defrosted.'

'OK'. I stand up and start putting the food back in the freezer. Trix puts her hands on my arms and moves me to one side.

'I think the food is defrosted too. I don't think you can refreeze most of this.'

'OK.' I leave the food on the worktop and go and sit down on the sofa. There is still a wet patch on the kitchen floor where Trix hasn't cleared it up properly. I shall have to mop it later. I don't want to do it now. She might think I'm criticising what she's already done.

'Where did you go this afternoon?'

'Here.'

'Well I can see that. I mean, are you poorly? Why weren't you at work?'

'Because I came home.'

She sits down next to me. 'I told Danny you were ill. I said I'd agreed that you could go home.'

'But you didn't say I could go home.'

'I know. I don't want you to lose your job though.'

I try, I really do try, to think about it from Trix's point of view. I know that I just walked out of work. I know that finding me sitting on the floor in a pool of water must look odd. I know that if I keep wandering off from work I could lose my job. I even know that that would be A Bad Thing. I just don't feel worried about it.

Trix picks my hand up off my lap. 'Do you think maybe you should see someone?'

'What for?'

'Well, maybe see a doctor, just to make sure that you're OK.'

'If you like.' I honestly don't mind one way or the other.

'OK. Shall I make you an appointment?'

'OK.' That seems to please her, which is nice. It's good to please people.

Chapter Forty-Two

Ben

'I'm coming. I'm coming.'

It's after eleven, so although I am coming to answer the door, I'm mainly shouting in the hope that whoever it is will stop knocking before the neighbours start complaining about the noise.

It's Danny. I haven't spoken to him since the wedding day. That's probably the longest we've been out of touch since I came back from Cambridge.

'What's up?'

'Can I come in?'

''Course.' He follows me through into the kitchen. 'Do you want a beer or something?'

He nods, and I dig two beers out of the fridge.

'Is Claudio around?'

'Gone to bed.'

'Right. Good.'

'What's up, mate?' I say 'mate.' That's probably a debatable point at the moment.

He sits down at the kitchen table. At least, there is definitely a table under the debris somewhere. He looks tired.

'John's gone.'

'Well, he's gone before...'

'No. He's gone properly. I chucked him out.'

'Bloody hell. Well done.' That didn't sound right, did it?

'No, not well done. Sorry. I didn't mean that.'

'Yeah. You did.'

'Well, yeah.' We've known each other a long time. If he

was looking for someone to say the right thing, he'd know better than to come here.

'I don't want to tell you the rest.'

'OK.' I wait. He's going to tell me. It's a myth that men don't talk to each other. We just pick our moments, and do a lot of preliminary beer-drinking first.

'I caught him coming on to Kingsley Berowne.' He drinks some more beer while I let this titbit sink in. Kingsley Berowne is a city councillor, a married city councillor.

'I'm sorry.'

'I don't think he even fancied him. I think it was just some sort of game. I'm humiliated, aren't I? How can I go into work and be in charge? They're all going to know about it.'

I hold back from pointing out that most of them probably already know what John was like. 'It'll be OK.'

He looks at me. 'I'm a black, gay department head. Half of them already think I only got the job to fill a quota somewhere.'

I don't know how to respond. I'm used to Danny being in control. 'I'm sorry.'

'I hate him for this.' He takes another swig of beer. There's more. I wait.

'What you said …' he starts but stops again. Time to rip off the band aid.

'Go on.'

'What you said about him coming on to Claudio, was it true?'

'Yeah.'

'Why didn't you tell me?'

'Would you have believed me?'

'He admitted it.'

'Coming on to Claudio?'

'The other stuff. Deano and Henri, and making sure

Claudio saw. I don't think he thought Claudio would actually cancel the wedding. I think he just thought it was funny to mess with him.'

That's when I look up and see my baby brother standing in the kitchen doorway.

Chapter Forty-Three

Henrietta

The doctor seems like a very nice lady. She's wearing a tweedy skirt and a cardigan, which makes her look older than she probably is. From her face, I think she's really only about my age. It must be hard being a doctor at this age. Probably no one takes her very seriously. I wonder if that's why she wears old lady clothes, to try to look older. And all the time I'm thinking that she's talking to me, and I'm not really listening to what she's saying, so when she stops talking I just sort of smile at her.

'So, would you say you were feeling particularly down about things at the moment?'

I shake my head. I don't want to worry her.

'Trix said you'd taken some time off work.'

I nod.

I feel sorry for her. I'm probably not being very helpful.

'Do you think some more time off work would be helpful?'

I lift my shoulders in a sort of half shrug.

'Sometimes when people are feeling like this it is better to keep busy.'

I tell her that I can keep busy at home.

'That's good. It's important that you try to feel active and in control of things.' I nod, to show I understand, and she signs a note saying that I can't go to work for the next three weeks.

'And what about medication?'

I shrug. I'm not poorly, but I suppose doctors probably like you to have medication, so it shows they're doing something.

'Maybe just a low dose. Just to lift you over this little hump.'

I nod. I don't want her to think I don't appreciate what she's doing.

Trix is waiting in the reception, and she puts her arm through mine as we walk back to the car. 'What did she say?'

I show her the note.

'Did she say anything else?'

'She says I have to keep busy.'

Trix laughs an odd little half-laugh. 'OK, but no more defrosting the freezer.'

I smile, so that she thinks I'm enjoying the joke.

She takes me home and goes back to work. I decide that, in the spirit of keeping busy, I'll clean the kitchen properly. I start in the corner behind the toaster. I brush up the loose crumbs, but there are a few right at the back, almost into the crack between the worktop and the wall, that I can't get to. I try running my fingernail along the join, but that just pushes them further down. I go into the bathroom and get a toothbrush, but that doesn't work either. Eventually I manage to suck them up with the attachment on the hoover. I go to put the hoover away and see my little handheld dirt devil on the shelf. Why didn't I think of that? It would have done the job perfectly. Trix says I over complicate things. She's right.

It's like with Claudio. He never called. He hasn't e-mailed, but I still check every hour on the hour. I won't let myself look more than that. A watched pot never boils, but he hasn't tried to get in touch, and it's not because he's been busy, or because he's been in a horrible accident, or because he's lost his phone and his computers had a virus; it's because he doesn't want to talk to me.

That's the simplest explanation. I'm stupid. I'm a silly

little girl, who can't even manage to clean a kitchen worktop properly, and he doesn't want to talk to me. I sit down on the floor next to the hoover cupboard, and consider this realisation. Then I remember what the doctor said about staying in control, and decide that I am going to take the initiative. Claudio doesn't want to talk to me because I'm silly and stupid. I need to stop being silly and stupid. One kitchen worktop isn't going to stop me from taking control of my own destiny. What I need to do, I think, is make everything perfect. I need to make me perfect, and make the flat perfect, and show that everything really is under control. Then things will be better. Everything will be better.

I take the dirt devil into the kitchen and run it over the worktop again, just to be sure.

Chapter Forty-Four

Trix

When I get back to work I head straight for Danny's office. That's not true. When I get back to work I skulk around in the staffroom for a bit and then stride around the library trying to look purposeful, whilst hoping to be able to 'accidentally' run into him. That way I won't actually have to go to his office and look for him. I'm not sure exactly what I said to him after the wedding, but I have a definite recollection that it wasn't good. He hasn't really spoken to me since. And he should have spoken to me, because he said some things too. He should really have come and found me by now.

I stick my head into the PA's office. 'Is he in?'

'Yes. You can go right in.'

Of course I can. I make it as far as his door, but can't quite make my hand do the knocking. I'm justifiably angry, I'm sure. Definitely justifiable. If only I could remember what he said, so I could be more precisely angry about it. And a little clearer about why he definitely shouldn't be angry with me. Maybe I could view this as a dry run and come back for a proper go later.

There's a small cough behind me. I turn back to Danny's PA. 'Normally people knock at this stage.'

Patronising cow. I'm working up to it, obviously. I knock too loudly, and too deliberately, on the door. Now she probably thinks I really didn't know how to work the door. 'Come in.'

I walk in briskly, adopting my best strictly professional face, and put the note down on his desk. 'Henri's signed off. Three weeks.'

He picks the note up. 'How is she?'

'I don't know.' I'm not in the mood to have him acting the sympathetic friend. Whatever was or wasn't said, I am sure that all of this is John's fault. 'She's not in work. Let me know if you have a problem sorting out cover.'

I start to walk out of the office. So far as I can tell there's nothing more to say.

'I'm sorry.'

'For what?'

'For believing John.' I look at Danny properly. He's impeccably turned out, as ever, but he does look tired.

'So, you don't believe him any more?' Even I can hear the scepticism in my voice.

'You haven't heard?'

Well, clearly not. I'm so out of the loop, I struggle with how doors work. 'I've been a bit preoccupied.'

And so he tells me. I'm guessing it's only the summary version, because we're at work and no alcohol has been consumed, but apparently after work on Friday, Danny and John and some of the City Council Cultural Services Department went to the pub, and Danny walked in on John propositioning a prominent city councillor in the gents' toilet.

'What about Claudio and Henri?'

'He set it up. Apparently he asked Deano to drop flowers around to Henri, and he arranged for Claudio to meet him to make sure he saw them together.'

'He told you?'

'The basics. I put the rest together with Claudio and Ben.'

'Claudio knows?'

Danny nods. 'I think he feels bad.'

'Good. He should.' However much he was set up, however much he was a victim too, Claudio just believed what John told him. I don't feel forgiving towards him.

'Are we OK?'

I nod. It isn't Danny's fault. John probably did more damage to him than anyone else. 'You're OK?'

'I will be.'

'You look good.'

'You know me. I bounce back.'

I lean across the desk and rub his hand with mine. He takes hold of it. 'There is one thing.'

I don't like the sound of this. 'What?'

'You and Ben.'

'We've just made friends; don't push it.'

'He just seems a bit lost.'

'I'm sure Ben's fine.' I really don't want to get into this. Since the wedding that wasn't I've been focusing all my energies on Henri, and trying to get her back to some sort of normality. 'Seriously, don't interfere in what you don't understand.'

'What if I think I do understand?'

'You don't.' It's intended to mark the end of the conversation. Cool and clear, and not inviting further discussion. To underline the point I stand up and step away from the desk.

Danny sits back and doesn't try to stop me. 'I know you're worried about Henri, but what about your own life?'

I hold my index finger up towards him. It's supposed to mean stop talking. Stop talking right now.

Danny never was one for quitting while ahead though. 'I'm just saying. I've known you both a long time. Apart, and together, and I just think ...'

I extend the rest of my fingers into the full-hand 'stop' sign, and arrange my features into my most severe 'not-amused' face. Danny raises his palms in submission, and I take the chance to make an exit.

I'm not having Danny telling me how to arrange my love

life. I think he's proved himself to be supremely unqualified in that area. And anyway, we're not even talking about my love life. Ben is not part of my love life. Ben is just some annoying guy I used to date, and with whom I had ill-advised one-time drunken sex. And a guy who winds me up so much that the police get called, and who's physiologically incapable of admitting that he might be wrong. I storm back through the library trying to concentrate on how unbearably arrogant he is, and not thinking about how he's also the guy who didn't once mention me ending the night retching over the toilet bowl, and who got up early the next morning to get me painkillers and food and clean underwear.

Chapter Forty-Five

Claudio

It takes me three days to work up the courage to actually ring Henri's doorbell. That's three days since I found Danny in the kitchen announcing what I should have already known. I almost set out to see her straight away that second, but Ben wouldn't let me. He said it was too late, and I should wait until the morning. Then in the morning, I decided to ring first but every time I started I didn't get as far as pressing 'Call'. So then I decided I needed to prepare what I was going to say. I got as far as driving past her house yesterday morning. Yesterday evening I parked the car and got out, but didn't make it as far as the door. So, it's not like I haven't been trying. To be honest, this is really a dry run. It's one o'clock in the afternoon, so Henri'll be at work.

I'm going to do it for real this evening though. Definitely this evening. Then the door opens.

Henrietta is wearing shorts and a vest top. Her hair is tied back. She looks knackered.

'Hi.'

We stand just looking at each other for a minute. I've been rehearsing in my head for days, and now I can't think of anything to say. I'm just staring at her. Henri starts talking, which is a relief, because I would have just stared at her until we both got old.

'Well, it's nice to see you. You'd better come in. Sorry I'm such a mess. I've been cleaning the flat. I just thought it would be nice to have things nice, in case, well just to have things nice. Would you like anything? A drink maybe? It's lunchtime, isn't it? Would you like something to eat? I don't know what I've got ...'

She continues the stream of consciousness through into the lounge. She's sorry about the mess and the state of her. She looks fine. Her flat always looks fine. She's worried that I might need feeding or drinking or making more comfortable. I refuse her insistent suggestions that I should sit down. This is good. Her nervousness is making me feel more and more in control. I reach my hand over to her and put my finger on her lips. She hesitates and stutters and then she's quiet.

'You look lovely.' I look round the room. 'There isn't any mess.'

I move my finger away and we're quiet for a minute, before she starts talking. 'I just, I'm not dressed properly. I didn't know you were coming. Just cos I'm off work, so bit scruffy. Sorry.'

I put my finger back over her lips. 'Why aren't you at work?'

I take my finger away. 'Oh, you know. Bit silly. Trix made me go to the doctors. I've been a little bit stressed, but I'm fine really. It's nothing. People overreact. I'm fine.'

I press my finger back over her lips. They feel soft against my hand, and I can feel the moisture from her mouth on my finger. I want to take my hand away and put my lips in its place. I know I'm supposed to say what I came to say first.

She's looking straight up at me, waiting to see what happens next. Her mouth is slightly open and I can feel her breathing. The talking can wait, I decide. I'll explain myself later. I move my hand to the side of her face, and bring the other hand up to her other cheek. I bend down to kiss her, very softly letting my tongue part her lips a little more. I mean to just kiss her for a minute, and then tell her that I'm sorry, and explain that I was tricked, and beg her to tell me it's not too late. But she starts to kiss me back. She stretches up on tip-toes and reaches her arm around my neck. I can't stop myself, and I don't want to stop myself.

He moves his hands down from my face and puts them round my middle, and then he lifts me up off the floor, and wraps his arms under my hips, tilting me so I can wrap my legs around his body, which I do. He carries me into the bedroom.

Part of me can't believe that he's back, but part of me knew he'd come back. I just needed to make sure I was good enough to deserve him. This is exactly like we used to be. He came in and kissed me and now we're going to bed together. I lift my arms up so that he can pull my vest off, and then he pulls his own T-shirt off over his head. He tugs at my shorts a bit, and I wriggle out of them, and lie down for him on the bed.

As he buries his face in my shoulder I can see a spider's web on the ceiling above him. That wasn't there this morning. It's another job the dustbuster is ideal for. I'm quite looking forward to zapping it. Apart from that one cobweb I think the flat is very nearly perfect, so my plan worked. I made everything perfect and Claudio came back. Now I just have to keep everything perfect so that he won't go away again.

He pushes into me and starts to move and I start to breathe more heavily so as not to discourage him. I bury my face hard into his shoulder, inhaling the scent of him, forcing it to fill my lungs. My fingers press into his back. His rhythm pounds into my body, and I try not to let any other thoughts come into this moment. I even let out a little 'Oooh' sound so that he'll know that everything is going absolutely perfectly.

Afterwards I lie very still and quiet resting my head on his chest. If I stay still and quiet I can't upset him, can I? He starts talking.

'So, I was thinking, maybe we could just have a quiet little wedding in Naples, rather than a big affair? Do you think that would be better?'

I feel my insides lurch a little bit. So we're still moving to Naples and getting married. I swallow the feeling. This is exactly what I was hoping for. He's back. We're together again. He still wants to get married. I'm still going to be Mrs Messina. It's all actually happening just like I wanted it to. I really am waking up and discovering that the last few weeks have just been a terrible dream.

'Ok.'

He strokes my cheek with his thumb. 'I'm sorry about the honeymoon. I'll make it up to you.'

'Ok.' I haven't even thought about the honeymoon to be honest. I'd completely forgotten we were supposed to have one. I guess Trix must have unpacked my suitcase while I was at Dad's.

'Where were we going to go?' The honeymoon was supposed to be a surprise. Claudio planned the whole thing. He is a lot cleverer than me about holidays and where to go at what time of year and stuff. It made sense to leave it to him.

'Tenerife. Some of the guys from Sorrento last season are repping out there. It would have been cool to catch up.'

'I'm sure it would have been nice.'

'I'll take you there, one day, I promise.' He sighs. I hope that the subject of the last few weeks won't come up again. It does feel like a bad dream that we can just gloss over. Talking about it just makes it seem closer and more real. 'What about the wedding presents?'

'What?'

'Did they get sent back?'

I just don't want to think about these sorts of details. 'I'm not sure. I think Dad or Trix must have sorted it out.'

'We should find out. I think really if we get married soon we should be allowed to keep them, don't you think?'

'If you like.'

He moves so that he's pulled up on one shoulder looking down at me. 'Sorry. I'm going on, aren't I?' He grins. 'Shall we do something more interesting instead?'

I don't object so he kisses me again passionately and warmly. I kiss him back and try to just think about making it a perfect kiss.

Chapter Forty-Six

Twenty years earlier

Henrietta

I try to pick up the telephone like I've seen Mummy do, but it's on the shelf so I have to climb on the chair to reach it.

'Hello.' I think Mummy says a number when she answers the phone too. 'Three.'

'Hello, darling.' It's Daddy. 'Is Mummy there?'

'Daddy!'

'Can I talk to Mummy please?'

I think about it for a minute. I don't think the phone will reach to where Mummy is. 'No.'

'Why not?'

I don't say anything.

'Give the phone to Mummy, darling.'

'S'asleep.'

'Asleep?'

Daddy's talking louder now. I don't like it. I don't like Mummy being so still. I don't like the way her pretty dress is getting all crumpled on the floor. I let out a big sob.

'Is Mummy asleep?'

Daddy sounds cross now. Another sob.

'Henrietta. This is important. Can you wake Mummy up for me?'

I don't know what to do. I know that if someone is sleeping I'm supposed to be a quiet girl. 'Sleeping. Shhhhh …'

'Henrietta listen to Daddy. Where's Mummy?'

I don't understand. 'Sleeping.'

'Where is she? Is she in bed?'

'No.' The sobbing has stopped now. Mummy looks funny. 'Funny. On floor.'

'Henrietta. Listen very carefully. I want you to try to wake Mummy up. Can you do that?'

'Sleeping. Shhhh ...'

'No. I want you to shout as loud as you can, like it's a game, Henri. Shout and see if you can wake Mummy up.'

I yell as loud as I can, but Mummy doesn't move.

'Is she waking up?'

'Sleeping. Shhh ...'

'OK Henri. I want you to keep trying to wake Mummy up. I'm going to come home now though, so I'll see you in a minute.'

The phone makes a clicky noise, and then Daddy isn't there any more. Mummy is lying very still on the floor. I sit down next to her and touch her with my fingertip, very gently like Daddy showed me with the baby goats at the farm park. She doesn't move.

There's tea spilled on the carpet next to where she's lying. Mummy doesn't like mess. I get my little plastic broom out of the toy cupboard and start sweeping the tea. It doesn't really work. The tea just gets more spread out.

Then Daddy comes back, and everything gets very busy. Other men come and kneel next to Mummy and then they and Daddy take her away in a special car called amamulance and I have to go and sit with Mrs Jackson over the road.

I sit at Mrs Jackson's house for ages. We eat cheese on toast and watch some of her programmes. Mrs Jackson always lets me watch her programmes when she looks after me. Daddy doesn't like me watching too much telly. Mrs Jackson's programmes are all about grown-ups shouting. I don't really understand them.

I fall asleep in the chair at Mrs Jackson's house and when

Daddy comes to get me it's very late and someone has put a blanket over me.

'Where's Mummy?'

'Mummy's not coming home any more.'

I start a really big cry, and can't make the words for a minute. 'Is Mummy cross with me?'

Daddy doesn't answer. He looks tired and sad. I couldn't wake Mummy up. I couldn't clean up the tea. I've made her so cross she doesn't ever want to come back.

Chapter Forty-Seven

Trix

I hate Henri being off work. It leaves me with mountains of extra stuff to do, most notably the stupid art competition. I made, what I thought, was a very impressive argument in favour of cancelling the whole thing, but apparently it's far too late for that. People are already working on their entries, and it's been in the paper, and Ben is coming in to judge.

That means that three afternoons a week are now taken up supervising Henri's after school art clubs so that the kids can finish their entries for the competition. Some of them have actually put a lot of work into it; if I wasn't resenting being there so much I'd be impressed. There'll be others that turn up with an entry on the day, which will split into two categories. Firstly there'll be the ones who've thrown some black paint at a piece of paper the night before; and secondly there'll be the ones with perfect displays that were clearly constructed over days and days of non-stop work by their parents (or possibly by their au pairs – it is a tad middle class around here).

The problem at the moment with having to supervise the project work during Art Club is that the kids keep asking me questions about what they're doing. I have eleven-year-olds trying to build infinity, and asking for my guidance on how to go about it. I'm rapidly growing to hate geeks, and I already hate looking stupid in front of schoolchildren. Hence the need to actually read Ben's book, thus breaching my no-thinking-about-Ben rule. This is a shame. It was a good rule.

Chapter 3: Beyond the physical: Zero comes of age
The third great leap in Zero's evolution was a long time coming. First it was merely a placeholder. Second it was a number in its own right, allowing us to state with confidence that 'there is nothing here.' Third, and most revolutionary of all, it became a trigger that fired the human imagination off into strange new directions.

That seems like a bit of a worry to me. I'm not sure how comfortable I am with Ben's imagination being fired off into strange new directions. An image of Ben keeps insinuating its way into my mind. Somehow the maths isn't engrossing me enough to make it stop.

From the outset mathematicians struggled to make Zero conform to their usual rules. If you accept that Zero is one less than one, you have to ask yourself what is one less than Zero? Then you end up with a whole new set of numbers that aren't anything to do with counting things. You can't really divide by Zero. If you try to multiply by it, you end up with nothing.

Accepting Zero means accepting that none of your rules for how numbers work are really rules at all. They're useful guidelines for those numbers that are all about counting physical stuff, but in the realm of nothing and everything all those rules break down.

And that's the big surprise that Zero offers us. Learning about Zero isn't learning about Nothing at all. It's about Everything. As soon as you accept Zero, you also have to accept the possibility of the Infinite. Everything begins with Nothing.

So even the maths doesn't conform to the rules. If I was speaking to him I'd point that out. Zero, I would tell him, is just like art and beauty and love after all. Of course I can't, because I'm not speaking to him or thinking about him at all.

I slam the book closed. It's not really as satisfying as shouting to his face is, but I feel I've made my point. The not thinking about him isn't going quite as well, unfortunately. I keep remembering university, which is insane. It's ancient history. Thinking about it is about as much practical use as … as writing a book about nothing.

I used to wind Ben up by saying that he was doing a degree in 'Sums'. That would make him go all pink and angry. Even then we argued a lot. I remember one time Claudio came to stay, and told Ben he thought I was scary, because we bickered about him drinking. It wasn't even a proper row that one.

Chapter Forty-Eight

Twelve years earlier

Trix

I knock on Ben's door. Normally I'd just walk in, but his brother is visiting and it would be just my luck to walk in on him in his pants. Given that he's only about fourteen, and is open-jawed with wonder at the fact that any girl is prepared to have sex with his brother, that would be properly weird on very many levels for both of us.

'Come in.' Ben yells over the range of music that's pervading the corridor. There's U2 from Ben's room (typical unimaginative man music), but in the corridor that gets mixed in with some sort of Bollywood thing from two rooms further down, and a hip-hop bassline thud pulsing the floor from downstairs. It's brilliant, and it's why I love living in halls.

Ben's room smells slightly of boy, so I lean over the bed and open the window. Normally we hang out in my room, which I have accessorised with tastefully cool posters and prints. Ben's room always makes me feel slightly like I'm in a monk's cell. There are hardly any personal touches. One picture of him and his brother and parents on holiday at Lake Garda, and one poster which proclaims: 'There are 10 sorts of people in the world: those who understand binary, and those who don't.' It's not funny. I don't even think Ben thinks it's funny. It's just one of those things that someone bought him, and he put it up rather than chuck it away. It could just as easily have been the other way around.

Claudio is lying on the bed, and Ben is sitting in the one and only chair, so I lean on the desk, trying to look comfortable and at home. Claudio is playing with one of those handheld game things. I don't really know what to say to him. I know I'm only five years older than him, but fourteen-year-old boys are a closed book. I don't have any brothers or sisters, and even when I was fourteen, boys only really talked to me to ask whether the carpets matched the curtains, and call me a Ginge. I was lucky to hit secondary school before 'minger' and 'minging' were common parlance. The rhyming possibilities would have made things even less bearable.

I look at Ben for support, but social unease isn't really something that he notices.

'So, what are we going to do this evening?'

Ben shrugs. 'Takeaway?'

Claudio perks up at this suggestion. 'Can we get pizza?'

Ben nods.

Claudio grins. 'Real pizza with orange cheese and processed ham, and thick white bread base?'

Ben laughs. 'Mum and Dad only ever let us have homemade pizza, with a proper Italian thin base, and lots of green stuff on it.'

'Well, it's good that they're looking after your health.' Weirdly, having Claudio there seems to be making me feel like I ought to be the grown-up.

'It's not our health they're worried about. It's our cultural heritage. Proper Neapolitan pizza only in our house.'

Ben and I walk to phone for the pizza. There's already a girl in the phone box so we wait outside. I take the chance to ask him what I ought to talk to Claudio about. He looks blank.

'Well, what do you talk to him about?'

'Dunno. Just whatever.'

'Well, what's he into?'

'Rocks.'

'What?'

'Rocks.'

'Rock music?' Please God, let him mean rock music.

'No. Actual rocks. Stones, pebbles, fossils, all that stuff.'

I clasp a hand to my mouth. 'Oh my god! There's two of you.'

Ben looks offended. 'I'm not into rocks.'

'Really?'

'Well, obviously, there are some interesting elements in geology. Actually a lot of what we know about the early days of the Earth comes from mineral deposits in rock layers, and that's fascinating.'

'But you're not really into it?'

The girl comes out of the phone box and Ben gives me a we're-not-finished-here look before he goes in to phone for pizza. I wait for him, and we continue without missing a beat when he comes out.

'There's nothing wrong with a wide range of interests, you know.'

'A wide range of interests. Hmmm … what A-levels did you do again? Physics, Maths, Further Maths, and what degree? Maths with Physics? I can see how you're broadening your horizons.'

'This from the woman who won't read a book that isn't make believe!'

'Did you just describe the wonders of the English fictional canon as make believe?'

'You know what? I think I did.'

We're back at Ben's room now. Claudio is still lying on the bed, and we make an effort to simmer down as we go in. Ben hits him across the legs.

'Shift. Let someone else sit down.'

Claudio wriggles upright and I sit on the edge of the bed next to him. He's still playing with his console thing, so I feel morally excused from talking to him. I look over at Ben, and find that he's looking at me. I look straight at him. He is actually quite sexy. It surprises me every time I realise that. In my head, he is a proper geeky boy. I'd never say it out loud, but sometimes in my head when I have to introduce him to people I can feel myself wanting to apologise, to explain and excuse him. But actually he is more than presentable. He's not trendy, but that's OK. I can't stand boys who look like they try too hard. I like clean and clean-shaven, but anything beyond that I consider to be excessive vanity in a man. His dress sense has improved quite a lot since I first met him, mainly because I threw away most of his wardrobe as a condition of agreeing to have sex with him the fourth time. It seemed like reasonable behaviour to me.

Anyway, I'm looking at him now, trying to make my eyes tell him how beautiful and gorgeous I think he is. It's a lot to get into a look, but I'm having a good shot at it.

'What?' Ben pulls a face at me, and sadly, it's not a 'Yeah baby' type of face.

'Nothing.'

'Then why are you looking at me funny?'

'I'm not looking at you funny.'

'You were.'

'Wasn't.'

'Were.'

Claudio has looked up from his game thingy to see what we're bickering over. I hope he's impressed with the level of argument a university education allows you to achieve. I feel that we are probably making him uncomfortable and should therefore stop, but if we stop now, Ben will have had the last word, and I can't allow that.

'Wasn't.'

Ben looks at his watch. 'I'm going to see if the pizza's here.'

This is the only downside of living in halls. When you order takeaway they deliver it to the porters' desk, so you have to go over there and loiter waiting for it to arrive. I have had conversations with porters in the past where they've sworn that no delivery guys have been in when you could actually smell the pizza in their office.

As Ben heads out of the door, I hear him mutter. 'Were.'

Being distracted by the bickering meant that I missed the opportunity to go with Ben, so now I'm stuck on my own with the fourteen-year-old rock boy.

'So Ben says you like geology?'

He makes an affirmative sounding grunt, which probably counts as advanced communication if you're fourteen.

'Any areas in particular?' I have no idea if there are different areas of geology, but at least I'm trying.

'Volcanoes.'

'Right. Good. That's interesting.' I mean, it might be interesting. I don't know. I sense that he's not going to tell me much more though. 'Well, I might get a drink then?'

I stand up. 'Do you want anything?'

'Sure. Wine.'

Wine? Can I give a fourteen-year-old wine? Is that normal? If it's not, is it really up to me to police this particular fourteen-year-old? And most worrying of all, am I proving myself to be horribly uncool by wondering whether it's OK? Claudio is still looking at me.

'It's OK. Mum and Dad let me drink.' He grins. 'Italian thing.'

That sounds plausible. I head off to the kitchen, feeling foolish, for having been made to feel provincial by a child. I fill three glasses with wine from the box in the fridge with the huge 'B' on the side in marker pen. It's not good wine, but it is cheap.

When I get back I put one glass down in front of Claudio. I would hand it to him, but that would involve him letting go of the games console and that doesn't look likely.

'It's not very good wine.' Now I'm apologising to him for the quality of the alcohol on offer. I suspect that his wine-swilling cosmopolitan Italian parents probably have slightly more expensive tastes than our student budget runs to though.

'It'll be fine.' He puts down the console, and picks up the glass and takes a big swig. He pulls a face. Ben walks in with the pizza.

'Food's here! Who gave you drink?'

Showing reactions clearly honed by hours playing computer games, Claudio is pointing at me before Ben has even finished the question.

'He said your mum and dad let him.'

Ben grins. 'Did he?'

He looks at Claudio, who is starting to look guilty. 'Well, they do. It's an Italian thing.'

'No. They don't. I'm your brother. They're my parents too. If you're going to lie, at least try to come up with an intelligent lie.'

Ben flips open the pizza box. 'Just don't get drunk. I don't want to end up delivering you home with a hangover.'

Claudio is clearly much taken with this new permissive society, but I'm less impressed.

'He lied to me.'

'So?'

'So, shouldn't we do something about that? Aren't you supposed to discipline children?'

'I'm not a child.'

'Yes. You are.'

'I'm not. I'm a young adult.'

Ben looks at him. 'Shut up and drink your wine.'

'No, don't drink your wine.' I glare at Ben. 'That's just rewarding him for lying.'

'It's only wine.'

'It's not. It's the whole principle of the thing.'

Ben shakes his head and bites into his pizza. 'I'm his big brother. I'm supposed to lead him astray.'

'I think he should have to apologise.'

Ben laughs. 'OK. Claudio, apologise to Trix for lying.'

'Sorry, Trix.'

It is actually quite funny now. I can remember being about the same age and getting caught fighting at school. There's a particular tone in which the forced apology is muttered that is just loud enough for you not to be in trouble for failing to do it, but not clear enough to be seen as a real apology. I peer down my nose at him. 'I can't hear you.'

Ben is sniggering behind me. Claudio pulls a face. 'Sorry, Trix.'

I nod primly. 'That's better.' I pick my glass up and take a swig. 'Now drink up. If we're going to lead you astray I don't want to get accused of being half-arsed about it.'

The next night, after a slightly grey looking Claudio has been delivered back to the bosom of his family suffering the effects of a sudden and apparently Claudio-specific stomach bug, Ben and I are in bed in my room.

'I'm not sure if your brother liked me.'

'He loved you.'

'Really?'

'Really. He did think you were a bit eccentric though.'

'I'm not eccentric!' I'm offended now. How can a teenage boy who thinks rock formations are a leisure activity think I'm eccentric? 'He didn't really say that?'

'Not exactly.'

'Good. You shouldn't make things up. It's mean.' I roll over and look Ben very seriously in the eye. 'You are a mean boy.'

'He didn't say eccentric. He said completely, fucking mental.'

'Oh. I thought you said he liked me.'

'He did.' Ben pulls me down on top of him. 'He's fourteen, Trix. That's high praise.'

Chapter Forty-Nine

Ben

I'm not sure what to do when I realise that Claudio didn't make it home last night. In my analysis there are, essentially, three possibilities. Either he finally managed to get as far as speaking to Henri and everything's OK again and he stayed there, or he didn't get as far as talking to her and sat in his car outside her flat all night, or he did talk to her and it didn't go well and then I'm not at all sure what he would have done.

I ring his mobile, and hear it ringing in his room, so that's no help. I'm wondering whether ringing Henri to see if he's there would be overly dramatic. Actually, my main concern about that idea is that I don't know what I'd say to her. I don't know if it's long enough since the wedding to just ring her and act normally or whether I'd still be expected to say something about what happened, and what would I say? I have a sense that asking if I can have back the towels I bought them would be wrong, but now it's in my head I can't think of anything else.

I decide that the best course of action would be to have a cup of tea and then think about it. Halfway through my tea I decide that if I had some toast as well, the situation would inevitably become clearer. Procrastination is a particular skill of mine. I'm in a state of prolonged procrastination at the moment. I've pretty much finished the active promotion for the book. I've got a couple of speaking things set up in the next couple of months, but basically no work on at all. I should, at this stage, be writing my next book. After the first one did well I signed a three-book deal, and number two should be getting underway this summer, which means that I should have definite plans for what it's going to be about by now, probably even a first draft. What will actually happen is that, in a couple of months' time, people will start hassling me, and I'll think about it then. I should also be writing articles for papers, and putting myself out there to comment on anything and everything vaguely maths related that hits the news. Part of me thinks that self-employment doesn't really suit me, but then I realise that the alternative would involve having to get out of bed and drag my arse into an office every single day, and I decide impoverishment through lack of motivation is a small price to pay.

And, demonstrating that procrastination works, and that you really should never do today what you can put off till tomorrow, just as I'm washing up my mug, Claudio walks through the door, with Henrietta in tow. 'In tow' seems like the right description. She's huddled under his arm. It's not clear whether he's unwilling to let go of her or vice versa. He bundles her into the kitchen. Claudio, at least, has a big grin on his face.

'So you finally got as far as talking to her?'

Claudio nods. 'And everything is sorted. My beautiful girl is going to come with me to Naples, and we're going to have a quiet little wedding in Italy, aren't we?'

Henri nods. I'm not an expert in this area, but I am surprised that everything's back on so quickly. Having said that, if I only have to deal with calm and rational people in my kitchen, that's not a status quo I'm keen to disrupt. I hope she gave him hell though. He deserved it.

Claudio sits down at the table, and pulls Henri down on to his lap. 'Now we just need to sort you out.'

'What?'

'I think that there should be romance for everyone. Danny too!' Claudio seems to have decided that sorting his own life out is insufficient and he's going to have a go at everybody else's too.

'I don't think Danny would particularly appreciate you interfering.'

'Right. Maybe leave that a while.' He pauses. 'That just leaves you then.'

'I'm fine.'

'You're lonely.'

'I'm fine.'

'You miss Trix.'

'What?'

He shrugs. Smug little shit. I give him a look which I intend to be the end of the conversation, but I can't quite let the subject drop. 'Don't be ridiculous. You can't miss stuff you never had, well not never, and …'

I taper off. Perhaps attack is a better form of defence in this case. And just in case Henrietta failed to give him a sufficiently hard time, it seems fair that someone should.

'Anyway, don't you think you'd be better off concentrating on your own relationships for a bit?'

Claudio's chin has dropped on to his chest, but he's still glaring up at me. He reminds me of when he was a teenager and someone would tell him off. It's a mix of defiance and contrition. Defiance seems to be winning. He mutters into his chest but it's clear enough what he said. 'You are still in love with her though, aren't you?'

I give him another look and walk out of the kitchen and out of the flat. Claudio is seriously taking the piss. He and Danny interfered enough with me and Trix before the wedding. And Claudio should have a better idea than anyone about the stupidity of interfering in other people's lives. As I leave, I give the door a proper hard slam. It feels good.

Chapter Fifty

Claudio looks really sad when Ben storms out. I can't have that. Claudio is supposed to be happy now. It's my job to make him happy. I press myself all against him and snake my arms around his back. He flashes a grin at me and raises his eyebrow. At first I don't get what he's driving at, but then he unpeels my arms from around him and drags me by the hand into the bedroom.

It is nice to be back with him. It's nice to be at his house too. I can relax a little bit more here. It's not my responsibility to keep it nice. I wish I hadn't thought that. Now the thought is in my head, I can't help but notice that it is a bit grubby in places. I close my eyes and try not to see it. I mean, it's to be expected, really, with just two boys living here. Claudio lowers me back on to the bed, and I try not to wonder when he last changed the sheets. I can't stop myself from tensing up a little bit though.

'Baby, are you OK?'

I open my eyes. 'I'm fine.'

I make my face into a smile to reinforce how I'm happy.

He grins. 'Let's see if we can get to more than fine.'

He starts kissing down my neck and chest, which normally I do really like. Well, I know that he really likes it, and I like making him happy, so I do really like it. I lie back and close my eyes again. Suddenly, he stops kissing me, and sits up. 'We should have a party.'

'What?'

'Well, for you, 'cause the wedding was spoilt, and as a goodbye before we go to Italy, and to celebrate that we're back together, and to make up for the fact that our friends won't all be at the wedding.'

I don't really know if I want to have a party. I think, maybe, I want to slope away to Naples and just live like the last few weeks never happened, because in any way that matters they didn't really. John's gone. Claudio's back. We're together. I think I want to act like this is how it's always been, and let everything else just fade down into a minor blip that's not even worth mentioning out loud.

'It'd be great. It'd be just like the party we had when I came back. That was a great party. You looked so beautiful. Come on. We should be celebrating.'

And he looks so excited, and I feel bad about not being excited straight away too. I'm sure a party would be lovely. It's sweet really that he wants to have one, to make up for missing out on the normal wedding party. It's considerate of him to think of that. I should be more grateful. 'That would be lovely.'

'Excellent. We'll ask everyone that came to my coming home party.'

I nod. That will be perfect. Obviously, that will be a little bit more Claudio's friends than mine, but we can't ask everyone that was invited to the wedding. That would be far too many people. I'm sure this will be much nicer.

Claudio grins at me. 'Sorry. I got distracted. Where were we?'

He starts kissing down my neck again, and I give a little moan to show him that I like it, and close my eyes.

Chapter Fifty-One

Ben

Storming out does have quite a nice dramatic feeling to it, but the anger only sustains me as far as the end of the road. I'm actually not great at anger. I know I come across as a miserable bugger, but actual fully-fledged temper is a bit tricky to maintain. I tend to default back to a sort of placid indifference fairly quickly.

It's a good example of regression to the mean actually, of how things tend to vary back towards an average or norm. It accounts for quite a lot of the effect of things like homeopathy. People consult a homeopath at the height of their illness, a situation which is intrinsically abnormal. Over the next few days or weeks they regress to the mean i.e. the illness gets a bit better, and the person, quite wrongly, attributes the improvement to the homeopathic medicine. I make a mental note to use my reversion back to placid indifference as an example in a book sometime.

I get to the end of the street unwilling to go straight home, but calm enough to realise that the obvious alternative is just wandering the streets. I count the days through my head, and decide that it's Saturday. That's another problem with being freelance – I never have a clue what day it is. Saturday means people with jobs might be at home. Excellent. I'll go and see Danny.

I decide to walk, feeling like a decent walk will probably do me good, and make up for having done nothing with my day but lie in bed and eat toast so far. I haven't done a great deal more than that with my week, and walking to Danny's seems like a decent substitute for real activity or achievement.

The universe doesn't agree, and it starts to pour down about ten minutes into the forty-minute walk. I'm still resisting going home where I could get dry, or get my coat, or even my car, so I power on. By the time I arrive at Danny's my hair is matted down to the side of my face; my clothes are drenched, and I can feel a channel of water forming from my hair straight down the back of my neck. Hopefully, Danny will be in and will lend me a dry T-shirt.

I run the last hundred yards to his house, revealing me to be deeply unfit, sending my breathing into over-excited asthmatic dog rhythm, and turning my face bright red. I add renewing gym membership to my mental list of things I can later put off, and ring the doorbell.

'Oh.'

'Oh. Hello.'

'Hi. What are you doing here?'

'Visiting Danny. What are you doing here?'

'Same.'

I stand in the doorway for a moment and look at him. It's the first time I've actually seen Ben since the horrible morning after. He's dripping wet and out of breath, but mainly I'm preoccupied with how he's here, now, in front of me, and I've had no chance to mentally prepare. I'd realised that I wasn't going to get through the rest of my life without seeing him; I know he's coming into work next week to judge the art competition, but if I'd seen him there it would have been under managed circumstances with time to prepare and other people around to hide behind. I was planning to be cool and professional, and then go home and neck a bottle of wine in self-congratulation.

'It's a bit wet.'

'Yeah.' I can't think of anything else to say.

He's looking at me very oddly though. 'I'm getting very wet.'

'Yeah.' Power of speech still not fully recovered.

'Can I come in, do you think?'

'Yes. Sorry. Do that.' Come in? Of course he can. Shit. That's what you do after you've answered the door. You ask them to come in.

He drips into the hallway. Danny comes downstairs from the bathroom at the same time, and makes much fuss about how wet Ben is. Danny rushes around finding towels and dry clothes, and bustling Ben off to the bathroom to change. I stand in the hallway watching all of this, glad of the activity, which reduces the need to think of words to say.

Danny and I were about to go out for lunch. He'll invite Ben now, which is normal. That's what we always would have done. If two of us were going somewhere and we ran into the other they would tag along. That's how we always behaved, back when things were normal. Things don't feel normal any more, and I don't want to sit through lunch with Ben pretending everything is OK. It's bad enough doing it with Danny, and that's just other people's lives.

Maybe that should never have been normal. Maybe there was stuff under the surface that it would have been healthier to get out and share and resolve, but we never did. I never did. I figured Ben never would. Even when we were together we argued about what we thought, not how we felt. He never tried to open the little box of unspoken things that always lingered in the hard to reach corners of our just-good-friends relationship, and I didn't either. I never really tried to get things resolved. Maybe because, if we're honest with ourselves, resolved is just another word for over.

So we go for lunch, and actually, it almost feels quite nice to be back here, the three of us just hanging out. We're not talking about anything that matters, but that's good. The last few weeks have all been big emotion and worry and constantly trying to hold everything and everyone together. It's nice to relax, well not quite relax obviously. There are still some subjects we're just not mentioning. But talking about nothing at all feels like a rest.

Danny and Ben are discussing their burgers. Ben has a cheese and bacon burger, whereas Danny has gone for the 'Ultimate burger', which has cheese, bacon, jalapeños, and beef chilli. Ben does not think chilli is a good addition to a burger.

'Burgers should be burger, cheese, possibly bacon, slice of tomato, lettuce, mayonnaise and a gherkin.'

Danny shakes his head. 'You can't like the gherkin.'

''Course not. You pick the gherkin out. It's still an integral part of buying a burger.'

It's a pointless conversation, but it's keeping us going, and nobody's stormed out, and nobody's cried. The conversation lulls for a moment, and we munch on our burgers without making eye contact. We haven't quite reached the level of easy silence yet.

Danny breaks the impasse. 'So Claudio and Henri are back on?'

Ben nods. 'They were all over each other in my kitchen this morning.'

'I can't believe she just took him back.' I can feel my temper rising as I think about her standing at the altar. I'm not sure I believe things can instantly be all better.

'How was she?' I have to ask. I really hope she's OK, but she's been spinning out for the last few weeks. I'm not sure I believe it can be all better that quick.

Ben pauses.

'Quiet.' He shrugs. 'What do I know though? I only saw her for a few minutes.'

Danny swallows. 'I hope they'll be OK.'

I can't help being worried. 'Maybe I should check that she's really OK.'

Danny shakes his head. 'Or maybe we should leave them to it. After all, I don't think any of us is particularly well qualified to advise on affairs of the heart.'

There's another silence. It's the first time that what happened with John, or, in a way, with Ben and me, has even been alluded to. I'm not sure how to react. And then Ben laughs, and Danny laughs too. So I join in, and after a second I find that I can't stop, because it is really quite funny. We're attractive, intelligent, successful people, well Danny and I are, certainly. It is sort of funny that we don't seem to be able to hold together any sort of adult relationship.

The laughter breaks the nervousness around the table, and Danny continues. 'The stupid thing is, I miss him.'

'I saw him.' Danny and I flip our heads straight at Ben.

'When?'

'Where?'

'Did you talk to him?'

I think I must have asked all of those, because Danny doesn't seem to have spoken at all.

'In town. He was really friendly actually. Like nothing had happened.'

'I can't believe you talked to him.' This behaviour clearly breaches some sort of friend code.

'I wasn't friendly to him.'

Danny shakes his head. 'It's OK. What did he say?'

'Not a lot. Just "Hi, how are you?" sort of stuff.'

'How did he look?' Danny is staring at the table, like he wishes he didn't care.

'Fine.' Ben shrugs. 'I asked him about Claudio.'

'What did he say?'

'Not much. Said it was just a bit of fun.'

'That was all?'

'That was all.'

Danny is looking down at his plate; I reach over and rub his arm.

'I know that he was a louse, and I know that we should have broken up years ago, but I miss him. It was good to have someone around.'

'Not at any cost though.'

Danny nods. 'I know. Everything feels odd at home though. The house is too big for one person.'

'You've been on your own there before.' Trust Ben to miss the point.

'But before I always figured he'd come back.'

I have to ask, just so I know how much of what I really think about John I'm allowed to say. 'And you're sure he won't be back this time?'

Danny's face twitches. 'I wouldn't have him in the house.'

'You've said that before.'

'This is different. It's good to have someone, but you're right. Not at any cost.'

Ben is breathing heavily beside me. 'Can I ask you something?'

Danny nods.

'Did John ever, I don't know, hurt you, you know, physically …?'

Danny pauses as if the answer might be yes. 'Of course not. What makes you think that?'

'Nothing.'

Danny pauses again. 'Good. Anyway, he's history. Let's talk of other things, to paraphrase the Walrus.'

'OK.'

'Actually, I need to heed the call of nature.'

Danny stands up and looks from me to Ben. 'It is good to be with someone though.'

He strides off towards the toilet. I look at Ben. 'Do you think that was a pointed comment at all?'

'Our friends trying to interfere and get us together? Surely not?'

'It just shows they care.' I'm feeling quite warm and fuzzy towards Danny at the moment.

Ben grins. 'S'pose he just wants us to be happy.'

'And being with me would make you happy?' Well, come on. I might as well score the point whilst I'm here.

'I didn't say that.'

'It was implied.'

'Not at all. I merely implied that Danny thinks you would make me happy.' He's smiling though. If it wasn't Ben I might almost think he was flirting.

'We should tell them about the wedding night. That'd shut them up.'

He opens his mouth, and closes it again, and opens it again, and closes it again. I think the wedding night was probably supposed to fall under the terms of our unspoken list of things that are not mentioned. I've thrown him on to unexpectedly unstable ground. In the end, he just shrugs. 'Tell who you like.'

This is very unstable ground. I can feel my certainties shifting. I'm not at all sure whether I like it or not. I laugh, keeping my tone light. 'And here was me thinking you were ashamed of me.'

He actually looks shocked. His mouth opens and closes and then opens again before he manages to shake his head. When the answer comes he sounds more upset than angry, I think. 'Don't be stupid.'

For a second I think he's going to continue, but then Danny comes back from the toilet. 'I want cake,' he announces. 'Do they have cake here?'

They do. They have chocolate fudge cake, so we order cake and pass another hour eating cake, and I'm sure it's good cake and I do like cake, but I really can't taste it, but we eat and we manage to keep talking about nothing very much. And the discomfort between the three of us has definitely eased. Well, the discomfort between me and Danny, and Danny and Ben has gone. I can't actually look at Ben. He actually looked shocked at the suggestion that he was ashamed of me. I don't think I've ever seen him shocked before. He can be goofy and he does get kind of stupid with strangers, but this time he seemed physically knocked back. I managed to stump the man who has an answer for everything.

Danny is carrying the weight of the conversation. He's chatting on about work, and maybe renting out a room at home, and probably a thousand and one other things. I'm barely managing to nod in the right places. I notice that Ben isn't doing much better.

Danny downs the last of his drink, and looks at the two

of us. 'Well, I've got some shopping to get so I'll head off. What are you two up to?'

Ben shrugs. 'Probably just head home.'

I nod. 'Me too.'

Danny laughs as he stands up. 'Well have fun. Try not to let the excitement overwhelm you.'

We sit for a moment after he's gone. I wonder whether to offer to buy him another drink. I wonder whether he might offer to buy me one. He doesn't, and I don't. I pick my bag up from the floor. 'Well then ... '

Ben nods. We both stand up, and I put my jacket on. Ben claps his hands together. 'Right.'

We walk towards the exit. 'The weather's brightened up.'

Ben nods again. How did we come to this? Me and Ben talking about the weather. At least when we were arguing, you could expect a decent quality of conversation.

Out in the street, we turn to face each other. I'm not sure whether to shake his hand, or kiss his cheek, or just run away. We've known each other for more than a decade. Why can't I remember what we normally do? In the end I sort of pat his shoulder. 'I'll see you then.'

I start to turn away. Ben takes a step after me. 'I could walk with you a bit.'

I nod. I was actually going to get the bus, but I don't say that. I just let him fall into step next to me.

We walk in silence for a bit. It's OK while we're in the city centre. The streets are busy and I keep getting bustled out of step from her, so it's hard to chat much anyway. By the time we hit the suburbs the streets are empty, and the silence is getting louder. I wish that Danny was still with us. He's a good man for keeping the conversation going. It's the old problem with small talk again. I don't have any insignificant chatter to offer. She tried to talk to me about the weather as we were leaving the pub. I just nodded. It's really the safest way. If I start talking about the weather I end up in a lecture about different sorts of cloud, and, apparently, that's not generally considered to be interesting.

Still, I have to say something. I know what I should say, and my useless brain has filtered out all other options. 'You don't really think I'm ashamed of you?'

She shrugs. Am I supposed to take that as a yes or a no? I stick with the silence, and hope that she expands her answer. 'Well, you don't exactly run around telling people about us.'

I'm not sure how to respond to that either. Does she mean the ten years ago 'us', or the wedding night 'us'? My mouth takes over, and, as always, adopts attack as the best form of defence. 'Neither do you.'

She stops walking and turns to look at me, but she doesn't look angry. To be honest she looks as if she's trying not to cry. We've reached the corner of her street. 'Well, I think I can find my way home from here.'

She turns and starts to walk off up the street, and I have a feeling like this is it. This is the moment. I have to say something, and it has to be the right thing. 'Wait.'

I shout after her and she stops and turns around. That's a good start. I walk the five paces over to her as slowly as

I can. I need the thinking time. I take a breath. 'I'm sick of this ...'

'Fine. I won't bother you again then.' She walks straight off again.

That wasn't a good start. 'No. No.'

I run round in front of her so she can't walk off. 'Not sick of you. Sick of this.'

Now this really is it. I tell myself to make it count. It's time to take the brakes off, and see if my inability not to say what I'm thinking might occasionally be a virtue. 'I'm sick of blaming each other for the fact that we're unhappy. I'm sick of you blaming me for one mistake, one ten-year-old mistake, which I can't change.'

I'm talking to a spot somewhere on her forehead. She's not looking at me. There's nothing for it now but to power on through. 'I can't go back and pick you. I can't go back and not leave.'

Now she looks at me. I could stop there, and if I did everything might turn out OK. She's looking hopeful, which isn't a look I've seen from her for a long time. I could stop right here, but I don't, because I can't. After ten years, I've chosen the truth, and because I am still me, that has to mean the whole truth.

'And even if I could change it, I don't think I would. It was a horrible mistake, and I did it in a stupid cowardly way, but if I hadn't done that, our whole lives would have been different. We wouldn't be here now. We wouldn't have been in the bridal suite that night. And we wouldn't have a chance to be together right now, as proper grown-ups, rather than kids who didn't know anything else.'

'Are you finished?'

I run over what I've just said in my head. I have no idea whether it's the right thing, whether I've said enough, but I have no idea what I would add to it anyway. Am I finished?

'I think so.'

I'm not sure how she's going to react. I think I just suggested that we be together right now as grown-ups. I'm not even sure that I am a grown-up, but maybe that's the point. When I was twenty-one I was sure I was grown-up. Maybe a total lack of certainty is the only true marker of maturity.

She's looking down at the floor again. She's very quiet when she speaks. 'You broke my heart.'

That's horrible to hear, but it's surprising too. Even back at uni, I never really felt like she needed me. She's always so in control. Friendly, approachable, warm, without a doubt, but somehow armour plated.

'I didn't know.' I stick with letting my mouth spill out the words. 'I'm sorry.' It's not enough, but it's true.

She looks up, and makes a fairly convincing attempt at a smile. 'But it was a long time ago.'

'It was.'

'And we're different people now.'

'We are.'

She glances down the road towards her house. 'Do you want to come in for a bit?'

'OK.'

We turn to walk towards her house and her fingers brush against mine. I take hold of them, and we walk down the street holding hands. It's slightly awkward.

Chapter Fifty-Two

Ben

'Well, you have to pick three.'

It's the end of the day on a fairly grey Thursday and I'm standing in the children's library looking at a table of what I guess I have to term 'artwork'. Henri has split them into three age groups and I have to pick a winner in each category and an overall winner. I don't really know where to start. There are only so many differences between pieces of paper covered in black paint that you can identify. I tentatively touch one sheet in the '7 and unders' section that has been drawn out like an old-fashioned counting board with counters drawn on it. I like it; at least it's different from the others. Henri shakes her head.

'What? Why not?'

'Clearly done by the parent. It's not fair. If the parent was going to do it, they should have entered the open-age section themselves.'

I laugh. 'You're hardline.'

She shrugs. She looks like she'd rather be somewhere else. Normally with Henri you'd expect her to be skipping about clapping her hands and talking incessantly about how wonderful everything is. The incessant talking was seriously annoying, but new cross Henrietta is making me nervous.

I look at the table again. This is going to be harder than I thought. I only agreed to do this by accident, and then went along with it because it annoyed Trix.

I glance at my watch – ten past five. She gets off work in twenty minutes, when she will be expecting me to meet her outside for our first official date in ten years. Actually, it's probably our first actual date ever. Eighteen-year-olds don't date. They just get drunk and forget to go home. It has the same outcome, for considerably less emotional and financial outlay.

When we went back to her flat on Saturday, we drank coffee and watched a DVD and then I went home. We chatted a bit, and I tried to explain imaginary numbers, and then we argued about whether imaginary numbers were silly, but there was no big falling into one another's arms, and no passionate volcanic sex. If I'm honest I was expecting either a door slammed in my face, or the sex.

Just before I went though she said. 'So you said about being together as grown-ups, and you know, if that's what you want, then maybe we could go out sometime, like for a drink or something, or food, if you want.'

And I said. 'Like a date?'

And she said. 'Yeah.'

So I'm meeting her after work tonight and taking her out for dinner, and maybe a film. 'Dinner and a movie' – I'm not an expert but that sounds like a date sort of a plan to me.

Henri lets out a little cough next to me. I smile in what I hope is an apologetic way and try to apply myself to the task. I plump for one of the black paint daubings in the '7 and unders.' It's not good, but does at least look like it might have been done by a small child.

The '8s to 14s' are easier. There's a standout model of a computer, with the screen covered in lots of little ones and zeros, and they've sort of built a section out of the screen so that the zeros spill out over the keyboard. I actually quite like it, you know, for a cardboard model of a computer.

The '15 and overs' are more difficult. One of them is actually knitted. I think it's an attempt to knit infinity, or maybe it was an attempt to knit a scarf that went horribly wrong. Either way, it's not going to win. There are two possibles I think. The first is a painting, a proper oil on canvas painting, of the cosmos. It's the grown-up version of the black paint on paper that won the kid's bit. It's very well done though, all swirling gas clouds with pin-pricks of starlight. The other possible is a cake. It's a regular Victoria sponge cake, but they've iced lettering on it. The lettering says 'Zeno's Infinity Cake', and underneath there are loads of speech bubbles saying. 'That piece was too big. Just half that size for me please!' and the speech bubbles get smaller and smaller until you can't see the actual lettering at all.

I point at the cake. 'I like this one.'

Henri glances at it. 'I don't get it.'

Trix pipes up behind her. 'It's a paradox.'

I look over at her. 'I didn't hear you come in.'

'Just wanted to let you know I've finished a bit early.'

I nod. 'Trix's right.'

'Of course.' Trix is still watching us from the doorway.

'Right about the cake. It's based on Zeno's paradox.'

Henri is looking blank, but we're technically still talking about the art, so she must be interested, mustn't she?

'Well, common sense tells us that if we keep cutting slices of cake and eating them the cake will run out, but mathematically if each piece is half the size of the piece before there's never an end point. If you have one hundred grams of cake and the first slice is fifty grams, then the second is twenty-five grams, the third is twelve and a half, the fourth is six and a quarter, but the numbers never quite add up to a hundred, so it seems like the cake will go on forever, with you just cutting smaller and smaller pieces.'

Trix walks over to look at the cake. 'So you can use cake to prove that maths doesn't work.'

'No. Obviously, there is a mathematical solution, but it hadn't been established at the time. That's why Zeno posed the question.'

Henri nods. 'So Zeno was from a long time ago.'

'Ancient Greece.' Hold on. That wasn't me. I look at Trix. She continues. 'And he didn't actually mention cake. He proposed the idea of a never-ending race, but it's the same principle.'

I'm impressed. She's almost right. I mean, she hasn't actually explained the solution, which is the really clever bit. It's all to do with there being a limit and numbers behaving differently as they move towards the limit, but I don't interrupt her or try to explain it at all. See how mature I'm getting. 'Bloody hell. Where did you learn that?'

'Read it in a book.'

'OK.' I find that I'm just standing grinning at her. She actually read my book. At least I assume it was my book. She might have been reading other books about Zeno's paradox. I hope not, not that I'd be jealous, but you know, I think she should have read mine first. I'm still grinning. Henri coughs quietly. She's looking at me and then back towards the art. The Art. Right. That's what I'm supposed to be doing.

'Right. The cake definitely has it. Can I make that the overall winner, or should I have one of the children's ones?'

Henri shrugs. 'Up to you. A kid is more likely to get us a picture in the local paper.'

'Computer kid is overall winner then.'

Henri nods. 'Fine. Now, could you sign the books for the runners-up before you go?'

She gestures towards a pile of thirty books. I hate signing books like this. It's worse than signing for actual people; at least then you get to rest your hand while they talk at you.

I glance at my watch and look at Trix, who has her impatient face on. 'Is it OK if I come in tomorrow to sign them?'

Henri nods. 'Are you going somewhere?'

I look at Trix. I can still remember her suggesting I was ashamed of her. I purposefully draw myself up to my full height. 'I am. I'm taking Trix out for dinner.'

Henri looks interested. 'Where are you going?'

'Probably Oscars.'

'I love Oscars.'

She sort of tilts her head at us. I don't say anything for a moment.

'Right then.'

Henrietta isn't looking like she's about to leave, you know, on her own.

'They have lovely puddings.'

'Yeah.' I have no idea why this conversation isn't over already. How do I make it stop?

'OK. So ...'

There's some silence but we're still not moving.

Trix jumps in. 'Why don't you sign those books now Ben? Henri and I need to have a little chat.'

She grabs Henri by the arm and drags her through to the main library. I try to concentrate on signing the books, but I keep hearing little bits of hissed conversation from Trix. After a couple of minutes I hear Henri squeal. She runs back into the room and picks her bag up. 'I've got to go. You have fun this evening.'

She dashes out again, and Trix comes in. I look at her. 'We are going to get a lot of stick for this.'

She nods. 'Do you mind?'

The question is asked casually, but I suspect there might be a bit of real concern behind it. I shake my head. 'Couldn't give a fuck.'

I put down my pen, and walk over to her. I offer my arm in what, I imagine, is a romantic gentlemanly fashion. 'Shall we?'

Chapter Fifty-Three

Trix

It's odd being on a date with Ben. To be honest it's odd being on a date at all. I'm not normally a dating sort of girl. Traditionally, I'm more of a 'meet boy, shag boy enthusiastically, shag boy slightly less enthusiastically, never call boy again' sort of girl. Although, there hasn't been much of that recently either.

I think I suggested the date thing, because I was scared of us just falling back into being us, when there hasn't been an Us for ten years. I'm telling myself that I'm being mature and sensible, and making sure we have a proper fresh start. And I'm nearly convinced. It hardly feels like I'm terrified of jumping in with both feet at all.

But actually, I am having fun. We're good company, and tonight we both seem to be making an effort to be nice to each other. We're disagreeing about everything, but it doesn't feel like we're trying to score points over it. We chose dessert over going to the movie, so clearly neither of us is too desperate to be able to sit in the dark without talking.

As the waitress clears away the dessert plates (chocolate toffee cheesecake, since you ask – at least if this doesn't work out I've got my comfort food of choice lined up) Ben leans forward. 'Do you want to know a secret?'

'OK.'

'I've always quite liked that you were into different stuff to me.'

I'm not quite sure what to say to that. 'What do you mean?'

He doesn't quite look at me. 'When I was at Cambridge, everything was so narrow, so specific. There's all these hugely, jaw-droppingly intelligent people but their field of knowledge is so narrow. And it's taken for granted that that knowledge is worthwhile. It's amazing, but in a way it was very cosy, too cosy.'

'And I'm not cosy?' I'm not sure whether to be offended. I suspect that, like me, Ben does not consider cosiness a good thing.

'No. Never cosy. You're ...' He pauses. 'More challenging.'

We've moved away from talking crap into actually talking. I don't want to stop, but I don't quite feel comfortable being here either. It's been a long time.

'But we row all the time.'

'Not all the time.'

'All the time we're awake.'

'Most of the time.'

'And I think you're a ridiculous little man.'

That might have been too much. 'I'm not little. I'm quite tall.'

'You're still ridiculous.'

Well, he is ridiculous. He's quiet for a second. 'But it doesn't matter.'

What an odd response. 'Doesn't it?'

'Does it make you like me any less?'

Does it? Do I like him less because he's ridiculous, and sometimes pompous, and quite deliberately miserable?

I shake my head. 'It feels like we've spent years trying to break whatever it is between us.'

He doesn't respond. I'm out on a limb here. Oh well.

'We didn't manage though, did we?'

He shakes his head.

'Good.'

He nods. 'It is. You are.'

'I am what?'

'You're good. You're a good thing.'

I nod. 'Very true. I am generally a very good thing.'

'You are. I love it. I love you.'

And then there's a silence. I can see his brain processing what his mouth just said. He's doing that thing he does where he sort of opens and closes his mouth as if he can swallow the words back and start again.

'What did you say?'

'I said I love it.'

'And after that.'

He looks straight at me. He seems to have decided that we're an all or nothing proposition. He might be right. 'I said I love you.'

I'm freaking out. 'Why did you say that?'

'Because it's true. I do love you.' He pulls a face. 'I hate it when Danny's right about things.'

'He is going to give us such a hard time over this.'

'Is he?'

'Of course he is. And Claudio too. Henri will be OK. She'll just think it's cute and romantic. Oh my God. We're going to be thought of as cute and romantic. We are going to get seven types of piss ripped out of us.'

'Are we?'

'Well, obviously.'

Ben takes a deep breath, and starts again using the special 'explaining it simply' voice he uses when Henri asks him about maths. 'Well, we would only get a hard time if we got together. And at the moment it's not at all clear whether that's happening.'

I'm confused. He says that he loves me, and then says he's not sure whether we're getting together. 'Why not?'

His head is in his hands now. 'Trix, I love you. I think

you're wonderful, but generally, I believe, this sort of thing takes two people.'

Seriously, what is he wittering on about? I nod gently. 'Yes.'

'Trix, do you think you might, at all, love me a bit too?'

And as a direct question it seems so much easier. I just nod.

Ben sighs. 'Shall we get out of here?'

I nod again. I do seem to have been temporarily relieved of the power of speech.

'I'll get the bill.'

We walk home holding hands. I lift his hand up in front of us. 'Did we used to hold hands?'

'I don't think so.'

'How do you feel about it? Bit couply?'

He nods. 'It is a bit.'

'OK, so we're not doing it when there are people around.' It's bad enough that we seem to be together. I'm not going to let him go all mushy on me.

We walk a bit further, and I have another thought. 'What about telling each other we love each other?'

'What about it?'

'Well, I think it's important to mention it.'

He nods.

I continue. 'But we don't want to be one of those couples that can't hang up the phone without saying "I wuv ooo", "I wuv ooo more" about seventeen times.'

'What if I promise never to say "I wuv ooo" at all?'

'You know what I mean.'

'OK. Well, what if we mention it once a week on a Sunday night, and then that'll see us through the week?'

I laugh. 'It's not very romantic.'

He nods. 'I know. Good, isn't it?'

'OK.'

He squeezes my hand a bit tighter. 'Only technically, I don't think you've told me you love me at all yet.'

I shrug. 'And now I can't until Sunday. You see, we've only been going out half an hour and I'm already in the lead.'

We continue the walk home covering important topics, like practising saying: 'This is Ben. He's my boyfriend,' and 'Have you met my girlfriend, Trix?' over and over again.

He walks me all the way home, and then stays over. It's exciting and new and warm and, as I start to get my head around his presence and proximity, surprisingly comfortable.

Chapter Fifty-Four

Ten years earlier

Ben

I drive myself to Cambridge. It's not like my first day in York, when my mum and dad brought me, with bags of food, and lots of muttered comments about why I couldn't keep living with them, when it was only fifty minutes drive. This is different. I'm a grown up now. I'm doing an MPhil, which will, naturally, become a DPhil when they see my intellectual capacity.

I am, as of today, a student of Gonville and Caius College, Cambridge. Even my mum's insistence on pronouncing it Ky-uss can't take the gloss off that. It does make me relieved that she didn't insist on coming down with me though. This is it. Getting here is what I've always been working towards.

I find my room and haul my stuff up the stairs. In addition to my existing student kit, I now have a full set of academic robes for college formal events. It's a different world. I pin my one poster up on the wall. It says 'There are 10 types of people in the world – those who understand binary, and those who don't.' Trix hated that poster. She was always trying to get me to buy stuff to make my room more personal. It's not a great poster, to be honest. I take it down again.

The photo of me, Mum, Dad and Claudio does make it up on to the wall. There are two other photos in the envelope with it. There's one of me, Danny and Trix at our Graduation Ball. Danny's wearing a purple bow tie and he's done his nails to match. The other photo is of me and Trix at the top of York Minster Tower. It was taken just before finals, when Trix decided we needed a day off revising. Or rather that I needed a day off revising, and she needed a day off intending to revise. We bought McDonald's and ate in the Minster Gardens. Then we went up the Minster Tower, because neither of us had done it before, and it seemed wrong to leave York without going up there. She got some tourist to take our picture at the top. We're both windswept and red in the face, but we're smiling.

I put the photo back in the envelope and place it my sock drawer. No point looking backwards.

Chapter Fifty-Five

'Stop eating that!'

Trix is dunking a carrot stick in the cheese and chive dip. She crunches unconcernedly, despite having been told not to. Now the top of the dip is all messed up. I start smoothing it over with a knife. 'It's supposed to be for the party. You've messed it up.'

'Sorry.'

'Well just don't eat anything else. It's supposed to be perfect for Claudio's party.'

'Your party as well.'

I nod. Of course it's my party as well, but that doesn't mean that I don't want it to be perfect when he arrives. I head back into the kitchen and start cutting bread rolls. I'm trying to concentrate on making even halves, but Trix doesn't seem keen to let me get on with it. 'Where is Claudio anyway?'

'He's coming later with Ben.'

Trix rolls her eyes. 'Leaving you to do all the organising.'

'He's keeping out of the way so that I can get on.' I look at her pointedly. 'He's being considerate.'

She laughs. 'He's being a lazy arse.'

I ignore that. I'm sure she knows he's not lazy. When we get to Naples he'll be working every day. I don't think it's too much for him to expect nice evenly cut bread rolls for his party, our party. 'He's very busy. He has a lot of packing to do.'

'So do you.'

'I've nearly finished mine.' That's not actually true. I've

279

hardly started. I've been busy with the party, and with work and things. I nearly tried a couple of times, but every time I get my suitcases out I don't know where to start. Normally I like packing. It's like a puzzle trying to fit it all into the space, without creasing things or putting delicate things underneath anything heavy. Anyway, that's not the point. I'm getting a bit tired of Trix's attitude today. 'I don't see Ben here helping.'

'Well, it's not his party. Anyway, who drove you to Sainsbury's yesterday to get all this stuff?'

She knows full well that Ben did. 'Claudio was busy.'

Trix puts her hand on my shoulder. 'I'm only teasing. Come on. It's going to be a great night.'

I nod. She carries on. 'Shouldn't you be getting dressed soon? I can cut those up.'

I hand her the knife but stay in the kitchen. She's not doing them right. The top halves are much bigger than the bottoms. 'They're not even.'

She turns around, still holding the bread knife. 'Go get changed. It's your big night. No one cares about uneven bread rolls.'

I go downstairs to my flat and start to get dressed. I start brushing my hair. I do thirty strokes on the right side first, then thirty on the left, and then the back. I put on the dress I wore on my first date with Claudio. He says it's his favourite.

I go back upstairs to see what Trix has done to the bread rolls. The later ones do seem a bit more even. I carry them through to put on the table. I want everything to be right, but I don't feel nervous. I don't have the butterflies-in-tummy pre-party feeling. I just feel like it has to be right, and then I'll have succeeded. I'll have done my duty.

The doorbell rings, and it takes a second before I recognise the noise. It's long enough for Trix to come past me and open the door. I hear Claudio and Ben in the hallway. Claudio comes into the living room, and puts his arms straight around me and his lips on mine. When he pulls away from the kiss, he looks around the room. 'This looks fantastic.'

I nod, even though it doesn't look fantastic at all. Even though her cutting got better, Trix has just bunged the bread on the plate in a big messy mound. You can still see the dent in the dip where she started eating, and the glasses don't match. That surprised me. I thought the glasses matched for the welcome home party, but Trix says these are the same ones.

More people start to arrive and the room fills up. I hang back watching Claudio greeting people. He's much better than I am at this sort of thing. I worry too much, and people can't enjoy themselves because I'm spoiling things. That's something else I need to get better at, if I'm going to be the perfect wife. Claudio is so much more relaxed than me. He comes over to me and wraps his arms around my waist. 'Are you having a good time, baby?'

I nod. He leans in closer to me and whispers. 'I can't believe we're flying out in two days.'

'Me neither.'

'It's going to be fabulous.'

I nod again. 'I know.'

I stretch up and put my arms around his neck. I have to stand up on tip-toes, which isn't very comfortable actually. I'm quite relieved when my dad comes over.

'Can I interrupt?'

Claudio unwraps his arms from my waist. 'Of course.'

Henrietta goes out into the hallway with her dad. I imagine it's one of those Father-Daughter chats. *You make sure he looks after you*, that sort of thing. I bet that's the sort of dad I'll be if we have girls. A proper protective old-fashioned Italian dad. I'll expect my daughters to wear polo necks and long skirts until they're twenty-one, and I'll give every boy they bring home a proper hard time. Maybe I could bring them up Muslim and then they could wear the full hijab?

It's weird thinking about me as a dad, but not terrifying. It feels like life is right on track. And I know Henri wants children, and she hasn't got a job in Italy yet, so why not get started straight away? 'You look pleased with yourself?'

'What's not to be pleased with?'

Danny shrugs. 'It's good. For a while there it didn't look like you two were going to make it.'

'All's well that ends well.'

'I suppose.'

If he has something else to say he doesn't say it. Henri and her dad come back. She comes over and I pull her close against my chest. Danny taps the side of his glass. 'Ladies and Gentlemen. A toast?'

The room simmers down to a quiet murmur and Danny continues. 'To Henrietta and Claudio! All the best on their travels!'

There's a chorus of 'Henrietta and Claudio' around the room. Danny continues before anyone manages to go back to their own conversations.

'Could I ask you to make a toast also to my very dear friends Benjamin and Trixabelle? It has only taken them a decade to admit that they fancy the pants off one another. So I am very confident that if we hang around for another twenty or thirty years they may one day get so far as wedding bells themselves!'

Ben and Trix are standing together at the other end of the room. As soon as Danny mentions them they take an involuntary step apart. When he mentions wedding bells they both start talking at once, and then look at each other, and then both start talking again, and then both look at each other, before Ben puts his hand out. 'You go first.'

'Just for the record I have absolutely no intention of getting married to that.'

'Good. Because I have no intention of asking you.'

She turns towards him. 'Great. I wouldn't expect you to. We're barely going out.'

He nods. 'Just friends.'

'Barely even friends.'

'I can't stand you personally.'

'Well it's mutual.'

By now they're both laughing rather than yelling. Ben grins. 'Well, I'm glad that's cleared up.'

And then he kisses her, and although on the one hand the idea of my big brother snogging anyone is just weird and gross in equal measure, you sort of can't take your eyes off them. It's not a romantic movie kiss. She's twisted round, which looks really uncomfortable, and they're sort of kissing and laughing at the same time and, I think, still arguing with each other. But they look good.

Danny lets out a big rumbling laugh and lifts his glass again. 'Well, to Ben and Trix anyway. To many years of contented mutual contempt!'

People raise their glasses to mutual contempt, and the party rumbles on. I talk to Danny for a bit, and then to Deano. To be fair, I don't think he ever knew that he had anything to do with what happened at the wedding. He's not the sharpest tool in the box – I don't try to explain it to him. It's ridiculous now I think about it anyway. As if Henri would look twice at him.

The party doesn't go on late, which is a relief, because I'm in the sub-group of people who live here, and therefore get stuck with the clearing up. Ben hangs around to help. Actually Ben tolerates having to help as a side-effect of retaining the possibility of getting laid later. I'm not sure that we're really helping though. Henri keeps telling us that we're not cleaning things properly. When she starts telling us we're putting things away in the wrong places I point out that it's my kitchen, and send her downstairs to bed. I think she's a bit reluctant to go, maybe because Claudio has cried off home claiming to still have loads of packing to do, but she scuttles away eventually.

Ben gestures at the rest of the clearing up. 'We are leaving this until the morning, aren't we?'

'Oh hell, yes.'

We head off to bed. He's stayed over maybe five times in the last two and a half weeks, and I've stayed at his twice, but we've already got the bedtime thing down to a slick routine. I hit the bathroom first. He sleeps on the left side of the bed. I get undressed while he's in the bathroom, but keep my undies on. Doing the whole mutual undressing thing every night is too much effort; doing the whole job yourself is a bit too 'old married couple' for this stage of the affair. Give us a couple more weeks though. We'll get there.

When he gets in bed he props himself up on his elbow to talk to me. He looks concerned.

'What's up?'

He swallows. 'What Danny said earlier ...'

Oh my God! 'Yeah?'

'You don't want to get married do you?'

I run the question back through my head. I'm pretty sure the intonation was 'You *don't* want to get married, do you?' rather than. 'You don't want to get married, *do you*?' I decide I'd better check. 'That wasn't a proposal, was it?'

I'm relieved to see that he looks horrified. 'You weren't expecting one, were you?'

'God! No!' And it's true. It's not that I don't want to be with Ben. I mean it's taken us this long to get together; I think if we're not pretty sure by now we're never going to be. I just don't really see myself marrying anyone.

'Right. I didn't think you were.'

'Don't get me wrong, I like having you around.'

His eyebrows flick up in his familiar quizzical look. 'You like having me around?'

'It's tolerable.'

'That the best I'm going to get?'

I nod. 'I just don't know if I want to get married at all.'

'I know what you mean.'

'Really?'

'Of course. I mean, I've been single for too long. I like things being disorganised in my personal way, as opposed to your personal way, which is obviously completely wrong.'

I've stopped looking at him now. I wonder if we'll ever get to a stage where we find the being nice parts of being together as easy as the being mean. 'I do miss you when you're not about though.'

He kisses my bare shoulder. 'Me too.'

Maybe we're getting the hang of it after all. I'm not quite comfortable settling in a touchy-feely mood though, so I laugh. 'Great. Can't live with you ...'

I tail off, and he finishes for me. 'Can't live without me!'

He wiggles his eyebrows in approximation of what he refers to as 'Claudio's Italian Stallion Look'. I choose to ignore it.

'So what do we do then? Just carry on like this, and buy spare toothbrushes?'

He shrugs. 'I guess so, unless you have a better idea.'

I shake my head. 'Do you?'

'No.' He lies down on the bed for a second and then sits straight up again. 'Actually yes. I think I might have ...'

Chapter Fifty-Six

Claudio

It's two days after the party. So far as I'm concerned today is the day. Naples here I come. Here we come. Ben is sitting in the kitchen looking chuffed with himself.

'You're not supposed to be happy to see the back of me.'

'Look outside.'

'What?'

'Just look outside at the front.'

I stick my head out of the front door. Planted up against the gate post is a bright red, in-your-face shiny estate agent's For Sale board. I walk out on to the street to look properly. There's a second smaller board stuck across it. 'Flat 2'.

'You're selling the flat?'

'I'm selling the flat.'

'But you love this flat!'

He looks at me a bit funny. 'It's just a flat.'

He's right. I don't really know why I said that. Ben doesn't do sentimentality about places or things, or, indeed, people really.

'Where am I going to go when I come back and visit?'

'I don't know. A hotel? Mum and Dad's? Maybe my new flat?'

He's speaking very slowly, like he's waiting for a small child to grasp the point.

'What about all my stuff?'

'Aren't you taking it all to Italy?'

'Not furniture. What about my furniture?'

'Technically, I think that would all be my furniture, so I'll either sell it, or take it to the new flat.'

'What?'

'Well, if I'm selling this flat I must be moving house.'

I hadn't thought of that. 'Yeah. Where are you going to live?'

He grins. This is clearly the bit he's been waiting for me to get to. 'I'm moving into Henrietta's flat.'

'You're moving in with Trix?'

'Don't be ridiculous. I'm moving into the flat. Trix and I are definitely not going to be living together. She'll just be slightly closer to hand.'

I shake my head at him. 'You're crazy. If you're serious about her, why don't you move in properly?'

'Don't want to. She doesn't want to.'

'But it's what people do. You go out with someone for a bit, then you move in. Some people even get married.'

Now Ben looks really confused. 'Good for people. We don't want to live together. We don't want to get married. We just want to be a bit more convenient.'

I really don't understand my brother. 'But you're crazy about her?'

He doesn't confirm it, but he doesn't deny the fact, which for Ben is real emotional development. 'Look, I think this is what'll work for us. That's what matters, isn't it? Just be happy for me, mate.'

I can't really argue with that, can I? 'Whatever works for you, mate.'

I can picture the two of them when they're ninety with him living in her basement and her banging on the floor when she needs seeing to. And there's a mental image I'm going to be stuck with all day.

Ben glances at the clock. I don't know why. It stopped about three months ago and neither of us bought new batteries. We both still look at it out of habit though, like it might make a recovery.

'What time's your flight?'

'Three. Two hour check-in though. I said we'd pick Henri up at half eleven.'

'Uh-huh. Are you ready to go?'

I nod. I couldn't be readier. Last time, when I went out to Naples it was an adventure. I knew I wasn't there forever, and I looked at it as a year in the sun. Now, it's like going home. It's been cool being back in the UK, but it's felt like a holiday. This feels like getting back to real life.

'What about Henri?'

'What about Henri?'

Ben shrugs. 'Dunno. New country. Different language. Is she excited?'

'Of course she is.' I stand up. 'Going to go pack my bathroom stuff.'

Of course she's excited. Why wouldn't she be? We've not talked about it that much. She's going to love it though. Once we get out there and she sees Naples, she's going to get all happy and Henrietta-ish about it. I know she is.

Chapter Fifty-Seven

Trix

I never thought I'd say this but I wish Henrietta would get into her control-freaky super-organised mode. She finally admitted this morning that she'd barely started packing, so now we're cramming stuff into her case any old way. Actually I'm cramming stuff into her case any old way. She's sort of wafting around the flat, picking up one thing at a time, and more often than not, putting it straight down again.

She's been funny all morning. I suspect it started when I told her about Ben moving in here.

'Are you sure you're not cross with me?'

She shakes her head.

'I mean, you're moving out anyway. I didn't think you'd mind.'

She gazes at me. Sorry to be unkind, but she looks kind of vacant.

'Did you drink too much last night?'

She keeps wafting round the room. 'No.'

'Right. And you're not cross about Ben moving in here.'

She looks at me again, and shakes her head.

'Are you sure you're OK?'

She nods, but she's still wandering around in her dressing gown, flitting from task to task. I know Henrietta. She's moving to Italy this afternoon. She should be marching around the place with lists and schedules and perfectly labelled matching baggage.

I go over to her and put my hand on hers. 'You know it's OK to be nervous. This is a big move.'

She nods again.

'Is that what it is? Are you nervous?'

She shakes her head and puts her mouth into a smile. 'It's very exciting.'

It sounds like she's reading from a script, like she's rehearsing someone else's words. 'It's a big step. It's OK to be a bit freaked out.'

'I'm fine. Anyway, talking about big steps, you're the one letting Ben move in with you.'

I let her change the subject. 'He's not moving in with me. He's moving in down here.'

'Right. Of course he is, Miss Independence.' She pauses. 'You don't worry that it's a bit quick?'

'It's been ten years.'

'You know what I mean.'

'It feels like the right thing to do.'

She nods. She seems to have switched her brightness back on. 'Like going with Claudio's the right thing for me.'

'Exactly.'

'Exactly.' She peers at the suitcase I've been packing, and wrinkles her nose. 'You're creasing things.'

That's more like it. 'Well you shouldn't have left it till the last minute should you.'

Henri pulls the case towards her and starts re-folding. 'Just because it's done quickly, it doesn't mean it can't be done properly.'

I resist the urge to laugh at her. She seems to be cheering up and I don't want to discourage her. 'What do you want to do with all the kitchen stuff?'

Her brow wrinkles up again. 'What do you mean?'

'Well, you're not going to take all your pots and pans and things on the plane, are you?'

She shakes her head. 'Claudio's rented a furnished flat to start with.'

'So what do you want to do with all that stuff?'

I can see her bottom lip starting to quiver, so I put my arm round her again. 'It's OK. What if I just box it up and put it in my loft for the time being?'

She nods.

I smile. 'And then it'll all be there, if …' I tail off. It's one of those sentences I shouldn't have started. What was I intending to say? If, this all turns out to be a terrible mistake? If it doesn't last the month? '… if you decide you want to ship it over, or anything.'

I think I pulled it back. It's the sort of thing Ben does all the time though. I'm beginning to understand how stressful conversation must be for him.

I go into the kitchen and start taking things out of cupboards. I suppose this isn't urgent. We can sort it out after Henri's gone, but it keeps me busy. I keep going until the doorbell rings.

I let Claudio and Ben in. Claudio hugs me effusively without me really needing to join in. 'The big day! Is she ready to go?'

'Just about, I think.' I have no idea. I've been keeping out of her way so she doesn't tell me I'm doing it wrong. She appears at the bottom of the stairs, and starts dragging a suitcase, which looks nearly as big as her, up the stairs. Ben runs down and helps her with it.

'Bloody hell! What have you got in here?'

Henri looks confused. 'Well everything really.'

Ben nods. 'Fair enough.'

Claudio and Henri hug. She looks absolutely tiny next to him. Not for the first time, I feel like her mum. I want to check that she's got everything she's likely to need, and give Claudio a lecture about how he has to look after her, and not let her run off on her own. Part of me still wants to kick him hard in the balls for the last time around. I don't.

We manage to gather Hen's stuff up and troop out to the car. Once Ben's wedged the luggage in, with Henri in the back, with Claudio's bags packed around her there isn't really room for me to go with them. I kneel on the front seat and manage to give Henri a sort of half-hug over the handbrake. 'Phone me lots, and e-mail, and come back to visit.'

She nods. I clamber out, and Claudio gets in. Ben gives me a quick kiss on the pavement. It's amazing how quickly we've slipped into the habit of casual affection. He promises to be back in a couple of hours, and then they're gone.

I go inside and head downstairs into Henri's flat. She's left the wardrobe open, so I can see that her clothes have gone, but once I close the doors it feels like she's just gone out for a bit. She's left the bed unmade, and there's rubbish in the bin. There are still a couple of books, and a big box of VHS videos in the living room, and all the furniture is just sitting here, like it's waiting for her to come home. She's hardly taken anything from the kitchen at all. It's probably the messiest I've seen the place since she moved in, which if Ben is going to be living here, is probably something I should get used to. It's not that he's actively gross. For a bloke he's pretty good at the cleaning and laundry stuff, well better than me, but mess he just doesn't really notice at all. Once he's finished with something it gets discarded on to the nearest flat surface, where he will cease to notice it, until he needs to use it again.

I go back upstairs to my living room and try to concentrate on watching TV, but my mind won't settle. It's another of those days, like the wedding, when you wake up knowing it's a Big Day, and then you end up with not a lot to do, and it makes you feel uncomfortable. In the end I run a bath, on the grounds that it should at least encourage me to sit still for a while, rather than just wandering from room to room. I always read in the bath. I can spend hours in there with a really great novel, or, if it's all there is, a really bad novel. Today I have another book to finish off though. I lie back and start to read while I wait for Ben to come back. Correction – while I wait for Ben to come home.

Nothing & Everything
Zero and infinity, far from being opposites are, in fact, one and the same. This relationship is hinted at in some of the most basic questions humanity asks about our universe. Has the universe always been here? If the answer is yes, then you have to embrace infinity. The universe is eternal, never beginning; it is infinite and has always been. If your answer is no, then what came before the beginning of the universe? That 'No' implies a starting point, and before that starting point, nothing. Zero or infinity? In this case, it looks as though one denies the other, but it's actually so much more complicated, and so much more beautiful than that.

So what do we mean by infinity? Infinity doesn't just mean everything. It means everything that ever was or will be or (and if this doesn't blow your mind you need to adjust your dosage) ever could be.

You can subtract anything you want from infinity and you won't make a dent. Infinity minus 1? Still infinity. Minus 47 million? Still infinity. Infinity doesn't get smaller, no matter how much you subtract. You can try to take away from it, to subtract from its wholeness for a lifetime, for a million lifetimes, but infinity is what it is. No matter what you try to take away, it remains all encompassing.

If you have something, and you break it, somehow you take a piece away, and it becomes less, then that something wasn't infinite. It was finite. However big it might have looked or felt, it had a beginning and an end. However hard you tried you wouldn't be able to make it infinite by continually adding one. The infinite and the big may look the same, may sometimes act and feel the same, but are as different in their nature as infinity is from the smallest least significant single grain of sand.

Chapter Fifty-Eight

Henrietta

I quite like being wedged in the back of the car, with Ben and Claudio chatting away to each other in the front. I can't really hear their conversation well enough to join in, but their voices are forming quite a pleasant background lull. I'm sort of perched in the seat surrounded by bags. It makes me feel like a little girl, all packed up for a family holiday.

I look out of the window most of the way. We drive through the city, and then out into the suburbs. We pass the turning for my dad's house, which I wave at, just a small little wave, so that the boys don't see and laugh at me. My dad said last night that he wasn't going to come and wave me off. He said it would be too upsetting. I can imagine him at home now. He'll be mowing the grass, or doing something involving his toolbox, I bet. He always comes over all Mr Handyman, when he wants to take his mind off stuff. It's like the summer after Mum died, he built a set of swings and a climbing frame for me for the garden, and then in the winter he made this massive doll's house for my Christmas present.

We had a little chat during the party though. We sat on the end of my bed, just like we did before, before the wedding thing. He said I'd done very well to get everything back together. He said he was sure I was going to be a wonderful wife for Claudio, like I've always been a wonderful daughter to him, which was nice of him to say. Wonderful wife. Wonderful daughter. The words feel nice and warm. In my head I can see myself wrapping those words around me all tight and safe.

Then he said that he was proud of me for being so courageous, and going all the way to Italy with Claudio.

'You're very brave to follow your heart,' he said. He said it must have been a very hard decision to go, which it must have been I suppose. I keep trying to think about that, but I can't really remember actually deciding. That's a strange thought, so I put it away, and think about being a wonderful wife instead.

The car moves out of the town and on to the dual carriageway. Now Ben isn't having to stop and start for traffic the constant sound of the engine is quite restful. It makes me want to close my eyes and be still. The stillness is really pleasant for a moment. But then the idea of just being still makes me think of being at Dad's house the day after the wedding, and I can almost feel the duvet on top of me, and I have to force myself to turn my head so that I don't become paralysed here forever.

I try to lean forward to listen to Claudio and Ben talking but I still can't really hear them over the engine noise, so I sit back again. I close my eyes, but keep tapping my fingers against my thigh so I'm not completely still. The thoughts in my brain run to the rhythm of the engine noise. Wonderful wife, wonderful wife.

It's a relief when we arrive at the airport and I can finally get out of the car. I hug Ben goodbye while Claudio goes and gets a luggage trolley. Ben leaves us outside the airport. It's a two hour check-in, so we all very sensibly agree that there's no point him waiting around. Claudio hugs him and does a lot of very Italian cheek kissing which Ben pulls a face at. Then we sort of stand for a moment and look at each other, before Ben makes a sort of muffled. 'Well, then', noise and gets back in the car. It's very sensible that no one is actually going to see us off. I don't think you're even allowed through security now if you're not flying anywhere. But seeing Ben drive away still feels anti-climactic.

At least now there's lots of activity to concentrate on. There's finding the right check-in and then queuing and finding all our paperwork and checking-in. Then we have to go through all the security stuff, which involves another queue, and then taking our shoes off, and Claudio getting sent back about three times until he's finally emptied his pockets properly and taken his belt off. We manage to fill nearly an hour just doing the stuff you have to do before they'll let you near the aeroplane. Once we're finally through security, Claudio puts his arms around me. 'This is it then. We're on our way.'

He drags me over to some free seats and manages, rather uncomfortably to keep his arm around me, despite the fixed plastic armrest in between us. He looks at me. 'Are you excited?'

I nod. He keeps looking at me. 'Really?'

'Of course.'

Claudio smiles. 'Good. It's going to be brilliant.'

I know it's going to be brilliant. I've looked at pictures of Naples on the internet. It looks lovely. Claudio rubs my back. '*Come vá l'Italiano?*'

I just look at him. He repeats it in English. 'I said, "How's the Italian coming along?"'

I shrug. 'Still lots to learn.'

To be honest, I've not really tried since we got back together. I started before the wedding a bit, but not really since then.

'Never mind. You'll pick it up once we're out there.'

'Sure.'

'Anyway, you'll have me. You'll barely need to speak Italian at all, and the children will be bi-lingual.'

'Children?'

'I thought you wanted kids.'

'I do.' Well, I do. It's just not something we've talked about recently.

Claudio squeezes me a bit tighter. It makes the armrest dig into my side. 'Well, why wait?'

I close my eyes. So this is it. This is what I've been dreaming about. I'm going to be Mrs Claudio Messina. We're going to live in a beautiful place, and raise our beautiful children.

When I open my eyes I notice that there's a big sticky dirty patch just opposite me on the floor. It looks like someone's spilt coke or something and it's not been cleaned up. I pull my feet in closer to me so I won't get contaminated by the grime. I try to force myself to keep thinking about the future.

I'm going to marry Claudio. I'm going to have the chance to make all those promises that I didn't get to make last time. No. Don't think about last time. This is all new and all perfect. I'm going to become Mrs Messina at a lovely service in an Italian registry office. Then I notice the dirty floor again and I can't stop the thoughts from coming any more. I'm going to make different promises that I won't understand in a service in a foreign language. I'm going to be stuck in a rented flat, apparently full of screaming children, while Claudio is out at work all day. And when he does come home he'll be able to talk to my children in their own special language, and I'll be all on my own. And however hard I try and however clean I make it, I won't ever be perfect enough. I feel sick.

Claudio is still talking. 'I've always imagined that we'd have a boy first, and then a girl. I think three or four is better than one or two though. You said you wanted a big family?'

I nod. It's true. I loved growing up just me and Dad, but

I always wanted a sister. Maybe it was because Mum wasn't there, but I used to imagine what it would be like to have a sister to play with and gossip with. What I really wanted was someone I could get into trouble with and share secrets with, and not have to try to be good. I swallow the nausea and try to find the right thing to say. 'Maybe having children straight away is a bit quick though?'

Claudio looks surprised. 'You always said you wanted to start a family as soon as you were married.'

'Did I?'

'Yeah. We talked about it on e-mail, when I was in Naples before.'

I don't want to make him cross. The thought of making him unhappy makes my throat constrict, so I need to be very careful what I say next. 'It's just that we've not had that much time together. Maybe it would be better if it was just us for a while before we think about having a family.'

He looks confused. 'But we know everything about each other already. Last year when we were e-mailing I told you stuff I've never told anyone. Seriously, no one knows me better than you.'

'Yeah.'

'And I know you. I know that you want a big family. I know that your first single was S Club 7.'

He pulls a face as he says that. 'I know that you loved working with children at the library, so I know you'll be a brilliant mum. I even know that you can't relax if there's dirt behind the toaster.'

'I never told you that.'

'It's kind of obvious. You're the only woman I've ever been out with who gets up in the night to wipe her surfaces.'

'I thought you were asleep.'

'I know.'

My sense of nausea is starting to subside. Maybe it will

be OK. He's right. We know all sorts of facts about each other. Probably I just have pre-'moving to another country with man who jilted you at the altar less than twelve weeks ago' jitters. It's probably very common. I just need to concentrate harder on making sure everything is right.

Claudio still has his arm clamped around me. 'So you are excited?'

I nod.

Claudio continues. 'And you'd tell me if you were having second thoughts?'

I nod again. Of course, I wouldn't tell him though. That would just make him unhappy. Why would I do that?

'OK.' Claudio wriggles his arm free and points at the departures sign. 'They're boarding our flight.'

He stands up and turns back towards me. 'Shall we?'

I take his hand and let him lead me to the gate.

It's busy at the boarding gate. There are a lot of families. School holidays start next week, and it looks like a lot of parents have decided to make the most of this week's cheaper prices. It's hot and noisy. I stay close to Claudio in the queue, and try not to get in anyone's way.

We're about seven people from the front of the boarding queue when he turns to me. 'You wouldn't though, would you?'

'What?'

'You wouldn't tell me if you were having second thoughts.'

'Of course I would.'

Claudio stops dead still. 'No. You wouldn't.'

People behind us are starting to look, wondering why Claudio is holding the queue up. I pull on his hand. 'Come on. People are looking.'

'I don't care.' Claudio puts both his hands on my shoulders. 'I'm sorry.'

'What for?'

He closes his eyes. 'I don't think you should come with me.'

People are definitely watching now. I lean towards Claudio and whisper. 'You can't do this again.'

'Again?'

'Like … like…' I can't even say it.

'This isn't like the wedding.'

'Yes. It is.' And it is. He's leaving me again. I've messed it up. I tried so hard to be perfect but I wasn't good enough. I wasn't excited enough. I wasn't enthusiastic enough about having children. 'I've done something wrong, haven't I?'

Claudio seems to realise that people are watching. He pulls me out of the queue and gestures to the people behind us to go in front. 'You haven't done anything wrong. It's me.'

I don't understand what he's saying at all, but he continues. 'It's me. I'm doing something I should have done before.'

'You don't want me to come?'

'I do. Of course I do. I want you with me, but it's not just about what I want, is it?'

Of course it's about what he wants. 'I just want to make you happy.'

'And I won't be happy if you're not.' He takes a deep breath. 'I want you to come with me. I want to marry you. I want to have children with you. But, I can't just decide that, can I?'

Why can't he just decide? I thought he had decided.

Claudio leans down and kisses me on the lips. 'I love you. But I have to do this.'

He takes his hands away from my body and looks at me. 'I'm going to board the plane now. If you want to come too, I'll be sitting on there waiting for you, but if you decide not to, I'll understand.'

'What?'

'I realised, I never really gave you a choice, did I?'

I'm still telling myself that I don't know what he means, but the sick feeling has come right back, and I don't know whether I can ignore it any more. I just look at the floor and wait for something to happen.

'I suppose I knew you'd do what you thought would make me happy.' His voice is shaking, like he might be going to cry. I don't know what I'm supposed to do to make it better. He carries on. 'And I didn't think about what would make you happy, so I'm doing that now. I'm sorry I left it so late. It's up to you, Henri. It's your choice.'

He walks past me and joins the back of the dwindling queue. He doesn't turn back. He doesn't look at me. I sit down on another hard plastic chair and watch him. I think about ringing Dad or Trix and asking them what I should do, but somehow I think that isn't what Claudio would want. Then I wonder whether worrying about what Claudio would want is what he would want either. However I do it though, he's expecting me to make a choice.

I sit and watch the queue go down. Claudio doesn't look at me at all until he's actually going through the doors on to the plane. Then he just throws me a little smile before he disappears.

There are only a couple of people left in the queue now. I close my eyes. What would make me happy I think would be if we'd got married when we were supposed to, and then if Claudio had wanted to stay here in England with me. That doesn't seem to be one of the choices though.

I picture Claudio standing at the altar before everything changed. If I'd married him then, would everything have been OK? Or would it just have been the same, but we'd have taken a lot longer to notice? Because Dad was right. You do have to be brave to follow your heart, rather than following someone else's.

A woman from the airline touches me on the arm. 'Sorry Miss. But you have to board now.'

I shake my head. She smiles. 'Nervous flyer? Don't worry. There's really nothing to be scared of. Did your boyfriend already get on the plane?'

'He's not my boyfriend.'

She rolls her eyes. 'Sorry. Shouldn't assume! You do really need to board now though.'

And I know what I have to do. Because he never actually said sorry for the wedding. Because I'm tired from trying so hard to make things perfect. Because, despite the fact that he loves me enough to give me the choice, him loving me isn't enough. Because there's a choice where we do what he wants, and a choice where just he does what he wants, but no choice where we do what I want.

What I have to do is shake my head, and then stand up and walk away without looking back. I turn to the woman, hand her my boarding pass, shake my head. 'I'm sorry. I won't be getting on the plane.'

And I stand up ready for my dignified walk off into the distance, but apparently it's not that straightforward. Apparently, if you've already checked your baggage, you can't leave the airport until it's been removed from the plane and searched, and apparently the plane can't take off until the baggage has been removed and sniffer dogs have done another check of the hold.

So it doesn't end with me walking wistfully out of the terminal, and him being flown off into the sunset. It ends with me sitting in a security interview room, and him sitting strapped into a hot plane on the tarmac waiting for a new take-off window. We never had our perfect wedding, and now we don't get our perfect end.

Epilogue

Three months later

Henrietta

'Are you ready?'

Danny's shouting up to me from downstairs. I check the wall clock that Trix bought me as a room warming present, and walk out of the freshly-painted boudoir I now rent in Danny's house. I lean over the banister.

'We've got plenty of time. But we can go now if you want. I don't mind.' I'm babbling. I can hear myself doing it.

Danny is leaning on the wall at the bottom of the stairs. He shakes his head. 'I just thought we could go for a drink before we meet the love birds.'

'All right. I just need to get my shoes.' I gesture back towards my room. 'Where do you want to go?'

He shrugs, very very casually. 'The Graduate maybe. It's near the curry house.'

Now I understand. 'Trix thinks the bar manager in there likes you.'

Another shrug, but he can't keep it up, and his face breaks into a suddenly unguarded smile. 'What did she say?'

I shake my head. Was what Trix told me a secret? Would she be cross if I told Danny? I take one of my deep breaths. Trix won't mind, and even if she does, she'll forgive me. It's OK. Everything is OK.

'She just said you always get served first in there.'

Danny looks sheepish. 'I went out with him once.'

This is new information. This might even be gossip that Trix doesn't know. 'When? What happened?' I run down the stairs so I can interrogate him properly.

'About a year ago.' He pulls a face. 'The time before the time before I last split up with John.'

We both make an exaggerated cough-spit motion at the mention of his name.

'And what happened?'

He looks at the floor. 'We went out once. It was great. He was lovely. We went back to his place and I basically freaked out and did a runner. Three days later John came back and that was that.'

'And you still like him?'

He nods. 'It might be too soon, but yeah. I think so.' He stands up straight, seemingly shaking the melancholy away as he does. 'And faint heart never won fair barman!'

'I'd better get my shoes then.' I run back up the stairs and into my room. As I sit down I notice the feeling in my tummy, the absence of feeling in my tummy. It's not empty or anxious. It's normal. I think I like it.

Shoes on. I lean over to switch off my laptop and notice the 'New Mail' symbol. I click on my email and there it is.

You have one new mail.

From: Claudio Messina

Subject: Sorry. New start?

And those two little buttons. Open or delete.

Open or delete?

About the Author

Alison May was born and raised in North Yorkshire, but now lives in Worcester with one husband, no kids and no pets. There were goldfish once. That ended badly.

Alison has studied History and Creative Writing, and has worked as a waitress, a shop assistant, a learning adviser, an advice centre manager, and a freelance trainer, before settling on 'making up stories' as an entirely acceptable grown-up career plan.

Alison is a member of the Romantic Novelists' Association. She writes contemporary romantic comedies. *Sweet Nothing* is her debut novel and first in the *21st Century Bard* series followed by *Midsummer Dreams*.

Follow Alison on
www.twitter.com/MsAlisonMay
www.alison-may.co.uk
www.facebook.com/pages/Alison-May

More Choc Lit

From Alison May

Midsummer Dreams

Book 2 in the 21st Century Bard series

Four people. Four messy lives. One night that changes everything ...

Emily is obsessed with ending her father's new relationship – but is blind to the fact that her own is far from perfect.

Dominic has spent so long making other people happy that he's hardly noticed he's not happy himself.

Helen has loved the same man, unrequitedly, for ten years. Now she may have to face up to the fact that he will never be hers.

Alex has always played the field. But when he finally meets a girl he wants to commit to, she is just out of his reach.

At a midsummer wedding party, the bonds that tie the four friends together begin to unravel and show them that, sometimes, the sensible choice is not always the right one.

A modern retelling of Shakespeare's Midsummer Night's Dream.

Visit www.choc-lit.com for more details, or simply scan barcode using your mobile phone QR reader.

Holly's Christmas Kiss

Book 1 – Christmas Kisses

Happy Holidays? Not for Michelle ...

Holly Michelle Jolly hates Christmas and she has a good reason to. Apart from her ridiculously festive name which made her the brunt of jokes at school, tragic and unfortunate events have a habit of happening to her around the holiday season. And this year is no different.

After the flight to her once-in-a-lifetime holiday destination is cancelled, Michelle faces the prospect of a cold and lonely Christmas. That is, until she meets Sean Munro. Sean loves Christmas, and he wants to share the magic with Michelle.

With Sean's help, can Michelle experience her first happy Christmas, or will their meeting just result in another year of memories that she'd rather forget?

Visit www.choc-lit.com for more details, or simply scan barcode using your mobile phone QR reader.

Cora's Christmas Kiss

Book 2 – Christmas Kisses

Can you expect a perfect Christmas after the year from hell?

Cora and Liam have both experienced horrible years that have led them to the same unlikely place – spending December working in the Grotto at Golding's department store.

Under the cover of a Father Christmas fat suit and an extremely unflattering reindeer costume, they find comfort in sharing their tales of woe during their bleak staffroom lunch breaks.

But is their new-found friendship just for Christmas? Or have they created something deeper, something that could carry them through to a hopeful new year?

Another heart-warming Christmas novella from Alison May! Keep your eyes peeled for characters you may recognise from Alison's previous novella, Holly's Christmas Kiss.

Visit www.choc-lit.com for more details, or simply scan barcode using your mobile phone QR reader.

Introducing Choc Lit

We're an independent publisher creating
a delicious selection of fiction.
Where heroes are like chocolate – irresistible!
Quality stories with a romance at the heart.

See our selection here:
www.choc-lit.com

We'd love to hear how you enjoyed *Sweet Nothing*.
Please leave a review where you purchased the novel
or visit: **www.choc-lit.com** and give your feedback.

Choc Lit novels are selected by genuine readers like yourself.
We only publish stories our Choc Lit Tasting Panel want to
see in print. Our reviews and awards speak for themselves.

Could you be a Star Selector and join our Tasting Panel?
Would you like to play a role in choosing which novels we
decide to publish? Do you enjoy reading romance novels?
Then you could be perfect for our Choc Lit Tasting Panel.

Visit here for more details...
www.choc-lit.com/join-the-choc-lit-tasting-panel

Keep in touch:
Sign up for our monthly newsletter Choc Lit Spread for
all the latest news and offers: www.spread.choc-lit.com.
Follow us on Twitter: @ChocLituk and Facebook: Choc Lit.

Or simply scan barcode using your mobile phone QR reader:

Choc Lit
Spread

Twitter

Facebook